THE REGENCY COLLECTION

Your favourite historical authors
invite you to be whisked away into a
magical world of rakes, rogues and romance…

D1396089

The Regency Large Print Collection

A MODEL DEBUTANTE

Louise Allen

First published in Great Britain 2005
by Mills & Boon, an imprint of Harlequin (UK) Limited,
Large Print edition 2011
Harlequin (UK) Limited,
Eton House, 18-24 Paradise Road, Richmond, Surrey TW9 1SR

ISBN: 978 0 263 23056 7

Harlequin (UK) policy is to use papers that are natural, renewable and recyclable products and made from wood grown in sustainable forests. The logging and manufacturing process conform to the legal environmental regulations of the country of origin.

Printed and bound in Great Britain
by CPI Antony Rowe, Chippenham, Wiltshire

Chapter One

February 1816

Miss Talitha Grey shivered delicately and risked a glance downwards. A single length of sheer white linen draped across her shoulder and fell to the floor at front and back: beneath it her naked skin had a faintly blue tinge. Tallie strongly suspected that it was marred by goose bumps.

With a resigned sigh she flexed her fingers on the gilded bow in her left hand and fixed her gaze once again on the screen of moth-eaten blue brocade that was doing duty for the skies of Classical Greece. Perhaps if she thought hard enough about it she could imagine that she was bathed in the heat of that ancient sun, her skin caressed by the lightest of warm zephyrs and not by the whistling draughts that entered the attic studio by every door and ill-fitting window frame.

Tallie exerted her vivid imagination and summoned up the distant sound of shepherds' pan pipes floating over olive groves to drown out the noise of arguing carters from Panton Square far below. She was concentrating on conjuring up the scent of wood smoke and pine woods to counteract the distressing smells of poor drainage and coal fires when a voice behind her said peevishly, 'Miss Grey! You have moved!'

Taking care to hold her pose and not turn her head Tallie said, 'I assure you I have not, Mr Harland.'

'Something has changed,' the speaker asserted. Tallie could hear the creak of the wooden platform on which Mr Frederick Harland had perched himself to reach the top of the vast canvas. On it he was depicting an epic scene of ancient Greece with the figure of the goddess Diana in the foreground, her back turned to the onlooker, her gaze sweeping the wooded hillsides and distant temples until it reached the wine-dark Aegean sea.

There was more creaking, the muttering that was the normal counterpart to Mr Harland's mental processes and then the floorboards protested as he walked towards her. 'Your skin colour has changed,' he announced with a faint air of accusation.

'I am cold,' Tallie responded placatingly without turning her head. Frederick Harland, she had discovered, took no more and no less interest in her naked form than he did in the colour, form and texture of a bowl of fruit, an antique urn or a length of drapery. When in the grip of his muse he was vague, inconsiderate and sometimes testy, but he was also kindly, paid her very well and was reassuringly safe to be alone with—whatever her state of undress.

'Cold? Has the fire gone out?'

'I believe it has not been lit today, Mr Harland.' Tallie wished she had thought to insist on a taper being set to the fire before they had started the session, but her mind had been on other things and it was not until the pose had been set and the artist had clambered up onto his scaffold that she realised that the lofty attic room was almost as chill as the February streets outside.

'Oh. Hmm. Well, another ten minutes and then we will stop.' The boards groaned again as he walked back to the canvas. 'In any case, I need more of that red for the skin tones, and the azure for the sky. The cost of lapis is extortionate…'

Tallie stopped listening as he grumbled on, his words indistinguishable. A slightly worried frown creased her brow as she resumed her own thoughts. At least in this pose she did not have to guard her expression, for she was standing with only a hint of her right profile visible from behind, her long, slightly waving, blonde hair falling free to midway down her back.

Her feet were bare. A fine filet of gold cord circled her brow, its trailing ends forming a darker accent in her hair, and the linen drapery revealed her left side, the curve of her hip, the swell of her buttock and the length of her leg. All of which normally delightful features were now unmistakeably disfigured by a rash of goose bumps.

Still, at half a guinea a sitting she could hardly complain, for Tallie had no option but to make her own living and the guineas from Mr Harland paid the rent. The fact that she was engaged in an occupation that was entirely beyond the pale for any lady, and which would be regarded by almost every right-thinking person as scarce better than prostitution, did not concern her.

She entirely trusted Mr Harland's intentions towards her, for it was not even that he was *making* himself behave in an entirely proper manner. No, she knew he was entirely uninterested in not only her but, apparently, all females. She had heard that some men preferred their own sex, but this did not appear to be the case either. It seemed that his mind was filled with a single-minded obsession for his art and it allowed no room for any other strong feeling.

The second ground for Tallie's lack of concern about her employment was that she was well aware that no work of Mr Harland's in which she featured was ever likely to grace the walls of an exhibition. It was not that his obsession for the classical ran counter to the modern taste, as the excitement at the news that the Elgin Marbles were to be exhibited showed. No, it was simply that his canvases were too vast and his perfectionism too obsessive to allow him ever to finish one, let alone submit it to critical judgement.

The Diana picture was the fourth in which Tallie had featured: each had reached a stage of near completion when the artist had flung his brushes from him with a cry of despair at ever realising his inner vision. They were stacked away now and from time to time he would attack one of them again for a day or two, then give up in frustration.

It was fortunate, both for the artist and for Tallie, that he was not only the possessor of a modest inheritance, but also had a flourishing and lucrative business in portraiture, an occupation he despised as mere craftsmanship. On three days a week he indulged his classical passion. For the rest of the time he painted Society portraits in the rather more salubrious studio on the first floor of the ramshackle house. It was a tribute to his work that the *ton* were prepared to make the journey to the shabby house in the decidedly unfashionable street just off Leicester Square to have their likenesses taken.

Tallie was mentally casting her accounts in an effort to decide whether she could see the winter out without replacing her hair-brown walking dress and pelisse or whether her other, publicly acknowledged, occupation required her to make an investment in a new outfit.

This financial review was more than enough to account for the crease between her brows, but the frown vanished to be replaced with an expression of real anxiety at the sound of the knocker thudding four floors below, soon followed by the sound of a number of male voices echoing up the uncarpeted stairwell.

With an exclamation of impatience at the interruption, Mr Harland cast down his palette with a clatter and, clambering down from his post, flung open the attic door.

Tallie ran to his side and out onto the tiny bare landing, clutching her flimsy draperies around her. Clearly up the stairway from below she could hear the voice of Peter, Mr Harland's colourman. Peter inhabited the ground-floor rooms with his pots and jars, his bags of pigments and flasks of oils and there magically ground vivid colours out of strange materials.

'Mr Harland doesn't receive clients on Wednesdays, gentlemen. Tuesdays and Thursdays are his days. You can't go up there now, sir!'

'Dammit, I wrote to say I would call to arrange my aunt's portrait and I have no intention of trailing back another day at Harland's convenience.' The drawling voice was arrogantly dismissive of the colourman's protests. 'Are you saying he is not here?'

'Yes, sir, I mean, no, sir, he is here, but he—'

'Perhaps he is with someone?' It was a new voice, carrying easily up to Tallie far above. A coolly sardonic, rather bored voice that made the previous speaker sound affectedly high-handed.

'The man has just said that Harland does not have clients on a Wednesday, Nick. Step out of my way, fellow, I have no intention of standing here bandying words with you all afternoon.'

'But the master's working with a model, sir! You can't go up there!' From the rising note of Peter's voice, the speaker had pushed past him and was already on the stairs.

'What? A female model? Now that is more the thing! Come on, you fellows, this should be good sport.' The voice had lost its drawling arrogance and held a note of excitement that made Tallie's chilled skin crawl. They were coming up, and it appeared that there were several men in the group.

Tallie had disrobed in a room on the floor below, having learned from experience of the effect that the dusty attic had on her small wardrobe, and her only covering was the fragile length of linen. She cast round wildly, her heart thudding. The attics, although essentially one large open space, rambled around corners made by the construction of racks of canvases and piles of dusty props, and in one corner, shielded by the largest rack, there was a large cupboard with a door to it.

'I will hide in the closet,' she said urgently to the artist, who was exclaiming in irritation at the interruption. 'Whatever you do, Mr Harland, do not let them know I am here or I will be quite ruined.'

He nodded distractedly. 'Yes, yes, into the closet with you. I wonder if any of the gentlemen would care to buy an historical canvas?'

Tallie did not stop to argue, but ran on bare feet across the splintery boards. She whisked round the corner of the racking as the voices outside neared the attic and jerked open the cupboard door. The key that had been on the outside clattered to the floor.

Tallie scrabbled for it, but it was nowhere to be

seen. With a sob of frustration she abandoned the search and pulled the door to behind her. The closet was lit by a tiny window, begrimed with dirt and cobwebs, but sufficient for her to see that the space contained nothing in which she might cover herself and nothing to wedge the door with. Not, she realised despairingly, that wedging it would have done any good for it opened outwards.

The men had reached the attic now. Through the warped boards that framed the closet she could hear at least four voices. The arrogant man and the sardonic man she recognised from their voices far below;
their companions had equally well-bred tones and in them she could recognise a kind of febrile excitement at the thought of what they were going to find in the studio.

Tallie felt quite ill with apprehension and scrabbled to pull her linen draperies around herself in some gesture towards a decent covering. Her fingers closed on air and chilled skin. The length of fabric had gone. Wildly she cast around the little closet as though three yards of white cloth could be hiding in an empty space, then she recalled the slight tug at her shoulder as she had hastened around the racking.

Harland's voice was clearly audible as she stood

there, shivering with cold and fear, her ear pressed against the door panels. He sounded flustered. 'Gentlemen, as you can see, I am alone, but really not in a fit state to receive. However, now you are here, what can I do for you, Mr Hemsley? Something about a portrait of your aunt, I believe you wrote?'

'Alone?' The owner of the arrogant voice—Mr Hemsley, she deduced—appeared to take no notice of the artist's question. 'Your man said you had a model up here.'

'He is mistaken. I was working from the nude earlier, but—'

'Nude, I'll say! See here, you fellows!' This voice was younger, excited.

'Take care, my lord! That platform is not very stable!' So, one of them had climbed up to the canvas.

'Bloody hell.' It was Hemsley, his voice strangely flat with what even Tallie in her innocence could recognise as lust. Then the excitement came back to his tone. 'I'll bet she's still here, Harland, you dog. Come on, men, yoicks and tally-ho!'

'For heaven's sake, Hemsley.' The sardonic man sounded utterly uninterested. 'How much longer do you intend hanging around in this squalid attic? Oh, very well, if nothing will satisfy you but to search, let us search. I will look over here, you and the others take the rest. Doubtless we will discover some large spiders, a dead starling or two and any number of mice.'

The voice was getting closer as he spoke. Tallie thought wildly of seizing the door handle and holding on if he tried to open it, but the possibility of being dragged out into the open in such an undignified way only added to the horror. The approaching footsteps halted. From the far side of the attic there was the sound of boisterous searching, excited cries and the occasional 'Do be careful of those canvases, gentlemen!' from the agitated artist.

The footsteps resumed, rounded the corner of the racking if her straining ears were correct, and stopped outside the closet. Tallie turned her back on the door, moved as far away from it as she could and, wrapping her arms around her shrinking body, awaited the worst.

Her hair fell on either side of her bowed head giving her the fragile illusion of shelter and anonymity. But even that vanished as the door creaked open, sending light from the studio flooding into the small space. It defeated the glimmer from the closet window and spilt the shadow of a man across the floor beside Tallie's feet.

He did not move. Tallie could hear his breathing,

steady and even, but she had also heard the sudden catch in it when he had first seen her. He was under control again now, standing there silently watching her. She could not drag her eyes away from the long shadow.

The unseen regard felt as though it was burning into her back. Tallie was well aware of just what he was seeing and a wave of scalding humiliation washed up her body. She was going to be sick, she knew it.

Oh, get it over with! she screamed silently. *How can you torture me like this?* At any moment he was going to call out and the whole pack of them would be there, leering, touching, jeering. Like an animal at bay she turned in upon herself, her mind too frozen with terror and shame to allow her coherent thought.

The shadow at her feet shifted. The man moved and something touched her shoulders lightly. It was a hand resting warm on the shrinking skin. The soft whisper of cloth brushed down her back and over her buttocks. Tallie choked on a scream and his voice—very soft, quite dispassionate—said, 'Here, your wrap was caught on a nail. Be very quiet and everything will be all right, I promise you.'

I promise you. She believed him. The hand was lifted, but she realised he was standing very close just behind her, close enough to whisper in her ear without the sound penetrating outside, close enough for her to feel the warmth of his breath. There was the sound of a long indrawn breath and Tallie had the strange sense that he was inhaling the scent of her. When he spoke again there was an edge to the controlled voice, the merest hint that he was finding her proximity unsettling.

'I am putting the key in the lock on the inside; as soon as I am gone, turn it.' No, she was imagining it: he sounded practical, aloof, unaffected by the sight of the naked girl shivering before him at his mercy.

The door shut, cutting off the bright light. He had gone, leaving the tiny space feeling vast and empty. Over the sound of her own pounding heart she had not heard him move. The voices of the other hunters sounded suddenly loud outside. 'What are you about, Nick? Run her to earth, have you?'

'That closet is locked.' He seemed to be speaking rather louder than necessary and Tallie, wrenching herself out of her frozen state with an effort, twisted the key in the lock, the sharp click masked by the noise outside. 'The key was outside,' the man Nick said.

Oh, clever, Tallie thought as her legs gave way under her and she sank slowly down the wall until she was huddled on the floor. *The closet is locked and the key was outside, so it couldn't have been locked from the inside. All perfectly truthful and all perfectly deceiving.*

'Gentlemen, gentlemen, will you not come down to the first floor, where you will be more comfortable, and we can discuss the question of Lady Agatha's portrait, Mr Hemsley.' The voices, the excitement dying out of them now their hunt had ended in disappointment, receded down the stairs as the men followed Mr Harland.

Tallie stayed huddled on the floor until her breathing settled a little and the wave of nausea subsided. Then she realised that she was so cold that she could hardly move. With agonising slowness, like an old woman recovering from a fall, she clawed her way up the wall until she was on her feet again. The sharp noise of the key in the lock as she turned it made her jump, but with ears straining she pushed the door open and tiptoed out into the cold attic. Far below she could just make out voices. Mr Harland had them all safely in his first-floor studio, thank goodness, probably offering them the good Madeira he kept for clients.

Tallie crept down the stairs to the next floor and into the near-empty bedchamber that she used to change in. The water in the basin on the washstand was icy as she rinsed her dusty fingers, but the blessed security of her clothing as she pulled it on warmed her from the inside, even though the old wool dress was chill from the room. The scent of the jasmine water she habitually wore touched her nostrils. In the absence of her body heat it was a faint ghost of an aroma.

Her hair snagged and tugged as she pulled the comb through it, but she had to braid it tightly and pin it up so that her hat covered the pale blonde shimmer of it modestly. To an onlooker familiar with the detail of ladies' fashions, the bonnet that she set on her now-subdued hair would have seemed surprisingly elegant in contrast to the shabby gown and pelisse. The straw was the finest pale Luton plait and the trimming, although modest enough, was of elegantly pleated grosgrain ribbon.

Safely and respectably dressed at last, Tallie ventured out onto the landing and peered over the rail. In the hall beneath she could see the tops of the hats of four gentlemen, a variety of well-tailored shoulders and the bare heads of Mr Harland and Peter, who had poked his dishevelled grey head out of his workshop door as the visitors left.

The last man paused and Tallie could hear his voice clearly. It was the sardonic tones of the man the others had called Nick, the man who had found and protected her hiding place. 'Good day, Mr Harland. I trust we have not caused any of your household too much disturbance.' The cool voice did not sound as though it was overly concerned, but Tallie was left with a strong impression of a gentleman who regarded his companions' behaviour with fastidious distaste.

'Thank you,' she whispered, unheard. She felt she had been rescued by him as surely as though he had plucked her from a burning building.

But he had not been unaffected, she knew. This man was no Frederick Harland, impervious to the female form. The sudden, soft sound of that intaken breath when he had opened the closet door and seen her, the very control of his stillness, told her that. The sensation that he was inhaling the scent of her body was a disturbingly sensual memory that shivered through her.

Her mind probed the hideous scene that would have followed if one of his companions had been there and instead decided that it was simply too horrible to think about yet. She needed to be safe at home with a hot cup of tea, a warm fire and some reassuring feminine companionship.

Frederick Harland came up the stairs, a look of surprise on his face when he saw Tallie standing there fully clothed. 'Are you going already, Miss Grey?'

Tallie knew him far too well to be surprised that he appeared to have already forgotten the peril she had been in. 'The light is going, Mr Harland,' she said simply. He gave an exclamation of irritation and continued up the stairs to the attic studio. With a sigh Tallie followed him. 'Did the gentleman have an interesting commission for you?' She needed her money for the day's sitting; although he never prevaricated when asked, or quibbled about how much she told him he owed her, the artist seemed to vaguely suppose money was of as little interest to her as it was to him and always had to be reminded.

'Hardly that. A Society dowager, Lady Agatha Mornington. Her nephew Mr Hemsley is paying for it. He doubtless sees it as an investment,' Mr Harland added suddenly, showing a surprising awareness of those around him.

'How so?' Tallie asked, pulling on her gloves. Mr Harland's portraits were hardly dagger cheap.

'He is none too plump in the pocket and I have heard from reliable sources that he has taken out a post-obit loan on his aunt's life. He is no doubt investing in a portrait because he needs to keep her sweet so she does not change her will.' He noticed Tallie was holding her purse and the discussion about money jogged his memory. 'And how much do I owe you, Miss Grey?'

'Two guineas, please, sir. Today, and three days last week, if you recall.' She took the coins with a smile and thanks. 'Do you think Lady Agatha knows he has a post-obit on her? Would she not be upset to think he was borrowing against her death?'

'She would cut him out, I should think,' the artist replied, beginning to scrape down his palette with a frown of concentration. 'He is a wild rake, that one. He'll end up having to rusticate to escape his debtors if he doesn't have some luck soon.'

'How dreadful that anyone could regard the death of a relative as good fortune,' Tallie observed, thinking that any relation, even a formidable dowager, would be pleasant to have in one's life. 'Who were the other gentlemen?'

'Um? Pass me that rag, would you be so kind? Oh, Lord Harperley and young Lord Parry.' Tallie bit back a gasp. She knew Lord Parry's mother and it was even possible that his lordship would also recognise her, for he had seen her once or twice. She swallowed and made herself concentrate on Mr Harland as he continued. 'I did not recognise the quiet gentleman. He may have been abroad, he had a slight tan.' Tallie smiled inwardly—trust Mr Harland to notice skin tone and colour. 'Striking-looking man,' he added dispassionately. 'I wonder if he would sit as Alexander.'

Tallie said her goodbyes and slipped downstairs, leaving Mr Harland musing aloud on his chances of enticing a member of the *ton* to model for him naked and brandishing a sword. As she stepped out onto the narrow street she found that she too was musing on that image and was finding it alarmingly disturbing. *Home and tea for you, Talitha*, she reproved herself. *And time for some quiet reflection on a narrow escape.*

Chapter Two

The walk back to Upper Wimpole Street where Tallie lodged was not inconsiderable, but even with two guineas in her purse she was not tempted to take a hackney carriage. As she walked briskly through the gathering gloom of a late February afternoon she tried to put the frightening events of the afternoon out of her mind by contemplating her finances. She only succeeded in making herself feel even lower than before.

Talitha Grey and her mother had found themselves having to eke out a life of shabby gentility when her father died suddenly five years previously. James Grey had left them with no assets other than some shady investments, which proved to be worth less than the paper they were printed upon, and a number of alarming debts. With Mrs Grey's small annuity and Tallie's one hundred pounds a year they managed, although Tallie's modest come-out was perforce abandoned and her mother sank rapidly into a melancholy decline.

When she followed her husband to the grave three years later, Tallie discovered that the annuity vanished with her mother's death and she was faced with the very limited options open to a well-bred young woman with little money and neither friends nor connections.

A respectable marriage was out of the question without dowry or sponsor. The choice appeared to be between hiring herself out as a lady's companion or as a governess. Neither appealed: something behind Tallie's calm, reserved countenance revolted at the thought of any more time spent entirely at another's beck and call, cut off from all independence of action or thought. She had loved her mother and had never grudged the fact that her entire life since her father's death had been devoted to her, but she had no intention of seeing the rest of that life disappear in the same way in the service of those to whom she had no ties of blood or affection.

Tallie had reviewed her talents once again with a rather more open mind. All that it seemed that she possessed was a certain aptitude with her fingers and good taste in the matter of style. Donning her last good gown, she had sallied out and had called upon every fashionable milliner that she could find in the *Directory*.

The famous Madame Phanie dismissed her out of hand, as did several others. It seemed that impoverished gentlewomen were two a penny and could be depended upon to give themselves airs from which their humbler sisters were mercifully free. But just when Tallie was about to give up, she found Madame d'Aunay's exquisite shop in Piccadilly, not four doors from Hardin, Howell and Company, the drapers.

Madame was graciously pleased to interview Miss Grey and even more gracious when she had a chance to view Miss Grey's work. Tallie joined the hard-working team in the back room. But one day, having heard a paean of praise of a particularly fetching Villager bonnet that Tallie had produced entirely by herself, Madame was moved to call her out of the workroom to discuss with the customer the minor changes to the trimmings that were required.

Word spread that Madame d'Aunay's establishment boasted a young lady of charming manners and gentility who was an absolute magician with a hat, especially one to flatter a lady on the shady side of forty. Soon Tallie had her own clientele. Madame charged a handsome supplement to send

Miss Grey into private homes for personal fittings, and, as Madame, once Mary Wilkinson of All Hallows, was a sensible woman, she paid Tallie a good portion for herself.

But it only just made ends meet. Tallie sighed as she climbed the steps to the front door of Mrs Penelope Blackstock's private lodging-house for young gentlewomen in Upper Wimpole Street. It was not like her to be so despondent, but it was beginning to dawn upon her lately that she was never going to earn enough to do more than scrape by and even that depended entirely on her ability to keep working. And now she had received an all-too-clear warning that one of her sources of income was perilous indeed. If Lord Parry had recognised her, then even her respectable employment would be in jeopardy.

'Tallie! You must be frozen.' Mrs Blackstock's eighteen-year-old niece Emilia, usually known as Millie, appeared from the parlour at the sound of the key in the door, her head wrapped turban-fashion in a shawl. 'Do come in and get warm by the fire. Aunt has just made some tea and we are toasting muffins.'

Thankfully Tallie dropped bonnet and pelisse on the hall chair and followed her in, pulling off her gloves as she did so. All the residents of the household, with the exception of Mrs Porter the cook and little Annie the maid of all work, were gathered round the fireplace.

Suddenly Tallie's vision swam and she found she could not find her way to her chair. Her sight was so blurred she had to grip the edge of the table to steady herself.

'Tallie dear, what is the matter? Are you ill?' Zenobia Scott, the other lodger, leapt to her feet and guided Tallie to her seat. 'You are frozen! Please, Mrs Blackstock, may I ask Cook to bring a hot brick for her feet?'

'I'll go.' Millie was already on her way and Tallie found herself a short while later wrapped snugly in a blanket with the blissful heat of one of the bricks that Cook always kept on the back of the range in the winter glowing by her feet.

She curled her fingers tightly around the teacup and smiled gratefully at her friends, thankful as always for having found this cheerful feminine sanctuary.

'Have you walked all the way home, Talitha?' Mrs Blackstock asked. 'I do wish you would not; it is so cold out there, and dark now. What occurred to upset you so? Has some man offered you an insult?'

'No, not exactly.' Tallie made herself think. She could hardly pretend now that nothing had happened—and in any case she badly wanted to talk about it—but although the other women knew she sat for Mr Harland, they had no idea it was in a scandalous state of undress. They knew how she had begun to sit for the portraitist and had unthinkingly assumed that the supply of Society ladies who required someone else to model their less-than-perfect or pregnant figures was constant. But Tallie had failed to tell them that after the first commission, undertaken at the behest of one of her millinery customers wanting a portrait to remind her husband of her pre-childbirth slenderness, she had succumbed to the temptation of far more lucrative modelling.

'I was at the studio,' she began, 'and a party of gentlemen arrived unexpectedly and insisted on coming up. They guessed Mr Harland had a female sitter and began the most dreadful hue and cry, looking for me.'

'How dreadful!' Mrs Blackstock and her niece said in one voice. Millie, a ravishingly pretty blonde with a lovely figure and a charming, though light, singing voice, was employed as a dancer at the Opera House. Despite all popular prejudice about her profession, she maintained both her virtue and an endearing innocence, whatever lures gentlemen threw out to 'Amelie LeNoir'.

'Did they discover you?' Mrs Blackstock added

anxiously. She kept a concerned eye on her three young ladies, although hard experience since she had been widowed had taught her that no lady of limited means could afford to be over-nice about her employment.

'No, fortunately the ones who were making such a hunt of it were diverted and all was well. But it was frightening and I was so very cold...'

Mrs Blackstock clucked. 'Make sure you have a good dinner tonight, Talitha dear, and go to bed early. My goodness, just look at the time! Millie, if we are to take out those curl papers and dress your hair for this evening's performance, we must bustle!'

She swept her niece out of the room, pausing to pat Tallie's shoulder as she went.

Zenobia shifted her position to regard her friend closely. Three years older than Tallie, she was a governess who chose to live independently and to go out to households daily. She had a small but appreciative clientele amongst those rare families who took the education of girls seriously and who wished to have their children's regular learning with their own governesses supplemented by Miss Scott's tuition in Italian, German and, in two radical households, Latin.

'Well?' Zenobia demanded abruptly. Years of

dealing with children had given her a sure sense for prevarication and careful half-truths. 'Who was he?'

'He? Who?'

Zenobia rolled her brown eyes ceilingwards. 'The man, of course. The one who was *not* hunting you.'

'How did you…I mean, what makes you think…?'

'Your choice of words was odd, that is all. And I know you very well. There is something about you, some little suppressed excitement. Come on, tell Zenna.'

'But I did not even see him, Zenna,' Tallie protested. 'Only his shadow on the floor. You see, they all came trooping up and I ran and hid in the closet, but the key fell out, and my draperies, er…'

'Tallie,' Zenna said, her face a picture of appalled realisation, 'you do not mean to tell me you were posing *unclad*?'

'Um…yes. But you see, Mr Harland is utterly immune to any interest in the female form. Why, I am as safe with him as I am with you; no one will ever see or buy his classical canvases, for they are never finished and, besides, they are vast in size.'

'Well, one group of men appears to have seen all too much,' Zenna retorted grimly. 'Just how many of them were there?'

'Four. But even if they saw me again, they would

never recognise me from the picture, for the pose was from the back.'

A little whimper escaped Zenna's lips. 'But what about this closet you hid in? Did none of them find you there?'

'Well, yes, one of them opened the door. But he did not see my face and he was a perfect gentleman. He gave me my drape back and the key, and told the others that the door was locked so they went away.'

The whimper became a moan. 'You were in a closet, with no clothes on and this man came in?' Tallie nodded. 'And he did not say anything, or touch you or…?'

'He caught his breath,' Tallie admitted, a *frisson* running down her spine again at the recollection of that soft sound.

'As well he might,' Zenna said grimly. 'By some miracle you appear to have encountered the only safe man in London.'

'Well, he saved me,' Tallie admitted, 'but he did not make me feel safe.' Zenna's rather thick brows rose interrogatively. 'His voice was so…so cool and sardonic, as though he did not care what anyone else thought. And he is…powerful somehow.'

'How on earth can you tell?' Zenna demanded, attempting to pour some cold water over what she felt were becoming dangerously heated imaginings. 'You did not see him, did you?'

'No, he just emanated this feeling. I can't describe it, but I suppose power is the best word. And Mr Harland wanted to ask him to pose as Alexander the Great.'

'Goodness. Well, if he looks anything like the representations of Alexander that I have seen, he is an impressive man indeed. What a fortunate thing you did not see him,' she added slyly, 'or you would be imagining yourself in love with him.'

'Oh, nonsense.' Tallie laughed and tossed a cushion at her teasing friend. She was suddenly feeling better. Alexander the Great indeed!

The next morning, refreshed by a good night's sleep, undisturbed by dreams of hallooing gentlemen and Carthaginian generals, Tallie woke to a sunny day, feeling considerably more optimistic than she had for some time.

'Better?' asked Zenna over the breakfast table. They were alone, for Mrs Blackstock was out marketing and Millie was tucked up in bed—as she rightly said, beauty sleep was essential in her profession.

'Mmm.' Tallie spread preserve on her toast with a lavish hand and contemplated the advertisements on the front page of the morning paper. 'How much money would it take to set up in one's own shop, do you think, Zenna?'

'As a milliner?' Zenna bit thoughtfully into a forkful of ham. 'Rent for the shop—and that would need space for a workroom, redecoration and fitting it out. Girls for the workshop, materials. A lot of money. Not as much as I would need for a school, but a lot. You would need a loan, or,' she added with a wicked twinkle, 'a protector.'

'I suspect that was how Madame D'Aunay got started, by prudently investing a farewell present from such a person,' Tallie confessed. 'But I have absolutely no intention of taking a lover so I can borrow money for a hat shop from him!'

Zenna choked back a gasp of laughter. 'It would certainly be a most original reason for abandoning the path of virtue. What are you doing today? I have the two Hutchinson girls all day and I plan to go for a nice walk in Green Park with them, conversing in Italian throughout.'

'That does sound pleasant, they seem such an amiable family from what you have told me. I have rather a pleasant day too, for I have hats to deliver to both Lady Parry and Miss Gower and they are quite my favourite clients.'

* * *

However, Tallie found it was hard to maintain such a cheerful mood. In the morning sunshine the hair-brown walking dress and pelisse were every bit as unsatisfactory as she had thought the day before. There was nothing for it but to purchase a dress length and make a new gown, for she really could not feel that she looked the part to be calling upon Society ladies. She looked in the windows of Hardin and Howell as she passed them and regretfully decided that the Parthenon Bazaar was likely to prove more suitable for her budget. Some economies were possible: if she did not take a hackney to her clients' homes but walked instead, that would save a few shillings.

Tallie was soon regretting the decision, for she had three hatboxes to collect at the milliners. Although her first call at Bruton Street was not far and the boxes were light, they were unwieldy, and the sight of a young lady carrying any parcel—let alone three hatboxes—in the street was sufficiently unconventional for her to attract several impertinent stares.

Feeling increasingly flustered, Tallie was tempted to change her plans and call at Miss Gower's in Albermarle Street first, for it was closer. But Miss Gower was eighty-three and would not be pleased to be disturbed before eleven o'clock. No, it would have to be Lady Parry and her two hats.

Tallie turned cautiously round the corner from New Bond Street, thankful that her destination was almost in sight. Inelegant though it was, she had found that, by balancing two hatboxes on top of each other and then holding the ribbons of the third twined in her fingers, she could just manage. It did nothing for her vision forward, however, and she was already getting a crick in her neck from peering around her pile of gaily striped boxes.

The collision happened just as she reached the entrance to Bruton Mews. For one startled moment she thought she had walked into the wall, for the obstacle she had hit was certainly solid enough and equally unyielding. One hatbox was driven into her diaphragm, making her whoop for breath, the top one fell off and rolled into the road and she managed to drop the other at her feet.

Doubled up, making unseemly gasping noises and with her eyes streaming, Tallie was conscious of an immaculate pair of boots in front of her. Rising out of them were well-muscled legs in buckskin breeches. Her eyes travelled upwards past a plain waistcoat revealed between the flaps of an equally plain riding coat, past a crisp white stock to a firm, well-shaven chin and the enquiring and frankly appreciative gaze of the owner of these altogether admirable attributes.

It was too much. Coming on top of yesterday's shock and the knowledge that she had made a serious error of judgement in deciding to walk, Tallie found she was swept with an irrational wave of anger. How dare this man stand there, looking cool, calm and assured and openly scrutinising her while she made an exhibition of herself?

'Look what you have done!' she gasped indignantly as her breath returned. 'Just look at that box in the road!'

Before the man could respond to her attack, a carriage clattered out of the mews rather too fast and drove straight for the gaily striped cerise-and-white hatbox lying in its path.

'Oh, no!' Tallie took a hasty step forward to try and snatch it up by its trailing ribbons, only to find herself unceremoniously yanked back onto the footway. She struggled against the grip on her arm, but to no avail. The carriage's nearside front wheel caught the box and rolled it over, flipping the lid off. Lady Parry's exquisite new promenade hat fell out into the mud of the gutter and came to rest there like a wounded bird of paradise.

'Ouch!' Her arm hurt and at her feet the result of hours of work and the product of the finest materials lay, its curling feathers reduced to a sodden mass.

The man released her arm without apology. 'It appeared to be preferable to have the hat under the wheels of the carriage than to have you in that position.' He stepped into the road and picked up the hat, dropping it into its box and handing that to Tallie before removing a large white handkerchief from his sleeve and rubbing the mud off his gloves with it. 'My valet insists on checking that I have a clean handkerchief before I go out; how gratified he will be that for once it was needed.'

Considering that she had collided with him and harangued him, he sounded politely unconcerned. He also sounded, to Tallie's incredulous ears, hideously familiar. No, surely not—it couldn't be! Tallie felt her jaw drop and she covered her confusion by groping in her reticule for her own handkerchief.

'Yes, of course, you are quite right, I am so sorry, sir,' she managed to stammer as she pretended to wipe her eyes. 'I must suppose I walked into you, sir. I do apologise.' She was blushing, she knew she was, the wave of heat was rising up her throat, try as she could to control it.

'You did, but it is of no matter. Can *all* these be

yours?' He gestured at the tumbled boxes, one dark brow raised.

'I was delivering them.' Tallie was certain that she was crimson. Her mind hardly seemed to be functioning at all, but somehow she had to end this encounter and remove herself and her hatboxes before something triggered his memory. Because with every word he spoke she was more than ever convinced that this was Nick—Mr Harland's Alexander the Great—the man who had found her hiding naked in the closet.

He never saw your face, you never spoke, she told herself frantically.

'Hmm. I hardly imagine your employer will be very happy about that,' he observed dispassionately, glancing at the boxes that Tallie had gathered up and were now piled beside her feet, each with at least one unpleasant stain on it.

Tallie glared at him, her anger returning as common sense asserted itself. Of course he would never recognise her—as far as he was concerned she was a humble milliner's assistant, someone of a class so far removed from his as to be virtually invisible. 'No, she will not be happy,' she agreed between gritted teeth. 'Have you any idea how much that hat that just fell out costs?' She knew she should not be addressing a gentleman in such a way, let alone one who had behaved with such chivalry to her the day before, but instinct screamed at her to keep him at a distance. She picked up the hatbox and held it, an insubstantial barrier between herself and all that maleness.

He lifted the lid of the box she was cradling in her arms and looked in. It brought him very close to her; close enough to see that his lashes were quite ridiculously long and dark for such a masculine-looking man, close enough to smell a peppery cologne with a hint of limes and certainly close enough to see a flash of wicked amusement in his dark grey eyes as he looked at her flustered and indignant face.

'Madame Phanie's establishment?' he enquired.

'No, Madame d'Aunay's.'

'Ah. Five guineas, then.'

This was so accurate that Tallie was betrayed into speech. 'How on earth do you know that, sir?'

She was answered with another lift of that expressive brow. 'One receives bills from time to time, my dear,' he drawled.

'Oh!' Tallie was furious with herself for asking and even more so for blushing hectically again. Even if he was merely referring to hats bought by his wife or sisters, her response to the remark showed clearly that she thought he meant he had been buying hats for a mistress. 'Well, I made it and it took *hours* and now it is quite ruined—and if you had not stopped me I could have saved it.'

'So it is all my fault?' he enquired drily. 'In that case I had better pay for it.' Before Tallie could respond he reached into his pocket, drew out a handful of coins and counted five bright guineas into her hand. Then he set the lid back on the ruined bonnet, stooped to pick up the remaining hatboxes and placed them carefully in her arms. 'Good day, my dear. And next time, ask your employer to send you in a hackney.'

Chapter Three

The man called Nick strode off up the street towards Berkeley Square without a backward glance,
leaving Tallie standing staring after him. Then she
realised that she was attracting no little attention.
A kitchen maid, her head just visible through the
area railings, stopped shaking out a rug to stare
open-mouthed; a footman in livery raised super-
cilious eyebrows as he strode past bearing his employer's messages; a hackney carriage driver called
out something that was mercifully unintelligible
to Tallie and a very smart matron, her maid at her
heels, fixed her with a look of scandalised outrage.

With a gasp Tallie clenched her fingers around the
coins and walked on as fast as she could with her
unwieldy burden. To be seen on the street taking
money from a man! No wonder people stared—she
must have appeared no better than a common pros-
titute. Tallie almost turned tail, then realised she

must at least call upon Lady Parry and apologise for her tardiness and for the damaged hat.

Feeling that everyone was staring at her and expecting at any moment to be accosted, either by some buck with a proposition or an outraged householder ordering her from his respectable street, Tallie finally reached Lady Parry's door. It was opened with merciful promptness by Rainbird the butler. He allowed a faint expression of surprise to cross his thin face at the sight of the flushed and flustered milliner standing before him with her pile of soiled hatboxes.

'Miss Grey! Have you been in an accident? Please, step inside at once.' He stood aside to let her in and snapped his fingers imperiously to the footman, who hurried forward. Tallie relinquished her boxes gratefully and regarded the butler with an expression of rueful apology.

'I am sorry to arrive in such a state, Rainbird, but I dropped the boxes in the street.'

'I will ring for the housekeeper, Miss Grey. You will want to wash your hands and have your gown brushed before you see her ladyship, I make no doubt.' Rainbird approved of Miss Grey, and had so far unbent as to remark on one occasion to Henry the footman, 'A milliner she might be now, my lad, but she's a lady for all that she has come down in the world. You just observe her manners: always easy and polite to staff. That comes from breeding and consideration and there are many with a hundred times her income who will never manage that naturally.'

Tallie was just gratefully accepting his offer when a small dark lady wearing a most fetching cap with floating ribbons and a jonquil morning dress, which almost made Tallie forget her woes, emerged into the hall. 'Miss Grey, good morning. I thought I heard your voice.'

'Good morning, my lady.' Tallie bobbed a neat curtsy, conscious of the snapping brown eyes assessing her appearance. 'I must apologise for arriving in such a state, ma'am, but I had an accident with the boxes.'

'I was just about to send for Mrs Mills, my lady.'

'Excellent, Rainbird. You run along with her, Miss Grey, and come down when you feel quite comfortable again. There is no hurry.' Lady Parry vanished as abruptly as she had appeared and Tallie surrendered herself into the care of the housekeeper who, despite tutting about ruinous mudstains, restored the tired old gown to as good a condition as Tallie could hope for with sponge and badger-bristle brush.

Her cheeks cooled by a splash of water, her hands

rinsed and her hair tidied, Tallie hurried downstairs and tapped on Lady Parry's morning-room door.

'Come in, Miss Grey, and let me have a look at you.' Kate Parry was a widow on the wrong side of forty with a son of twenty, a tidy personal fortune and apparently boundless enthusiasm for whatever took her fancy. 'Sit down and have a glass of Madeira. No, show me no missish reluctance, you have obviously had a shock and coddling your insides with tea or ratafia will not help at all.'

She peered closely at Tallie's face. 'Have you been crying, my dear? Were you hurt?'

'Oh, no, ma'am, only I had the breath knocked out of me for a moment.' Tallie took a sip of the strong wine, choked a little, then took another. It was certainly soothing to her nerves. 'It made my eyes water, you see.' She hesitated. Rainbird had placed the two hatboxes for Lady Parry upon a side-table, having first carefully spread a sheet of the morning paper to protect the polished surface from the mud. 'I am afraid I dropped your new hats.'

'How provoking for you! And has your handiwork been spoiled? I do hope not. Never mind, it is more important that you were not hurt. We will look at the hats in a moment: you drink your wine and tell me all about it.'

Thus encouraged by Lady Parry's warm interest,

and perhaps rather more by the unfamiliar glow of the wine, Tallie began her tale.

The foolish decision to walk was easily enough admitted to, and, although Lady Parry shook her head, she did not lecture. She was quite well aware of Tallie's circumstances, having taken care to draw her out, little by little, during the year that she had been visiting Bruton Street. As a matter of course Kate Parry took considerable interest in most people who came her way, but she found herself particularly in sympathy with the reserved young woman who created such elegant hats for her.

Tallie was as discreet about her own affairs as she was about her other clients, but from the little she did let drop, careful study of the *Landed Gentry* and a thorough gossip with her old friend Miss Gower, Kate had a clearer picture than Tallie would ever have suspected. Tallie would have been even more surprised to discover that Lady Parry had a scheme in mind for her, but it was not something of which she had the slightest inkling since, for it to come about, something had to happen first to which Lady Parry looked forward with sadness.

She thought about it now and gave a little sigh before fixing her attention on Tallie's misadventures once again. 'So you were attracting some unwelcome attention?' she prompted as Tallie broke off.

'Yes, but by the time I realised how foolish it was to be walking I was halfway here, so there was no advantage in turning back. Then—' She broke off, took a deep breath and resumed. 'I walked straight into a gentleman. And I dropped all the boxes; the one with your special promenade hat rolled into the roadway—and I was quite...' she searched for a ladylike expression, failed and blurted out '...winded.'

Lady Parry suppressed a smile. Poor Miss Grey, it must have been most upsetting for her, but the scene itself sounded not a little amusing. 'Who was he?' she enquired, attempting to sound suitably grave.

'I have no idea,' Tallie said, then flushed. She could hardly say she knew his first name only— what would Lady Parry think?

'An elderly gentleman?' It was said with a wicked twinkle, which Tallie did not fail to notice.

'No, ma'am. About thirty, perhaps, or a little younger?' Tallie speculated, wrinkling her straight nose, which Mr Harland always compared favourably to those of the best Greek statues.

Enchanting, Lady Parry thought, watching the play of emotion on Tallie's face. *To have a daughter like that! So attractive, so intelligent. And she would so repay dressing well...* 'And did he assist you?'

'Yes, ma'am, although he stopped me rescuing the box from the road until it was too late and a carriage struck it.'

'Yet this gallant gentleman displeased you, and for more than his tardiness with the hatbox, I imagine?' Now Tallie was blushing in earnest. 'My goodness, Miss Grey, whatever did he do? Did he take some liberty with you?' It might well have occurred, for the sort of man who would think nothing of fondling a kitchen maid if she took his fancy would probably be equally free with an attractive young milliner if the chance arose, and he certainly appeared to have ruffled the normally calm and self-controlled Miss Grey.

'No. Not if you mean did he try and kiss me or make an improper remark, ma'am. But...but when I was cross because of your hat, he looked in the box and guessed how much it cost and he *paid* me for it, in guineas, right there on the street!' She swallowed. 'And people saw him.'

'Dear me, that was a thoughtless thing for him to have done,' Lady Parry exclaimed. 'No wonder you are so angry with him.' Now what had she said? The girl was as pink as a peony.

'Yes, but I should not be angry with him, it is

very ungrateful of me and I am sure it was just thoughtlessness.' Tallie was finding herself more confused by the minute about how she regarded Nick. Gallant and quick-witted rescuer or heartless rake, not above trifling with a respectable working girl?

'I do not think that having the courtesy to pick up your boxes entitles him to sufficient gratitude for you not to be angry at such an imprudent act on his part as to make you the cynosure of all eyes on a public street.' Rather out of breath with the effort of such a convoluted declaration, Lady Parry sat back and watched Tallie with interest. There was more to her distracted mood than she was revealing, she was sure of it.

Tallie rummaged hastily in her reticule for her handkerchief. There really was nothing more she felt she could safely say, for the turmoil of her feelings increased the more she thought about the encounter.

To have seen the man who only yesterday saw her naked body…to feel such anger when she knew she owed him a considerable debt for his tact and quick thinking and that in any case the reaction was out of all proportion to his offence just now… And she was making a positive exhibition of herself in front of her kindest and most influential patroness.

'I beg your pardon, ma'am,' she started to say when there was the sound of the front door opening and footsteps in the hall accompanied by male voices.

'Oh, good,' Lady Parry said, 'William is home. I have absolutely no hope that I will succeed, but I intend asking him to escort me to Lady Cressett's soirée tonight. I declare the wretch knew I was going to ask him, for he made himself scarce just before I came down for breakfast! Would you be so good as to pull the bell for Rainbird, Miss Grey?'

Tallie did so, remaining standing in the shadowy corner by the bell-pull. She had glimpsed young Lord Parry on occasions, but only fleetingly as they passed in the hallway. She had no real fear that he would recognise her from the picture yesterday, but she had no desire to come to the notice of *any* of the men who had seen it. In any case, it would be most unbecoming of her to put herself forward.

Rainbird entered and informed Lady Parry that their lordships had gone into the study. 'Would your ladyship wish a message conveyed?'

'Yes, please ask them both to come in, Rainbird. My nephew must be here as well,' she added for Tallie's benefit.

'I will wait in the hall, ma'am; you will wish to be private.'

'Not at all, Miss Grey, please, come… William, my dear boy! And my favourite nephew as well. Now that is fortuitous, you may both escort me this evening.'

William, Lord Parry, was twenty years old. Born to a large fortune and rather girlish good looks, he had grown up, much to his mama's relief, a thoroughly nice, unspoilt young man, if a touch young for his age. A suitable wife would mature him, she was sure; in the meantime she was happy for him to sow his harmless wild oats under the apparently careless eye of his guardian and her trustee, her nephew Lord Arndale.

William grinned disarmingly at the rallying note in his mother's voice. 'Escort you, Mama? Er…I think I am engaged; in fact, I feel sure I am.'

His companion followed him into the room and came across to take Lady Parry's hand in his. 'Aunt Kate.' He bent to kiss her cheek, a tall dark man in immaculate riding wear. 'I hope I find you well this morning, ma'am? I am happy to inform you that William has absolutely no engagements of note this evening and will be delighted to escort you to whichever concert of ancient music you have in mind.'

Lady Parry laughed, ignoring her son's outraged protestations. 'No such thing, you wicked man. I would like you both to come with me to Lady Cresset's soirée. I can promise absolutely no ancient music and several tables set out for cards.'

Tallie stood stock-still in her corner. Lady Parry's nephew was none other than the man she had just collided with in the street, the man who had protected her yesterday in the studio. To her horror she realised that Lady Parry had remembered her and had turned on the sofa to look for her.

'Miss Grey, do, please, come and sit down again.' Tallie hung back in the shadows. 'Miss Grey was kindly engaged on an errand for me and has had a distressing accident in the street.'

Both men looked in her direction and Tallie realised there was nothing for it but to emerge. She stepped forward, keeping her eyes down and her hands clasped in front of her.

'Nicholas, this is Miss Grey. Miss Grey, Lord Arndale, my nephew. I believe you have met my son on occasion before now.'

Tallie dropped a neat curtsy without looking up. Was she blushing again? Her heart was certainly pounding. 'Lord Arndale, Lord Parry.'

William Parry stepped forward with the eagerness that typified him. 'I say, Miss Grey, are you hurt?'

'No, no, not at all, my lord.'

'Perhaps if you were to move, William, Miss Grey could resume her seat,' Nick Stangate observed drily, watching his cousin with suppressed amusement. 'I believe this was your chair, Miss Grey?' He indicated a bergÈre armchair on which a reticule lay, its drab plainness in startling contrast to the charming toile upholstery fabric.

'Thank you, it is, my lord.' So, this unusual young woman must be the lady milliner who had been concerning his Aunt Kate to the point where he had felt it necessary, as Lady Parry's trustee, to take a hand and make some enquiries himself. He should have realised when he ran into her in the street just now and scattered her hatboxes. Doubtless he would have done if his mind had not been preoccupied with another young woman altogether.

Nick took a seat beside his aunt, which had the effect of bringing him opposite Miss Grey. She was certainly well spoken, and elegant in her deportment and appearance, despite the dreadful gown, unflattering coiffure and downcast eyes. Her present demeanour was in startling contrast to that of the angry girl who had scolded him in the street.

She was sitting quite still now, seemingly composed, yet he sensed a desire to burrow backward into the chair cushions out of sight.

'But what happened?' William was persisting. 'Are you quite sure you are not injured, Miss Grey? Perhaps we should send for the doctor, Mama.'

Despite the self-effacing meekness of the slender figure in front of him and the fact that she had spoken hardly a word, Nick was quite certain he knew exactly what the young woman's problem was. It was not often that his conscience pricked him, but he felt its unfamiliar sting now.

'I believe Miss Grey is wounded in spirits, not in her person. She collided with a gentleman in the street and had the misfortune to choose one who was not only so slow that he allowed her possessions to be crushed under the wheels of a passing carriage, but who then had the impertinence to recompense her for the damage in a way that was, I believe, very ill judged.'

He felt a stirring of interest as Tallie's eyes flew to his face. There it was again, that mixture of spirit and—could it be—fear flashing out from behind the subdued front she was presenting.

'Ill judged!' she snapped, then appeared to recollect herself. He found himself both intrigued and amused. 'Yes, my lord, you are correct,' she added softly, and he realised her eyes were on his face, reading what little emotion he allowed to appear there. 'Although I am sure the gentleman's actions sprang from a genuine desire to make amends and not from the wish to—shall we say, tease—an inferior.'

'Touché,' he murmured, enjoying the emerald flash of her eyes. *So, Miss Grey, you are prepared to duel, are you?*

'Nicholas,' his aunt demanded, 'are you the gentleman in question?'

'I have to confess I am, Aunt,' he admitted, turning slightly to meet her indignant look. 'And I am justly reproved by Miss Grey. I had no idea that she was a young lady kindly undertaking an errand for you. I mistook her for a milliner's girl—'

'I *am* a milliner's girl, my lord,' Tallie said in frigidly polite tones. So, Miss Grey was not attempting to presume upon her patroness's friendly treatment. And she was certainly not going to toady to Lady Parry's nephew. How refreshing. He let his gaze linger on her face as she continued. 'If you will excuse me, Lady Parry, you will wish to speak in private to their lordships, I am sure. I will take the undamaged hat upstairs and leave it with your dresser. I will naturally make every effort to have the other one replaced within the week.'

She stood up, dropped another curtsy to Lady Parry, picked up the hatboxes and walked briskly to the door before Nick could get to his feet and step past her to open it. As she reached for the door handle it turned and Rainbird stepped into the room.

'Mr Hemsley is here to see his lordship, my lady,' he announced. Nick stopped where he was with an inward flash of irritation. Damn Hemsley; he was showing not the slightest sign of becoming bored with William, despite Nick's persistently accompanying his cousin to every gambling den and sporting venue that Hemsley invited him to. He had made no attempt to fleece William while Nick was there. Possibly Nick was misjudging him and he was not the Captain Sharp he suspected, but he rather feared the combination of William's innocence and large fortune and Hemsley's financial embarrassment and lack of scruple was every bit as dangerous as he thought.

Either way, he was getting more than a little weary of chaperoning his cousin. Beside anything else, it was putting a decided dampener on the more sophisticated pleasures with which Nick Stangate normally entertained himself when in London.

Beside him his aunt nodded assent to the butler

and Rainbird stood aside and ushered the visitor into the room.

Nick saw Miss Grey step back, but even so she could not escape coming face to face with the man who was entering the room. Why the devil was she blushing? Nick could see the colour staining her throat from across the room. Damn the man, had he murmured some remark? Could Hemsley not restrain himself from flirting with every woman who crossed his path? He schooled his face, resisting the temptation to take a hand. It was not part of his tactics to cross swords with the man yet.

'Lady Parry, ma'am! A thousand apologies for disturbing you...'

Flustered, Tallie found herself alone in the hall with Rainbird. 'I will just go up to Miss Hodgson with this hat, Rainbird.'

'There is no need, Miss Grey, I will have it taken up directly. May I call you a hackney carriage?'

This time Tallie had no hesitation in accepting, despite the very short distance to Albermarle Street where Miss Gower lived. She sat back against the squabs and contemplated the stained hatboxes on the seat opposite in an unsuccessful effort to keep her mind off those two unsettling encounters.

Infuriating man! If only she did not feel such

a strong sense of obligation to Nicholas Stangate for the chivalrous way he had behaved yesterday, she could feel thoroughly and justifiably cross with him. And as for Mr Hemsley—well, he was just as much of a rake as she had imagined from what she had heard at the studio. The gleam in his blue eyes and the swift wink he had sent her as they passed in the doorway confirmed her in that opinion. A very good-looking rake, of course, if one had a penchant for that style of rather obvious blond handsome-ness. And if one were prepared to tolerate such an insolent regard. Now she had been seen, but not recognised, by three of the four men from the studio; she closed her eyes and gave thanks once again for Nick Stangate's chivalry.

The hackney pulled up in front of Miss Gower's dark green front door and Tallie jumped down with one box. 'Please wait, I will not be above ten min-utes.'

Miss Gower had not been well for several weeks now and her maid had told Tallie that the doctor had forbidden any but the shortest visits, but even ill health was not enough to stop the indomitable old lady's interest in her appearance. Of all her little indulgences, pretty hats were perhaps her favourite, and the more frivolous the creation that Tallie could show her, the happier she was.

On this occasion, however, Tallie saw with dismay that the heavy brass knocker was wrapped in baize. She knocked gently and the door was opened by Smithson, Miss Gower's butler, whom Tallie suspected was nearly as old as his mistress.

'Oh, Miss Grey,' he said lugubriously. 'The mistress cannot see you, I am afraid. Very poorly she is this morning, very poorly indeed.'

'I am sorry to hear that, Smithson.' The old man looked so shaky and distressed that Tallie wished she could give him a hug, but she knew he would be scandalised. 'Will you tell her I called and that I sent my best wishes for her recovery?'

'No hope of that, Miss Grey. No hope of that. Doctor Knighton called yesterday and warned us all.' He sniffed. 'Slipping away…slipping away.'

Tallie hesitated. 'Should I leave her new hat, do you think, Smithson?'

'Yes, please, Miss Grey. I will put it on the stand next to her bed so she can see it. That will give her so much pleasure. Is it a pretty one, Miss Grey?'

'Very,' Tallie assured him. 'Her favourite pink ribbons, and ruched silk all under the brim, and just one pink rose tucked above the ear.'

'Oh, she'll like that, Miss Grey.' The old man took the box in both tremulous hands.

'Goodbye, then, Smithson, you will let me know when…when she gets better?'

Thoroughly depressed, Tallie gave the driver Madame d'Aunay's direction and climbed back into the cab. One could hardly hope that a frail old lady would live for ever, but Miss Gower had seemed so indomitable and had had such a love of life that it seemed impossible that the years would ever catch up with her.

'Well, that will teach you to refine upon encounters with gentlemen and worry about what they think and say,' Tallie scolded herself out loud as the cab turned into Piccadilly. 'There are much more important and serious things happening than your foolish adventures. Poor Miss Gower, and without even any family to support her now.'

Chapter Four

Tallie spent a week engaged in exemplary hard work at Madame d'Aunay's, activity that entirely failed to distract her mind from worrying about Miss Gower or, when all self-discipline failed her, brooding about Lord Arndale. She was dwelling upon him, she told herself, because he had proved so infuriating. It was nothing to do with their encounter at the studio and most certainly had not the slightest connection with the fact he was an extremely attractive man.

As she had feared, Lady Parry's special hat proved beyond rescue, so it had to be entirely remade from scratch. Faced with the sale of it twice over, Madame was not moved to scold Tallie for the accident and instead recommended her personal service to a certain Mrs Leighton. 'A cit, of course,' she confided, 'but newly married and her husband is as rich as they come and denies her nothing. I expect her to spend at least as much as Miss Gower ever did and I would not want you to suffer from the loss of a client.'

But Tallie was not concerned about the size of Miss Gower's orders, and her grief when she heard the news that the old lady had finally slipped away two days after her last hat was delivered was as genuine as if she had been a relative.

On Saturday evening the residents of the lodging-house in Upper Wimpole Street found themselves together in the parlour before dinner. Although they were each engaged upon some small task, Tallie sensed a palpable air of relaxation amongst all of them with the end of a busy week.

'This is pleasant to be all together,' Zenna observed cheerfully. 'Do you not go to the Opera House this evening, Millie?'

'No, the run finished yesterday and they are staging a masquerade tonight. The new production begins on Monday—it is called *The Lost Italian Prince* and is a very affecting melodrama.'

'And do you have a good part?' Tallie enquired. She was sorting through a pile of coloured silks, which had become, through some alchemy of their own, hopelessly tangled whilst untouched in a closed box. Millie was a rarity in the world of the theatre—a genuinely chaste young lady—and her aunt and her friends did their best to support her, while living in constant anxiety about the bucks and roués she inevitably encountered.

'Yes!' Millie glowed with pride. 'I have a speaking line all to myself and I sing in a trio in the second act. I play one of the village maidens who, with her friends, helps hide the Prince whilst he is fleeing his Wicked Uncle.'

'What happens in the end?' Mrs Blackstock enquired, looking up from the account book she was filling in at the other end of the table from Zenna, who was marking her pupils' French vocabulary work.

Millie put down the sheet she was hemming, curled up more comfortably on the rather battered sofa and prepared to explain the plot. 'Well, the Prince falls in love with this village maiden—only she isn't really, she's the daughter of the Duke in disguise because he wants her to marry this awful man—and when the Wicked Uncle—the Prince's uncle, that is, who is trying to murder him—finds where he is hiding, she sacrifices herself by throwing herself from the battlements in front of his troops and—'

The sound of the front door-knocker thudding with great force in a resounding tattoo brought each lady upright with a start, for one moment convinced that the Wicked Uncle himself must be at the door.

'My goodness, who can that be?' Mrs Blackstock demanded, putting down her quill.

'Someone's very superior footman, I should imagine,' Tallie replied, getting up to edge the curtain aside and peep out into the dark, wet street. 'That was a fine example of the London Knock if ever I heard one. It is too dark outside, I cannot make out who it is. Oh, yes, now Annie has opened the door I can see the livery. Why, surely that is one of Lady Parry's footmen! I wonder why she is sending me a message here, she always sends orders to the shop.'

Annie came in, her sharp face flushed with importance. 'There's this footman, mam, and he's brought this letter for Miss Grey, mam. Cor, he is tall, mam.'

'Thank you, Annie,' Mrs Blackstock said repressively. 'Wait and see if Miss Grey has a reply for him.'

Tallie turned the letter over in her hands, then, realising that she was never going to find out what it was about until she opened it, cracked the seal in a shower of red wax and spread out the single sheet.

'But how strange!'

'What?' Zenna demanded at last, when, after the one exclamation, Tallie fell silent.

'Why, Lady Parry asks me to call at ten on Monday morning upon a personal matter. Annie, please say to the footman that Miss Grey will be happy to call as Lady Parry asks. Can you remember that?'

'Yes, miss.' The maid closed the door behind her, mouthing the words of the message silently.

'What can it mean, Zenna?'

Tallie handed the letter to Zenna, who scanned it and handed it back with a shrug. 'I have no more idea than you, goose.' Her friend laughed. 'Perhaps she wants to set you up in your own millinery business, producing exclusive hats only for her and her circle of bosom friends.'

'Now that would be wonderful,' Tallie agreed, smiling back. 'But somehow I do not think it likely.' Rack her brains as she might, she could think of no plausible explanation for the mysterious note and she could not help but feel a twinge of apprehension at the thought of another visit to Bruton Street so soon. What if she met Lord Arndale again? 'I wish tomorrow were not Sunday,' she said with a little shiver. 'I hate mysteries and being kept in suspense.'

* * *

Sunday did indeed drag, despite Matins at St Marylebone Church and a damp walk in Regent's Park. By mid-afternoon Tallie was disgusted to find herself apprehensive and, as she described it to Zenna, 'all of a fidget'.

'But what on earth is the matter with you?' her friend enquired, looking up at Tallie quizzically from her position on the hearthrug where she was burning her fingers roasting chestnuts. They had the parlour to themselves and had settled down to an afternoon of comfortable relaxation before the chilly walk to church for evensong.

Tallie considered confessing that her wild imagination was conjuring up images of Lord Arndale denouncing her to Lady Parry as an immoral and wanton young woman who posed nude for artists, but the words would not form on her lips. 'I am afraid I may have done something to displease Lady Parry and she is summoning me to say that she no longer requires my services,' she blurted out at last.

'What nonsense,' Zenna stated. 'Ouch! Oh, do pass that bowl, Tallie—these are so hot.' She dropped the nuts into the dish and gave the matter some thought while she sucked her fingers. 'Even if you *had* displeased her, surely she would write to Madame d'Aunay, not ask you to call?'

Not if Lord Arndale had told her such a scandalous story, Tallie thought miserably. Lady Parry was too kind to spread such a tale abroad, but she would certainly not tolerate continuing contact with such an abandoned young woman.

Zenna twisted round on the rug and studied Tallie's face thoughtfully. 'Has this anything to do with that incident at the studio the other day?' she demanded.

'Oh! How did you guess? Zenna, I met the man who found me in the closet—I would know his voice anywhere. And he is Lady Parry's trustee and nephew and he came to the house when I was there last.'

'And did he cry, "There is that beautiful woman I saw in a state of nature the other day"? Or did he quite fail to recognise you face on, fully clad, with your hair up and a bonnet on your head?'

'He did not recognise me then, I am sure of it. But, Zenna, he may have thought about it afterwards and something might have jogged his memory…'

'What nonsense. You told me you had your hair loose and it was falling around your face, did you not? It is a lovely colour, but not such an unusual shade that he could recognise you from it—and you look very different with it up, in any case. Besides,

I somehow feel it would not have been your hair he would have been looking at.'

Zenna got to her feet and took the bowl of chestnuts from Tallie's limp grasp. 'If you are not going to eat these, I most certainly am. Do you really think that he took so much notice of you? At Lady Parry's, I mean? He would have had to be made of stone not to take notice before, of course.'

'No, you are quite right, Zenna. I am being foolish. All he saw at Lady Parry's was a milliner, not a young lady, or an artist's model.'

'Ah, but you rather wish he had.'

Tallie made a face at her friend, but some treacherous part of her mind did indeed wish that those lazy grey eyes had looked at her and seen neither a naked model nor a humble menial, but the real young lady beneath those guises. *Stop it*, she thought. *He is dangerous*, and leaned over to take a still-hot chestnut from the bowl.

But a long night tossing and turning did nothing to calm Tallie's nervous apprehension. She dressed with care and penned a note to her employer explaining that she had been called away for the day unexpectedly and sent little Annie off to deliver it, keeping her fingers crossed that Madame would not take exception to this rare absence.

Tallie took a hackney carriage, reluctant to risk arriving either late or windswept on Lady Parry's doorstep, but even a safe and punctual arrival did not make her feel any better.

Rainbird opened the front door with his usual stately demeanour, although a spark of something more than welcome showed in his eyes as he regarded the shabby visitor. 'Good morning, Miss Grey. Her ladyship asked me to show you through to the library.'

Tallie followed across the hall to a door she had never entered on her previous visits and was startled when Rainbird opened it and announced with some emphasis, 'Miss Grey.' It was not treatment she was used to and Tallie looked around the room with interest as she entered.

The first person she saw was Lord Arndale standing by a heavy mahogany desk set in the window embrasure. He had apparently been leaning over studying a document spread before the other occupant of the room and had glanced up at Rainbird's announcement. Tallie's heart gave a hard thump at the sight of him and she looked in confusion at the other man, a complete stranger to her.

The two could hardly have been a greater contrast. Nick Stangate towered over his seated companion, broad shoulders filling his riding coat, everything about him seeming to exude life and ruthlessly controlled energy. The other man was more than twice his age, his hair scant and greying, his face thin and of an unhealthy shade. His eyes, though, were sharp and intelligent and Tallie almost stepped back as he fixed them on her face.

There was no sign of Lady Parry and, in the few seconds of silence as the two men regarded her, Tallie felt the colour ebbing out of her face. Why she should feel she was on trial in some way she had no idea, unless it was her guilty awareness of her scandalous secret.

As Mr Dover rose to his feet Nick Stangate straightened up and studied the young woman who had been shown in. The same shabby gown and pelisse as before; the same rather elegant bonnet, but this time she looked as though she had passed a very indifferent night. He stopped speculating as his companion spoke.

'Miss Grey, good morning. We have not met: I am James Dover, Miss Gower's attorney at law. I believe you are acquainted with Lord Arndale, who is her executor?'

Now, what the devil had there been in that introduction to cause her to go white to the lips? Nick stepped forward and took her hand. 'Miss Grey, you have gone quite pale. Are you unwell? Please, sit here.'

She did not resist him as he urged her gently into a chair. 'I am sorry, my lord, I am being foolish. It is just that meeting a lawyer brought back the memory of the last encounters I had with members of Mr Dover's profession. You must forgive me, sir,' she added, turning to the older man. 'I mean no disrespect, Mr Dover. The situation when my father, and then my mother, died was…difficult.'

Nick realised that he was still holding her hand lightly in his. Her wrist felt cold under his fingers and she looked up to meet his eyes. Hers were candid, green and intelligent. He realised that although she must be deeply puzzled she had asked no questions. Her reticence was refreshing and also disconcerting. 'I am sorry we alarmed you, Miss Grey, your pulse is racing.' Her gaze dropped, and on an impulse he added, 'For a moment I thought you had a guilty secret.'

There was a silence. Then her eyes flew back to his face and to his surprise Nick saw the colour staining her throat, rising up to her cheeks. Without meaning to he had touched a raw spot and some hunter's instinct in him stirred. Instinctively his grasp on her wrist tightened and she pulled her hand free, leaving Nick staring down at her bent head in wild speculation. He thought he had found out all there was to know about Miss Talitha Grey. Had his investigators been so careless as to have missed a scandal?

With a rustle of skirts his aunt swept in. 'I am sorry to have kept you all. Good morning, Miss Grey. I do hope you did not get wet—it is a perfectly dreadful morning is it not?'

'Indeed, my lady,' Tallie agreed. She stood up and bobbed a curtsy. Nick saw her hand go to the wrist he had been grasping. Had he hurt her? She had made no protest. 'On days like this one wonders if spring will ever come,' she added politely.

'Do sit down, everyone.' Lady Parry took the chair next to Tallie, and regarded the men. 'You have introduced yourselves? Excellent. Well, Mr Dover, you had better explain to Miss Grey, who is doubtless wondering what on earth this is all about, why she has been asked to come here this morning.'

Mr Dover inclined his head, adjusted his spectacles, coughed and flattened the document before him with one hand. Nick, to whom none of this was new, watched Talitha from under hooded lids. Her first reaction was going to be very instructive.

'Miss Grey, as I told you, I was the attorney at law to Miss Gower and, with Lord Arndale here, it falls to me to administer her will.' He paused and regarded Tallie benevolently. 'I have to tell you that you are remembered in that document.'

'Oh, how very kind of Miss Gower!' To Nick's surprise he saw her eyes were filling with tears. Why had he thought her so composed that she would not give way to emotion? She hastily pulled her handkerchief from her reticule. 'I beg your pardon.' She dabbed her eyes, tried to speak, tried again and with an apparent effort managed to say, 'I will treasure any keepsake that she has left me; I was very fond of her.'

Nick chuckled softly to himself. If she thought she had inherited a pretty ornament or a book or two, Miss Grey was in for a surprise. He was startled as she shot him a reproachful glance. She was not going to pretend she was not affected by the old lady's thoughtfulness, the expression said as plainly as though she had spoken, even if his lordship found a milliner's gratitude for a trifling gift amusing. He absorbed the reproof silently. What very expressive eyes she had…

'It amounts to rather more than a keepsake, Miss Grey,' the lawyer said, smiling at her. 'I am happy to tell you that you stand to inherit fifty thousand pounds.'

'But…but that is…'

'Several thousand pounds a year if invested prudently. I must congratulate you.'

'I was going to say "impossible",' Tallie stammered. 'There must be some mistake, surely? Lady Parry?'

Appealed to, Lady Parry shook her head, laughing kindly at Tallie's confusion. 'No mistake, my dear. Miss Gower knew of your history, as I do. You must forgive us for looking into the past of such an unusual young milliner as you are. You must also forgive us for a little plot to restore you to the sort of life to which you were born and bred. It gave Miss Gower such pleasure to think of the difference this would make for you.'

Tallie looked from one face to another, her gaze skimming hastily over Nick's, set in an unhelpfully bland expression. She finally settled on the lawyer. 'But, Mr Dover, is this legal? I am no relative of Miss Gower's—surely someone else has a better claim to her fortune?'

'She was so devoid of relatives that she had to borrow me from my aunt to stand in as a nephew and executor,' Nick remarked, reaching the decision that she was as genuinely incredulous as she appeared and liking her for the lack of any sign of pleasure at the inheritance. No grasping little miss, this one. 'You are cheating no one of their dues.'

'But her servants, her friends…'

'Her servants have been left well provided with generous annuities and her few close friends such as myself have all been left keepsakes—pictures, jewellery and so forth.' His aunt leaned across and patted her hand. 'None of us need her money, my dear Miss Grey. It is quite all right. This is not a dream, and you are perfectly entitled to your inheritance.'

Mr Dover got to his feet and began to shuffle papers into a portfolio. 'You will need a day or so to recover from the surprise, Miss Grey, but I will write to confirm what I have said and you will doubtless be able to furnish me with the direction of your bank and your man of business.' He tied the cords around the folder and bowed to the ladies. 'Your ladyship, Miss Grey, I bid you good day.'

Lady Parry got to her feet. 'If I could just have a word, Mr Dover. There is the question of Miss Gower's house—the staff asked me for advice on several matters, which I am sure you are far better equipped than I to answer. Miss Grey, would you be comfortable here for a few minutes? There is something I would very much like to discuss with you.'

The door closed behind her, leaving Nick alone with Miss Grey. Now was as good a time as any to confirm what his agents had found out about this young woman who had so won the hearts of his aunt and Miss Gower. Was she all she seemed? And what was the guilty secret that made her blush so? He suppressed a stirring of interest, which he recognised as sensual. She was far from his usual type; possibly that other blonde in the studio had had more of an effect than he thought.

Tallie was unconscious of the regard bent upon her face. She found it difficult to concentrate on what she had just been told, it was too unbeliev-able. Instead she found her mind wandering to the *Peerage*, which she had rather secretively conned the day before. Nicholas Stangate, 3rd Earl of Arn-dale… The family seat in Hertfordshire, a town house in Brook Street. Unmarried, twenty-nine years old with no brothers or sisters…

'You do not appear very pleased by the news you have just received,' he remarked, sinking into the seat opposite hers and leaning back. Tallie looked at him: he appeared completely relaxed, but his gaze was anything but casual.

'I was not thinking about it,' she admitted. She waited for that dark brow to lift, and, as she had anticipated, it did. Despite everything she smiled slightly, liking the expression of dry humour.

'I have said something to amuse you?'

'No, it was just that I was expecting you to raise one eyebrow when I admitted to such odd behaviour—and you did.'

Both brows shot up and he grinned at her disarmingly, instantly subtracting years from his age as the cool reserve vanished. 'I am appalled that I am so predictable in my mannerisms. I can see that acquaintanceship with you will be a salutary experience, Miss Grey.' She dropped her eyes, suddenly conscious of how intimate the conversation seemed, alone in the room with him. 'Not only do you have a keen eye to depress affectation, but you have a mind above the acquisition of a fortune. Do tell me, how is it you can dismiss fifty thousand pounds with such ease?'

'Oh, no! I cannot do that.' Her eyes lifted swiftly. 'No, you misunderstand me, my lord. It is such a shock that it does not seem real. I cannot think about it without becoming confused, so I was just letting my mind wander until I felt more rational.'

'Then I think you should have a glass of sherry, which will restore the tone of your mind a little, and we can discuss it. You will have some practical affairs to consider almost immediately.' He saw her dubious expression as he reached for the decanter that stood on a table beside his chair. 'Now, what is disturbing you, Miss Grey? The thought of consuming wine at this hour of the day or my presumption in making free with my aunt's decanters? If it is the former, think of it as medicine for your shock; if the latter, rest assured that I take no liberties without my aunt's permission.'

Tallie bit her lip in vexation. Was she *so* easy to read that he could observe her every emotion in her face? 'Neither, my lord. It is simply that I do not feel that it is my place to be—'

'But what *is* your place, Miss Grey?' He reached over and handed her the glass before picking up his own. 'To your good fortune, and to your happy restoration to your natural position in Society.'

Tallie took an experimental sip and decided she liked the taste. It still felt very strange to be having such a conversation with a gentleman, let alone this one, but she refused to appear a simpering miss, so she retorted frankly, 'If I knew what that was, I might welcome my restoration to it, my lord!'

'I wish you would call me Nick.'

'Certainly not, Lord Arndale!'

'You could adopt me as an honorary cousin,' he suggested gravely. 'Miss Gower considered me as a nephew and, as you are her heiress, I am sure that makes us cousins.'

In spite of her efforts Tallie could not help but

laugh. 'I beg leave to tell you that this is ridiculous, *my lord*. I stand in no need of cousins, only of a recommendation to a bank and to a respectable man of business who is used to managing the affairs of single ladies, and I am sure Lady Parry will be kind enough to suggest how I go about finding those.'

At that moment her ladyship opened the door and sailed in with her usual energy, smiling gratefully at Nick as he stood to offer her the chair he had been occupying.

'I see the two of you are getting on famously, which is just as I had hoped,' she announced, sinking down and smiling at Tallie. 'Now, Nicholas, pour me a glass of sherry and be off with you; Miss Grey and I have plans to make.'

He handed her the glass and began to stroll out of the room but halted by Tallie's chair. 'I will bid you good day, Miss Grey. I have every expectation of seeing a great deal of you in the near future.' Lady Parry appeared to notice nothing odd in his voice, but Tallie was left uncertain as to whether she had just received a threat or a promise.

Chapter Five

Lady Parry regarded Tallie silently for a moment, then remarked, 'My nephew is anticipating a suggestion I am about to make to you, Miss Grey—Talitha, if I may call you that. Do I have it correctly?'

'Yes, ma'am, I agree it is very unusual. I was named for a great-aunt. Please, do call me that or better, Tallie, which is what my friends call me.'

'Tallie, then.' Lady Parry hesitated, an unusual occurrence for someone so decided, then said carefully, 'You must forgive me, my dear Tallie, if you find me interfering.' She waved into silence Tallie's immediate protest. 'I told you that Miss Gower and I took pleasure in our little plot to re-establish you to what, if it was not for the sad and untimely demise of your parents, would have been your natural position in Society.'

'But, ma'am, even if my father had lived, I would

not have expected one-twentieth of this fortune as my portion!'

'Perhaps not, but I am sure you would have been able to live a life of comfort and security and to make your come-out, would you not?' She waited for Tallie's nod of agreement, then pressed on. 'Now you find yourself all alone without the family to assist with your belated entry into Society and perhaps you are a little nervous of how to go on.'

'But I do not look to make a come-out, ma'am,' Tallie protested. 'I am much too old! I have not been able to give this any thought, but perhaps I should find myself a house, in a country town maybe, where I may live respectably with a companion—'

'And wither into an old maid?' Lady Parry interrupted. 'Nonsense! What a waste that would be. How old are you, child?'

'Five and twenty, ma'am.'

'Indeed, you do not look it, and you will look it even less when your hair is dressed and you are clothed as befits your station. There is not the slightest reason why you should not come out this Season, and even less why you should not find any number of most eligible suitors when you do. Not, of course, the young sprigs such as my son—they will all be too busy flirting with silly little chits just out of the schoolroom, as green as they are themselves. No, you will attract the slightly older men, those who are bored with vapid girls in their first Season and who look for character and intelligence as well as a pretty face and good breeding.'

Tallie blinked. This fairy-tale picture was so far from her imaginings that she could not believe Lady Parry was serious. 'But—'

'But me no buts! Really, my dear, are you attempting to tell me that you had resigned yourself to your life of industry and self-reliance; that you dreamed no dreams?'

'Why, no, ma'am, I mean, yes, I had resigned myself. What use are dreams when one must worry day to day whether one can continue to support a respectable style of living, however modest?' *Perhaps some dreams*, her conscience prompted her. *Perhaps some dreams about cool grey eyes and a lazily amused, deep voice...*

'Then you must learn to dream, Tallie. In fact, you must learn to make your dreams reality.'

'I would need a chaperon,' Tallie said doubtfully. 'I believe one can hire gentlewomen who arrange come-outs...'

'Shabby genteel, most of them,' Lady Parry said dismissively. 'What I was going to suggest was that you come here to stay with me and I launch you this Season. There, what do you say to that?'

Tallie felt her mouth fall open unbecomingly and shut it with a snap. 'Lady Parry…ma'am…I could not possibly impose upon you. Thank you so much for such a wonderful offer, but—'

'I have told you, Tallie, no buts!' The older woman leaned forward and took Tallie's right hand in hers. 'My dear, let me confide in you. I have no daughter, no nieces and I long for the fun of launching a débutante upon a Season. I want the company, I want to have a lively young person to shop with, to gossip with, to watch over and hope for. I want a daughter—and you need a mama. What could be more perfect?' Tallie stared at her speechlessly, feeling like Cinderella, whirled from her cold hearth into the glittering ballroom at the palace at the wave of a magic wand. 'Do say yes!'

Feeling as though she was stepping into space, Tallie whispered, 'Yes.' Then her voice returned to her. 'Oh, yes, your ladyship, if you are quite sure I would be no trouble…'

'I *want* you to be a trouble! I want to plot and plan and make lists and schemes. We must think of parties and dances and I must make sure all the most influential hostesses know about you. Vouchers for Almack's, drives in the parks. Gowns, a riding horse, dancing lessons… We will be worn out, my dear, never fear. Oh, yes, and will you not call me Aunt Kate?'

'I could never...' Tallie saw her ladyship's expressive face fall and smiled helplessly. 'If you really wish me to, ma'am...Aunt Kate. I will do my very best not to disappoint you and to be useful.'

'Then you may start by pulling the bell rope for Rainbird. Will you be ready to move here in a week, do you think? Ah, Rainbird, has my nephew left yet?'

'He is on the point of doing so, my lady. Shall I request him to step in here?'

Nick Stangate put his head around the door, sending a sharp glance from his aunt's animated expression to Tallie's stunned face. 'I see my aunt has outlined her scheme, Miss Grey.'

'And dear Tallie has accepted my suggestion,' Lady Parry responded gleefully. 'Will you drive Miss Grey home, Nicholas? You may tell her your thoughts on a suitable bank and man of business while you are about it.' Taking his assent as read, she got to her feet and enveloped Tallie in a warm embrace. 'Off you go with Lord Arndale and I will speak to the housekeeper about your room. I did not dare tempt fate by making anything ready before I had spoken to you.'

Dazedly murmuring her thanks, Tallie allowed

herself to be swept into the hallway and out to where a groom was standing patiently at the head of a pair of match bays harnessed to a rakish high-perch phaeton.

Nick Stangate helped her up into a seat, which seemed dangerously far above the roadway, and swung himself up beside her. 'Let them go, Chivers.'

They wove through the traffic in silence for a few minutes, then Nick remarked, 'Stunned into silence by your good fortune, Miss Grey?'

'Yes,' she admitted baldly. 'It all seems like a dream—the money, Lady Kate's wonderful offer, a Season... And last week I was worrying about whether I could afford a new gown and—' She broke off, biting her lip.

'And?'

'And Miss Gower and thinking about how shallow it was to worry about such a little thing as old gowns or muddy hatboxes when someone for whom you have affection and respect is reaching the end of their life.'

'And you had no idea of her intentions towards you?' He reined in to allow an old-fashioned closed carriage to draw away from the kerbside, then let the bays ease back into a trot, watchfully negotiating the Bond Street traffic.

'Why, no, not the slightest hint. It is so improbable, so like a fairy story I still cannot believe it.'

There was a hint of laughter in his voice as he said, 'Miss Gower as the fairy godmother—yes, I can imagine her in that role, wearing one of those outrageous hats you used to make for her.'

'She liked them as pretty as they could be,' Tallie said defensively. 'I am glad she saw the last one I made for her; it was quite impossibly pink with as much ruched silk ribbon as I could fit under the brim and a big rose.'

'I saw it,' Nick assured her. 'She had it on the stand by her bed and showed it off to all her visitors—' He broke off, then added, 'Do you have a handkerchief?'

'I am so sorry.' Tallie scrabbled in her reticule and blew her nose. 'You must think me a positive watering pot, I seem to be weeping on virtually every occasion we meet.'

'Not at all. No one can help their eyes watering after a blow to the…er, middle, and to shed a tear at the reading of a will is a most natural reaction, I am sure.'

He sounded indifferent rather than sympathetic and Tallie, who had began to warm to him for telling her about Miss Gower's hat, frowned.

'So my aunt persuaded you to come and stay in

Bruton Street?' he observed as they crossed Oxford
Street.

'Yes,' Tallie agreed, flushing at the coolness in
his tone. 'Do you not feel that is a good idea?'

'I am sure it will be very much to your benefit.'

Was she imagining the slight emphasis on *your*?
'You feel I am not a suitable person for Lady Kate
to sponsor?' she asked, keeping the anger out of her
voice with an effort. 'You think perhaps I am not
who I purport to be? Or perhaps you object to my
employment at Madame d'Aunay's?'

Nick shot her a hard glance. 'I know that you are
precisely who you say you are,' he replied. 'I made
it my business to find out. And I am sure that your
employment as a milliner has been entirely respectable.'

The furious retort that rose to Tallie's lips went
unspoken. *Of course* he had to check on her, he
was his aunt's trustee. It was his duty to protect his
widowed relative. How was Lord Arndale to know
that she was not an adventuress, ready to prey upon
Lady Kate's kind heart, or someone who would
bring scandal to the household?

Then as they crossed Weymouth Street into Upper
Wimpole Street her heart seemed to stop with a
sickening jolt. But she *was* just such a person! She
had kept her shocking secret about Mr Harland's

studio because she had feared disgrace and being branded immoral. But what would be simply a personal shame to a young milliner would be an utter scandal if it was exposed in the household of a Society lady.

Tallie realised that Nick had asked her a question. 'I am sorry, you said something?' Was her voice shaking?

'I asked if I am correct in saying it is the house just here on the left with the green front door?'

'Yes.' Of course he knew the address, he must have been checking on all of her circumstances and connections. He would know all about the humble lodging-house and its inhabitants and the fact that they were women earning their own way in the world. Did he know about Mr Harland? Surely not, he would have mentioned something as scandalous as that.

Nick reined in the horses and half-turned on the seat to look at her. 'Are you quite well, Miss Grey?'

'Yes. Yes, of course, my lord.' He looked at her for a long minute; Tallie stared back defiantly, expecting to see that cold grey, inquisitorial look in his eyes, but all they revealed was a concern and a warmth that completely unsettled her. The events of the day had overwhelmed her other senses and perceptions; now she was aware of him again as a man, a disturbing physical presence and an unreadable intelligence.

Behind her she was vaguely aware of the front door opening, but her eyes seemed locked with Nick's.

'Tallie! Thank good…I mean, Miss Grey, you are home.' It was Zenna, sounding uncharacteristically flurried. Tallie turned in her seat, conscious of a strange feeling; part relief, part resentment.

'Zenna! Please will you give me a hand down? I am sure his lordship will not want to let go his reins.' Zenna hurried down the steps and stretched up a hand while Tallie jumped down. 'My lord, may I introduce my friend? Zenobia, this is Lord Arndale, who has kindly driven me back from Lady Parry's. My lord, Miss Scott.'

Lord Arndale raised his hat. 'Miss Scott, good afternoon. Miss Grey, I will send details of a bank that I can recommend; should you wish me to accompany you to their offices, I am entirely at your disposal.'

Tallie tried to order her thoughts and behave like a young lady for whom a banker was a necessary adjunct to everyday life. Beside her Zenna was waiting silently; Tallie could feel the waves of antipathy coming from her like the heat from a fire.

Startled, she glanced from Nick Stangate to her

friend. He was sitting patiently awaiting her reply, his gaze resting on the two plainly clad young women. Tallie was beginning to be able to interpret his apparently indifferent regard; it appeared Zenna was able to do instinctively. There was assessment in those grey eyes regarding them—assessment and disapproval.

She collected her straying thoughts and said politely, 'Thank you, my lord, that would be most kind. Good day.' She dropped the slightest of curtsies and turned to mount the steps. 'Are you returning inside, Miss Scott?'

As the door closed behind them, cutting off the sound of Lord Arndale's carriage wheels on the cobbles, Zenna said furiously, 'Insufferable man! Is he the one who…?'

'Yes, Lady Parry's nephew, as I told you the other day. But why do you say he is insufferable?'

Tallie took off her bonnet and gloves and followed the still fuming Zenna into the parlour. His regard had certainly been cool, but Zenna's life as a governess had inured her to snubs and she had always seemed to shrug them off.

Zenna appeared flustered, then she said slowly, 'I really do not know, but something in his regard infuriated me. I could feel my hair rising like a cat seeing a dog!' She brooded for a moment. 'I have it: he disapproves of me as your friend, not in principle. He does not like seeing you on good terms with a humble governess.'

'Nonsense,' Tallie retorted. 'I am a humble milliner, if it comes to that.' Not for much longer, an inner voice reminded her. 'And in any case, what is it to Lord Arndale what company I keep?' Even as she said it, the thought intruded that as his aunt's trustee Nick Stangate had every legitimate interest in the company she kept—and that included Miss Grey's friends.

'Do have a care, Tallie, I am so worried about Millie; the thought that both of you might be the prey of rakes is too worrying to contemplate!'

'Lord Arndale's interest in me and my connections has nothing to do with any amorous intentions, I can assure you.' Tallie allowed herself one flickering moment's contemplation of being the object of such desires and hastily suppressed the thought. 'I will explain it all in a minute—but do tell me what is so concerning you about Millie.'

Zenna paced around the room, too agitated to join her friend on the sofa. 'I walked back from the Langton house across the Park and there was Millie, with no female companion at all, arm in arm with this man.'

'He may have been a perfectly respectable admirer.'

'You know as well as I that, given her profession, Millie cannot hope to make a *respectable* connection with anyone of the *ton*! And this man is nothing if not a member of the most fashionable set—his clothes, his air, everything about him. If his intentions were respectable, why did he not welcome an introduction to one of Millie's friends?'

'He did not, then?'

Zenna flushed angrily. 'I was comprehensively snubbed; not that Millie noticed, it was very smoothly done and she is obviously too entranced by him to see what is under her nose.'

No wonder Zenna had reacted so strongly to Nick Stangate's cold and judgemental regard. 'Do you know his name?'

'A Mr Hemsley. Millie calls him Jack.' Zenna, who was finally sitting down on the sofa, caught her friend's look of alarmed recognition. 'You know him?'

'Oh, yes,' Tallie said grimly. 'He is an acquaintance of Lord Arndale and the Parrys, and he was the man who led the pack of them hunting for me in the studio. I saw him again when I last delivered hats to Lady Parry. You are quite correct to be worried, Zenna, he is a complete rake and I am certain can have no respectable reason for paying attention to Millie.'

'What can we do? Should we speak to Mrs Blackstock?'

They regarded each other dubiously. 'It might have been a chance meeting,' Zenobia said. 'I would not wish to upset Millie by questioning her judgement.'

'And we would be suggesting that she might behave imprudently if we were to mention it to Mrs Blackstock...' Tallie's voice trailed away. 'We must keep a quiet eye on Millie. It is possible that, if his intentions are dishonourable, the realisation that she has attentive friends will deter him.'

Zenna nodded decisively. 'Yes, I agree, that is the best plan.'

An awkward silence followed their decision on what action to take over Millie's unsuitable admirer. Tallie knew Zenna would be expecting her to tell all about the mysterious request to call upon Lady Parry and she must be equally curious as to why Tallie was being driven home by the very man she was so wary of. But Zenna would not pry and Tallie found her own tongue stumbling over what should be a perfectly simple piece of news.

But it was not so simple, she realised. As the fog of shock and confused delight at the news cleared, things became more and more complicated and delicate.

All her friends were in very straitened circumstances. They would greet the news of her good fortune with unenvious delight, she was sure, but her immediate, unthinking instinct to give money away and make life easier for them was fraught with difficulties.

How could she do it without appearing to patronise and putting them in a position where what had been a friendship of equals would be shadowed by inequality? An outright offer of money would wound the pride of any of them, but she did so much want to help lift the anxiety of making ends meet day after day from all three, just as it had been miraculously lifted from her.

'Zenna,' she began tentatively.

'Yes? Do you want to tell me about this morning? Has something unpleasant happened?'

'No, nothing unpleasant—far from it. But I have had such a shock my head is spinning and I hardly know what to think or do.'

'Lord Arndale has proposed?' Zenna enquired.

'Proposed? No! Certainly not! Why should he do such a thing?' Tallie felt so hot and bothered at the very idea that she completely lost her train of thought and simply stared at her friend.

Zenna shrugged. 'Just a fancy that crossed my mind.' Tallie regarded her, astonished, until she retorted, 'Well, he is quite extraordinarily good-looking.'

'Zenna!'

'I might be a spinster governess, but there is nothing wrong with my eyesight and I can recognise an attractive man when I see one, even if I do not care for him,' her friend replied somewhat snappishly.

'Yes, of course you can,' Tallie apologised hastily. 'Do you really think him so handsome?'

It was Zenna's turn to stare. 'There appears to be something amiss with *your* eyesight, Talitha. But never mind Lord Arndale—what happened if it is nothing to do with him?'

'Dear Miss Gower who died the other week has left me a legacy in her will,' Tallie said cautiously.

'Oh, how thoughtful of her. What is it? A piece of jewellery or a small sum of money?'

'That is what I expected when they told me, but, Zenna—it is fifty thousand pounds.'

'Fifty thou…are you sure? Not fifty or five hundred?'

'That is what I thought at first, but there is no

mistake. She has left me her entire fortune, beyond legacies to friends and servants.'

'How wonderful!' Zenna hugged Tallie hard, then sat back with a face radiant with pleasure at her friend's good fortune. 'What are you going to do now?'

'I hardly know, it is such a surprise.' An idea suddenly struck her and, without giving herself time to worry about details, Tallie said, 'I must make some sensible investments, of course. Zenna, you know you have always said your dream is to have your own school? Why do we not go into partnership and do just that?'

'I do not have any money,' Zenna protested. But Tallie saw the sudden flare of excitement in her eyes.

'Yes, but you have all the skills and know how a school should be run. I will provide the money for the house and so forth, you manage the school. And,' she added as Zenna opened her mouth to argue, 'I would hope to find somewhere large enough for me to make it my home as well, if you should not object.'

'Object? Object! Tallie, do you really mean it? How wonderful, there are so many things I want to try, so many new ideas about the education of girls—' She broke off. 'But you have not given this any thought yet, have you? You must do so, and take advice. And, in any case, why on earth would you want to live in a girls' school? With this fortune you can be a Society lady.'

'I am too old, Zenna, and I know no one.'

'Nonsense.' Zenna leapt to her feet and began to pace the room. 'Lady Parry would advise you.'

'She already has,' Tallie admitted. 'She has invited me to stay with her and make my come-out under her aegis.'

'Did you not agree? That is a marvellous opportunity, you could not hope for anything more fortunate.'

'Yes, I did agree, but now I think I must tell her I have changed my mind,' Tallie said slowly. Her conscience was pricking her very badly and she knew that, whatever her views might be about Lord Arndale's opinions, she owed it to her kind patroness to ensure that she brought not a whiff of scandal to her household.

She met Zenna's bemused gaze and blurted out, 'I must tell her about my work for Mr Harland. I cannot risk the scandal if anything came out, it would be a dreadful way to repay her kindness.' She did not add the other consideration, which had been looming large ever since she saw Lord Arndale's inimical stare fixed upon her friend.

If a respectable governess was not considered a suitable acquaintance for the newly wealthy Miss Grey, what would Lady Parry make of a lodging-house keeper and an opera dancer?

'I must speak to her this afternoon,' she said resolutely. 'I will thank her for her kindness, but she will see that I am an unsuitable recipient of it. Better to do it at once, before she has the chance to make any further plans on my behalf.'

Zenna shook her head sadly. 'You must do as you think fit, of course, but it is such a shame that you will not make a come-out.'

'Never mind. Tomorrow we can start to make plans for the school—if that idea is still agreeable to you.'

'How can it be anything else? I cannot believe my good fortune—I declare I feel as dazed as you look, Tallie dearest.' She broke off at the sound of the front door opening. 'That must be Mrs Blackstock. What will you tell her?'

'Nothing yet, I think. I have no wish to embarrass our friends with the size of my inheritance, although I would value your advice about how I might help them at some point. I think perhaps tomorrow we can tell her of our plans and give notice. If she finds other tenants before the school is ready, we can always find lodgings together, or go to an hotel.'

'An hotel?' Zenna echoed, wide-eyed.

'Why, yes,' Tallie said recklessly. 'I can afford it, after all!'

This frivolity did not last much beyond luncheon. Zenna was distractedly making lists, breaking off to suck her pen, gaze into space and then resume her scribbling.

But Tallie was imagining how disappointed in her Lady Parry was going to be when she discovered that her protégée was so abandoned as to supplement her living by posing naked.

Chapter Six

Rainbird hid any reaction he felt at Tallie's second, unexpected, call of the day. 'Her ladyship is At Home, Miss Grey, and has no one with her at present.'

'Talitha! What a nice surprise.' Lady Parry put down the book she was reading and looked up with a pleased smile as Tallie was announced. 'Come and sit down by me.'

'I…I think I would rather stand, ma'am.' Tallie took a deep breath and said, 'I am very sorry to appear ungracious, Lady Parry, but I feel I should not have accepted your kind offer this morning and I thought I should come and say so immediately.'

'Why ever not? My poor child, stop standing there looking like a parlour maid who has broken the best Minton and sit down. There, that is better. Now, I know you must have had a shock this morning, but—'

'It is not that, ma'am. I had not considered what a difficult position I would be putting you in.'

'Because you have had to work for your living? If I do not regard it, be certain that Society will not—not when they learn of your family and fortune, and observe your ladylike deportment.'

'My friends, ma'am—'

'Your friends are more than welcome in my house, Talitha.'

'Lady Parry,' Tallie said with some emphasis, feeling she was being swept along faster than she wanted, 'my only friends are a governess, a lodging-house keeper and an opera dancer. I do not believe you could have been aware of that fact when you made your kind offer just now.'

'I have never met a governess who was not respectable and I am sure if the lodging-house in question is where you make your home, its proprietress is bound to be most acceptable.'

'The opera dancer is her niece and lives with us,' Tallie persisted.

'And is she a nice girl?'

'Very. And despite what the world thinks of actresses and performers, she is a modest, virtuous and respectable young woman into the bargain.'

'There now, so where is the problem?'

'You would not object if I were to continue my friendships?'

'Certainly not. Your friends are most welcome in my home whenever they wish to call upon you.'

'Thank you, ma'am. But not everyone will be of your opinion.'

'By everyone, I assume you mean my nephew?'

'Er…I…' Tallie had no wish to tell tales or to sound in any way critical of Lady Parry's family.

'And which of your friends has Nicholas been viewing with that chilly eye of his?'

'Miss Scott, the governess.'

'Foolish boy—he has always been overprotective. And has he set eyes upon the young lady from the opera yet?'

'I believe not.'

'He will,' his fond aunt prophesised cheerfully. 'At least, he probably already *has* met her if she is pretty. Never mind, Talitha. Whom I allow under my roof is my decision. Once Nicholas gets to know you better he will soon cease to worry.'

'That is not all, Lady Parry.'

'I thought we had agreed that you would call me Aunt Kate?'

'You will not wish me to when I tell you about the other matter, ma'am,' Tallie said, feeling ready to sink now that the moment for confession was upon her. 'I am not just a milliner, I have been earning my living in another way as well.'

'I know,' Lady Parry said calmly.

'You know? But, ma'am, you cannot…I have been sitting for an artist!'

'Indeed. Mr Harland, a most talented gentleman, I believe.'

'But, Lady Parry, how could you have discovered what I have been doing?'

Her ladyship held up a hand to silence Tallie as Rainbird appeared with a tea tray.

'Will you pour, my dear?' She waited while Tallie handed her her cup with a hand that trembled. 'A macaroon? No? You must not become so agitated, Talitha. I called upon Mr Harland a while ago as I am considering having my portrait painted. I observed a canvas and asked who the model was, for I thought I recognised her.'

'He told you?' Tallie was aghast, both at the thought that the compromising classical paintings had been displayed in the studio and that Mr Harland had been so indiscreet as to reveal her name.

'He was immediately very embarrassed at his slip. I am sure it was only because I said I thought I knew the model.'

'And you are not shocked, ma'am? The fact that

I was sitting for an artist at all, let alone the way I was…dressed.'

'Admittedly it was not the way in which one would normally wish an unmarried lady to be depicted, but under the circumstances I feel we should disregard it.'

'Circumstances?' Tallie said weakly.

'I can tell Mr Harland is a most respectable person and I am sure that his slip in revealing your name would not be repeated.'

Tallie was so taken aback that for a moment she could not find the words to continue.

Finally she ventured, 'But, ma'am, if it should be found out once I am launched in Society, it would reflect upon you. After all, I am of no account, but you are a leading member of the *ton*.'

'And have more than enough credit to carry off any little indiscretions of my protégée,' Lady Parry said with a chuckle. 'And it will not be long before you too are a figure in Society, mark my words. A fortune the size of yours is more than enough to cover up any number of indiscretions. Now then, you are still going to be able to move here in a week?'

'Yes, ma'am,' Tallie stammered.

'Aunt Kate, please, my dear Tallie. Goodness, is that the time? I am due at Lady Fraser's in an hour, and be seen in this gown I cannot and will not! No, there is no need for you to rush off, this is your home now. Just ring if you need anything.' Lady Parry sprang from the sofa on which she had been decoratively draped, fluttered across to drop a kiss on Tallie's cheek and was out of the room before the younger woman could do more than gasp,

'Goodbye.'

Tallie got slowly to her feet, too bemused to pull herself together and leave. She had been steeled to explain why she was an inappropriate person for Lady Parry to take under her wing and had found both her anxiety for her friends and her scrupulous confession about Mr Harland swept aside.

Which meant that in a week's time her former life also would be swept away and she would be making her come-out as a young lady of fashion. Her money worries would be about how to invest and spend it, not how to make enough to afford a new pelisse.

Tallie stood by the window and stared out at the fashionable street life bustling below her. She untied the ribbons of her bonnet and tossed it onto the sofa as though freeing her head would help her think, but things still seemed just as unreal and unbelievable as they had before.

'Back again, Miss Grey?' a voice behind her enquired. Tallie stiffened, but did not turn. He had entered without her hearing. 'Come to confess your secret?' Lord Arndale's voice sounded as uninterested as if he had enquired whether she had just returned from walking in the park.

Tallie felt the breath catch in her throat. She wanted… What did she want? Why had she had hardly a coherent, calm thought since this man had found her in the attic studio?

She found her voice suddenly. 'Confess? Yes, that is precisely what I have been doing, my lord.'

'You have?' Despite everything Tallie felt her mouth curve into a smile. So, she had managed to surprise the imperturbable Nick Stangate, had she?

'Yes, my lord.' Emboldened by the fact that she could not see his sardonic expression, Tallie wondered if it was safe to tease him further and decided against it. 'It appears that Lady Parry was already aware of the matter that was troubling me.'

'And?' He was coming closer; Tallie could see his reflection blurred in the window glass. How could she ever have said he made her feel safe?

'Lady Parry appears to feel I am refining too much about it. She does not regard it.' How her voice was staying so steady she had no idea.

Nick Stangate was standing at her shoulder, just behind her.

'And do you think I would share her opinion?' He had lowered his voice. It sounded faintly menacing in the quiet room.

'Without wishing to appear rude, my lord, your opinion does not concern me. But then you are Lady Parry's trustee, not her guardian, are you not, my lord?'

Had she overstepped the mark? It appeared not: there was a faint noise that she realised incredulously was a muffled snort of amusement. Then he was still.

'What scent are you wearing, Miss Grey?' The question was so unexpected it was all she could do not to spin round.

'Jasmine,' she replied. Was it her imagination, or was he so close that she could feel his breath on her nape?

'It reminds me of something,' Nick said slowly. 'No—somewhere, a place. But somewhere cold, dusty...'

'Really? How strange: I have always thought it a summer smell.' Then Tallie realised what he was remembering—the faint traces of her scent on her chilled, naked skin in the attic room. And he was standing as he had then, close by her left shoulder, close enough to touch, close enough to smell her fear and her perfume.

Talitha turned so swiftly that Nick had no opportunity to step back, even if he had wanted to. He stopped racking his memory for a trace of an elusive perfume as a far more intrusive sensation than curiosity flooded through his body. Simple desire. Damn it, why had he not realised the feelings that Talitha Grey evoked in him for what they were? It was not suspicion of the secret she openly admitted to him she was hiding. It was not even the perfectly natural protectiveness of his aunt that would mean he would take a sharp interest in any new acquaintance of hers.

His habitual honesty with himself answered his own question. He had been rather too preoccupied with another blonde young woman for him to have thought more clearly about this one until she had achieved this insidious effect on him.

Not that the two women were more than superficially similar, of course. That exquisite nymph huddling in the dirty attic closet was shorter than Miss Grey. Her hair had waved in tresses shot through with varied shades of gold, unlike the straight, pale gilt severity of the coiffure so close in front of him now. And she had quivered with fear, unlike the tense fierceness that this young woman showed in the face of his curiosity or disapproval.

Nick shook himself mentally. He had allowed his imagination to drift too often to that naked girl. She had proved a damnably uncomfortable preoccupation, so uncomfortable that he had been tempted to go back to the studio and ask for her name and direction. A natural fastidiousness had stopped him; to do so felt like an extension of Jack Hemsley's behaviour.

But how had he been so blind as not to appreciate the delicious feminine charms now standing so close to him? That reproof about not noticing a 'milliner's girl' was deserved. And how had he failed to look beyond that frightful pelisse to the charming figure beneath? Lord Arndale ruthlessly suppressed thought of just how Miss Grey would appear clad only in that length of sheer linen and smiled into the defiant green eyes.

'Naturally I bow to my aunt's good judgement. Can we not call it a truce, Miss Grey? After all, immediately after you heard of your good fortune we seemed to be on good enough terms, did we not?'

Yes, he had allowed himself to relax with her, succumb to the image she presented of the innocent young lady forced to fend for herself by harsh circumstances. And he had let her lull his suspicions at the way she had reacted to a confrontation with a lawyer. The sensation of her pulse fluttering under his fingers returned and he clenched his fist to banish the *frisson*.

Talitha nodded with apparent reluctance, but did not let her eyes drop from his. They were standing so close that she had to tilt her head back at what must have been an uncomfortable angle, yet she made no move away from him. Nick was suddenly struck by the fancy that she was attempting to hold his attention away from something else, something she was desperate to hide from him.

He broke the eye contact, abruptly stepping back and sweeping the room in a comprehensive glance. Nothing.

'Satisfied that I have not been stealing the silver?' she enquired icily, stooping to pick up her bonnet and tying the ribbons with a jerk. 'The truce did not last long, did it, my lord?'

'The truce will last just as long as I am satisfied you are hiding nothing that will embarrass or harm my aunt,' he replied, trampling firmly on a desire to rip open that bow, toss the bonnet to one side and kiss the anger off her face. Then the image of those green eyes fluttering closed in passion, that firm mouth softening beneath his, that delicately curved body yielding in his arms crashed into his mind with the force of a blow and he turned abruptly on his heel to hide the shock of arousal.

'I will ring for Rainbird. I regret that I am unable to drive you this afternoon, but he will call you a cab.'

'Thank you, my lord. Perhaps before you leave you would be so kind as to give me the direction of the bank you were going to recommend to me. I have no need to take you up on your kind offer to escort me—Miss Scott will do so, I am sure.'

Nick strode to the bureau and, pulling a sheet of paper towards him scribbled a few lines. When he turned, Talitha was standing closer to him, her hand held out for the note. 'Miss Scott? Ah, yes, the governess.'

'Indeed. My friend to whom you were introduced this morning. Doubtless your investigations will have unearthed the full list of her extremely respectable clients. Lady Parry has been so kind as to say that all of my small circle of friends are welcome here while I am staying with her.' She tucked the paper into her reticule and added, 'In addition to Miss Scott, there is Mrs Blackstock, the lodging-house keeper, and her niece Miss Blackstock, who is an opera dancer.'

'Are you attempting to provoke me, Miss Grey?' Nick was conscious that his strong desire to kiss

Talitha Grey until she was whimpering in his arms was rapidly being replaced by the need to shake her until her teeth rattled. 'An *opera* dancer?'

'Certainly, my lord. I am surprised your researches did not uncover that fact,' she replied placidly, slipping past him as Rainbird opened the door. 'Possibly you know her as Amelie LeNoir. Thank you, Rainbird. Good day, my lord.'

Nick threw himself down in the nearest armchair and stared at the closed door. *Damn it!* A little milliner with gilt hair and green eyes and a secret had undermined his self-control, his carefully maintained lack of emotion and his utter confidence that he had his world, and that of each of his dependents, firmly where he wanted it.

And no bad thing either, he told himself, his sense of humour returning as rapidly as it had left him. Bear-leading his cousin, assisting the failing Miss Gower, ruthlessly checking up on his aunt's new protégée—he would turn into a sanctimonious straight-laced Puritan if he carried on like this. *You need some fun, Nick Stangate*, he told himself. Whether having Miss Talitha Grey in the Parry household would prove to be fun, exactly, remained to be seen. It was certainly not going to be dull. And if that young lady thought she was going to keep any secrets from him for very long, she was seriously mistaken.

That small stiletto thrust about the opera dancer had been neatly delivered, he thought appreciatively. Presumably it was intended to repay him for the remark about buying hats, which she had risen to all too easily.

Amelie LeNoir. Could she really mean that she was friendly with an opera dancer? Presumably, if she was the niece of the lodging-house keeper, she shared the same house—unless she was in some man's keeping. No, even Miss Grey would not openly profess friendship with a kept woman. A virtuous actress would be a novelty—and possibly a means by which to tease Talitha Grey.

In a very short time he was becoming addicted to the stimulus of provoking the flash of green fire in those wide eyes. He would seek out Miss LeNoir and in the meantime he must have a word with his enquiry agent. Neither Miss LeNoir nor Talitha's secret had featured in the expensive reports that had arrived at regular intervals, systematically setting out Miss Grey's career from respectable gentry childhood through reclusive poverty with her dying mother to hard-working self-reliance. Lord Arndale disliked incompetence almost as much as he disliked not being in command of all the facts: Mr

Gregory Tolliver was going to have some explaining to do as to why a Society matron knew his target's secrets and he did not.

Chapter Seven

The next day Zenna accompanied Tallie to see first Mr Dover the solicitor and then to Martin and Wigmore, the bankers Nick Stangate had recommended. Tallie found herself expected at both sets of offices and at both of them found herself making decisions and issuing orders, which, if she gave herself time to think about it, seemed the stuff of fairy tales. Eventually they emerged blinking into the watery sunlight on the corner of Poultry and Queen Street, an obsequious clerk at their elbow to hail them a carriage.

'We were received with the most gratifying degree of attention,' she observed to her friend once they were alone and the cab was crawling down Cheapside towards St Paul's. 'But I still cannot believe that I was sitting there, making decisions about bank deposits and gilts, and being lectured on the absolute necessity to make my will.'

'You and your money were what was receiving the attention,' Zenna retorted. 'What a lowering thought that men who would have scarcely noticed us yesterday hung upon your every word and wish today, simply because of your acquisition of wealth.'

'That is the way of the world, I suppose.' Tallie looked sombre for a moment, then smiled wickedly. 'But reprehensible though it may be, I fully intend to enjoy it—we have been prudent and sensible too long, Zenna. We deserve a holiday!'

'We? But I have my plans for the school to draw up and house-agents to see, as well as my pupils to attend to,' Zenna protested.

'You cannot do both, not efficiently at any rate. Zenna, why do you not give notice to the parents of your pupils and concentrate on the school. No, hear me out.' She raised a hand as Zenna opened her mouth. 'This school is an investment—a joint investment—is it not? Then I should be investing in your time to set it up, and you should be concentrating on house-agents, and interviewing teachers and drawing up a curriculum and so on.

'Stop frowning, Zenna!' She laughed at her friend's dubious expression. 'I understand all your scruples. We will talk to Mr Dover and ask him to draw up a partnership agreement, then all will be set out and fair. Now agree, do, because I have lots of other plans I want to discuss with you.'

'Very well,' Zenna agreed with the air of someone being persuaded to do something they wanted to do, but felt they should not. 'I will be guided by Mr Dover, he does seem a very rigorous lawyer and will make sure I am not taking more than my fair share in this agreement.'

Tallie nodded decisively. 'And I have had another brilliant idea for investing my money. It concerns Mrs Blackstock. What if I should buy a town house or two? She could run them as select boarding-houses. I am sure she would soon be making a handsome profit for me and thereby a good income for herself.'

'An excellent idea,' Zenobia approved, grabbing the hanging strap as the cab once again jolted to a halt. 'What a crush! I had not realised the City would be so busy. What about Millie? I confess, I have not observed Mr Hemsley in her company again, but I know she is receiving notes from someone, for she blushes and hides them under her table napkin when the morning post arrives.'

'That is difficult,' Tallie agreed, peering out of the window. 'Why, no wonder the street is in such chaos, some yokel is driving a herd of sheep through! But I do not think it will be any faster to get out and walk, so we had better stay where we are. I had thought that if Mrs Blackstock was busy with the new boarding-houses, Millie might stay at home to help her. But she loves the stage—it is not as if she is doing it because she needs the money. Then I thought of giving her a dowry in the hope of attracting some respectable person to marry her, but I cannot think of a tactful way of doing that, so I confess I am somewhat at a stand.'

'Hmm. No doubt something will occur to us. What are you doing this afternoon? Shopping?'

A roll of banknotes had been burning a hole in Tallie's reticule for the past hour, but she wanted to take Zenna shopping with her when she went. Tallie had a plan to buy her friend some clothes so she could be invited to parties too. That was going to take some tact and cunning and Zenna was engaged that afternoon with pupils.

'I must go shopping tomorrow, for I cannot arrive at Lady Parry's with my wardrobe in the state it is. I am sure she will recommend me to all the right modistes once I am with her, but until then I need your advice, Zenna. Are you free tomorrow? Because if you are, we can look at house-agents as well.'

Zenna agreed, attempting to look as though she would enjoy the experience. She produced her tablets and began to add to her endless lists, while Tallie brooded on the interview with Madame d'Aunay she had resolved on having that afternoon.

She had already written to her employer, apologising again for her absence, giving a carefully edited account of her change in circumstances and informing her that she would be stopping work as soon as she had finished the hats on which she was working. She expected Madame to be unhappy about this, but she was unprepared for the atmosphere that greeted her when she arrived at the shop that afternoon.

The first shock was the fact that Madame curtsied as she entered the salon and ushered her through to her inner sanctum, the elegantly appointed private room reserved for the best clients.

'I must apologise, Madame...' Tallie began, only to be silenced by the expression of forced affability on Madame's face.

'Do not mention it, Miss Grey. Naturally you will wish to dissociate yourself from this establishment immediately. I have your outstanding wages here.' She reached for an envelope, a slight flush staining her neck.

'Goodness, no,' Tallie protested. 'I have given you no notice, I cannot take that.'

'Very well, ma'am.'

Tallie blinked. Had her former employer called her 'ma'am'? 'The hats on which I am working—'

'Sarah will take them over, Miss Grey.' There was an awkward pause. 'I will naturally be sorry to lose Lady Parry's business, but—'

'But why should you?' Tallie felt distinctly disorientated.

'I understood that you would be living with Lady Parry, Miss Grey, and naturally assumed—'

'Oh, good heavens, no!' Tallie realised her former employer thought she would be making the hats directly for her patroness from now on. 'Obviously if Lady Parry needed a trim changing or something of that nature...but I am sure she will wish to continue purchasing her hats from you.'

'I see.' Madame looked even more uneasy. 'I believe you said you will be making your come-out this Season, Miss Grey?'

'Indeed, yes, and I will need several hats...'

'What a pity that this salon produces hats so much more fitting for the older lady,' Madame said expressionlessly.

'But...' Tallie gathered her wits together. So, suddenly she was an embarrassment to Madame: neither a lady nor an employee, but someone who might prove a liability if there was a scandal when she made her début. Society ladies might take exception to the fact that one of Madame d'Aunay's artisans had the presumption to move above her station.

She glanced towards the door into the workroom. 'The girls are very busy, Miss Grey,' the milliner said hurriedly.

'I am sure they are, Madame.' Tallie got to her feet. 'I must thank you for having given me a chance when I needed employment: I will not forget that. Please be assured that I will do nothing to dissuade Lady Parry from continuing to buy hats here.'

She swept out, head held high before she saw whether she was receiving another curtsy or not. When she found herself on the pavement outside the shop she hesitated, unsure which way to turn along the crowded street, unable to think clearly about what she should be doing next.

Anger, sorrow and insecurity fought within her. Was it going to be this difficult with everyone she met in her new life?

'Miss Grey, good afternoon.' The cheerful voice at her elbow jerked her back to the present and an awareness that she was still standing on the pavement with passers-by flowing around her.

'Lord Parry. I do beg your pardon, I was wool-gathering.' Tallie pulled herself together with an effort and managed a smile. William was regarding her with unaffected delight and she was irresistibly reminded of a large retriever puppy. He seemed painfully young and, she suspected, was rapidly reaching the stage when young ladies were proving a mysterious, but irresistible, source of interest.

'May I escort you anywhere?'

'No, I thank you, but I was just going to…to walk home.' She supposed that would be the best thing to do. She hardly felt inclined to go window-shopping in her present distracted frame of mind.

'I say, that is rather a long walk, isn't it? Let me call you a hackney carriage.'

'I…no…thank you. I think I would like the fresh air.'

To her surprise, for in Tallie's experience youths were often far too self-absorbed to take much notice of anyone else's emotional state, William shot her a sharp glance, tucked her hand firmly under his elbow and began to steer her towards the end of Berkeley Street.

'Are you feeling a little out of sorts, Miss Grey? Never mind, I know just the thing.'

'What, my lord?' Half-amused despite her battered feelings, Tallie meekly allowed herself to be guided along the crowded pavement.

'Ice cream. I will take you to Gunter's and you

can have a nice lemon ice and a wafer and a cup of chocolate and you'll soon feel right as rain.'

Tallie suppressed a smile. Of course, food and the sweeter the better—the answer to distress for every very young person. 'That is extremely kind of you, my lord.'

They arrived at the fashionable tearooms in a slight lull and found a choice of tables available. 'Would you like to sit in the window?' William suggested. 'There is more to look at.'

And everyone can see us, Tallie thought, allowing herself to be seated. She could hardly feel that her presence in her drab pelisse was adding much lustre to young Lord Parry's carefully cultivated image. His clothing was immaculate, if a little on the exaggerated side when it came to cut, his hair was ruthlessly pomaded into elegant curls and his neckcloth, although lacking the exquisite folds achieved by a certain gentleman Tallie could think of, was highly creditable.

'I see you are admiring my neckcloth,' he confided, dropping his voice.

'I beg your pardon,' Tallie said hastily, 'I had no intention of staring…'

'Not at all.' He fairly glowed with pride and Tallie concluded that if his lordship *was* twenty years old his birthday must have been very recent indeed.

'My cousin Nick showed me how to tie it. I was trying for a Waterfall and making a complete mull of it, so he taught me this.'

'You are close to Lord Arndale?' Tallie enquired, moving her napkin to allow a water ice and a cup of steaming chocolate to be set in front of her.

William became quiet, obviously unused to discussing his feelings. 'He's the best of fellows,' he managed after some thought. 'Like a brother, only he doesn't lecture. Leastways, I don't have a brother, but I hear what the other chaps say and older brothers sound like the very de—are very strict. Always lecturing.'

'And Lord Arndale does not lecture you?' Tallie enquired, surprised. It seemed unlikely from what she knew of him that Nick Stangate would tolerate the foolishness of youth.

'No.' William took a large spoonful of vanilla ice and paused with it halfway to his mouth. 'He *looks* sometimes.'

'Looks?'

'Yes, just *looks*. And then you feel uncomfortable and wonder if whatever you are doing is a good thing. You know?'

'No, but I can imagine.' Tallie took a reviving sip of chocolate.

'You'll see, once you come and live with us.'

'Do you mind me moving in, my lord?' Tallie asked abruptly. This was an unlikely conversation to be having with a very young man who was virtually a stranger to her, but William with his natural confiding friendliness did not appear to find it so.

'No, of course not. It'll be like having a sister and Mama is having a wonderful time already. You will call me William, won't you?' He ate some more of his ice and demolished his wafer, then, with the frankness that Tallie was beginning to associate with him—so unlike his cousin—said, 'Are you feeling better now?'

'I…yes, thank you.'

'Good. What was wrong?' Then he blushed scarlet. 'Lord! I am sorry, it is just that it is so easy talking to you I just didn't think. Forget I asked.'

Perversely Tallie, who ten minutes ago would have walked on hot coals rather than reveal her wounded feelings, said, 'No, it is quite all right to ask. I had just had a very difficult conversation with Madame d'Aunay, who used be my employer.'

'Um?' William nodded encouragingly. 'Old tartar, is she?'

'It isn't that. She is embarrassed because a day ago I was a milliner and her employee; now she thinks she has to treat me like a lady and is afraid that if I make a scandal it will reflect on her busi-

ness. I do not think I know *what* I am any more.'
To her horror a lump appeared in her throat.

'Oh, I say!' William whisked out a large pocket
handkerchief and, leaning across the table, held it
out to her. 'You aren't going to cry, are you, Miss
Grey…? I feel an absolute clod…'

Tallie ducked her head and shot a rapid glance
around the still half-empty room. No one appeared
to have noticed them. 'Thank you, William, I am
quite all right, truly. And I'm not going to cry, it is
just that I do not know whether I am angry or hurt
or what I feel.'

His hand still hovered with the linen, and she
put up her own hand to touch his wrist and silently
urge him to put the handkerchief away. As she did
so a movement outside caught her attention. Lord
Arndale was watching them through the glass, one
dark brow raised in chilly incredulity.

'Good afternoon.' He appeared at their table with
what seemed to Tallie to be supernatural speed.
Glancing at William's face, she saw he had turned
as red as she knew she had. The pair of them must
have presented a perfect picture of guilt surprised.

This was ridiculous. William might be an awkward adolescent, but she was five and twenty and
a woman of the world. She was certainly not going

to allow Nicholas Stangate to put her out of countenance.

'Good afternoon, my lord,' she said affably. 'Will you not join us? Lord Parry has been treating me to the indulgence of an ice. I can certainly recommend the lemon, although I believe the vanilla is equally delicious.' William was rapidly collecting himself, stuffing the handkerchief back into his pocket and rising to move around the table and offer his cousin his seat.

'Thank you, William. No, nothing for me.' Nick waved away the hovering waiter with a careless hand and regarded Tallie with what she could only interpret as scepticism. 'It appeared that my cousin, far from treating you to afternoon tea, had reduced you to tears.'

'Oh, I say…'

'Did it appear so?' Tallie took another tiny taste of ice and smiled. 'A mote of something flew into my eye and Lord Parry was kind enough to offer me his handkerchief.' She smiled warmly at the youth, who blushed again, this time with pink-cheeked pleasure.

Lord Arndale was watching the byplay with little sign of either belief or approval. Tallie decided it was time to distract him from his cousin. 'I deserve a little indulgence, my lord. I have spent the morning in the City, paying close attention to Mr Dover and the gentlemen at the bank, just as you recommended me to.'

The dark brows snapped together. 'You went alone?'

'Certainly not, my lord.' Tallie managed a tone of modest outrage. 'Naturally I was accompanied by Miss Scott, as I told you I would be.'

'Ah, yes, your governess friend.'

'And my business partner,' Tallie corrected gently, watching him from under demurely lowered lashes.

'And what business might that be?'

'It is far too early to divulge the details,' Tallie said repressively, dapping her lips delicately with the napkin.

'If you are going to plunge into dubious investments, Miss Grey, I must tell you as your—'

'As my what, my lord?' Tallie gathered up her reticule and smiled at William. 'Do you know, I think I would like you to call me a hackney after all, Lord Parry, if you would be so kind.' She waited until he rose and went to the door before turning back to his cousin, who was watching her with smouldering eyes. 'You may be Lady Parry's trustee and you may be Miss Gower's executor, my lord, but you have no role in my life.'

William was on the pavement, head tipped back,

obviously asking the driver of the hackney carriage drawn up at the kerb to wait. 'What a thoroughly nice young man Lord Parry is,' she added, without thinking. 'His mama must be very proud of him.'

'He is indeed,' Nick Stangate said close by her ear as he pulled back her chair for her. 'Very nice, very young, very titled and very rich. And he is in no need of a wife, or any other romantic liaison at the moment.'

Vehement, furious denial rose to Tallie's lips, but she controlled it—just. Only a hesitation as she rose betrayed the anger that lanced through her. That he thought she could entertain the slightest desire to flirt with, let alone set out to ensnare, a lad five years her junior for the sake of title and wealth was utterly insulting and she half-turned to hiss a furious response. Then a wicked thought flashed through her brain and she bit her tongue.

She calmly straightened her skirts and turned to smile into the darkly handsome face so close to hers. 'And what were *you* doing when you were twenty, my lord? I cannot believe that romantic liaisons were very far from your thoughts. I am sure Lord Parry is quite old enough to know what he wants. I am *so* looking forward to getting to know him better.'

She kept her temper under control as she thanked

William prettily for her treat and for the hackney and sat stock-still while the vehicle rocked and bumped over the cobbles back to Upper Wimpole Street. She could hardly give way to her feelings in the middle of a public street. But when she got back to the house and found the parlour empty, she seized a cushion from the sofa and pummelled it until feathers started to leak from one seam.

'Insufferable man!'

'Let me guess.' Zenna appeared in the doorway, quill in one hand and Latin primer in the other. 'Lord Arndale.'

'Yes.' Tallie threw the cushion back onto the sofa and sat on it with emphasis. 'I declare, Zenna, that man has the most appalling effect on me. Did you ever know me to lose my temper before? Did I not always try to be calm and philosophical in the face of setbacks? Would I have stooped to mockery and deception in order to annoy another person? Was I able to sleep at night?'

'No, yes, no and usually,' Zenna said with a grin. 'Now, what has he done? Has he tried to kiss you?'

Tallie glared at her. 'I do wish you would stop this jesting of yours, Zenna. First you say you expect him to propose, then to kiss me. The wretched creature is suspicious of me, that is all. He knows I have something to hide and is busily investigating me.

And now he accuses me of setting my cap at his cousin.'

'Lord Parry? But how old did you say he was? Sixteen?'

'Twenty, and a very young and very charming twenty-year-old at that. I met him in Piccadilly and he took me for an ice cream and we talked until who should arrive but Nick Stangate, looking like the wrath of God.'

'Tallie!'

'I am sorry, I did not intend to blaspheme. He is like one of those Greek gods. You know, thunderbolts and eyes that turn people to stone,' she added wildly.

'I think you are getting thoroughly confused with your Greek myths and need a nice cup of tea.' Zenna put her head out of the door and called to Annie, then came back in and sat down.

'I don't think I can drink anything, thank you. I am full of lemon ice and hot chocolate.' She tried not to think about the episode in Gunter's, but it kept insisting on being worried at, like a sore tooth. '*Why* should he think anything so foolish as that? William is five years younger than I am.'

'Perhaps he's jea—' Zenna caught herself and bit off the word. 'Perhaps he is just abnormally suspicious,' she said soothingly. 'Tell me all about Gunter's, I have always wanted to try one of their ices.'

Chapter Eight

'There was a time—can it be just a few days ago?—when my only worry was earning my living,' Tallie lamented as the hackney carriage made its way along Oxford Street. 'Now I have to worry about my position in Society—or lack of it; how to invest a ridiculous amount of money wisely; how to keep an interfering, autocratic aristocrat from discovering my secrets and how to persuade *you* to allow me to buy you a dress or two.'

'Tallie, I simply cannot accept expensive presents…' Zenna protested for the third time that morning.

'I am not trying to give you expensive presents— just one evening dress so we can go to parties together. *Please*, Zenna. I need your support. Lady Parry is so kind, but it is not the same as a friend my own age. And it would give me such pleasure to give you a present.' She smiled hopefully at her friend, who sighed and smiled back.

'Very well, and thank you, Tallie. It would be very pleasant to have a nice evening gown, I have to admit, but as for the other gowns you were talking of, that is far too much.'

'Business expenses,' Tallie said firmly. 'We can put them down as business expenses. You must have some good day dresses for interviewing teachers and parents. We are aiming at the highest quality for this school, are we not?'

Zenna began to protest that arguing with Tallie was more exhausting than trying to handle a room full of six-year-old boys when the hackney pulled up outside the Pantheon Bazaar and Tallie got to her feet. 'We will start here, then I thought Hardin and Howell, Stagg and Mantle's and Clark and Debenham's.' She smiled at Zenna, who descended onto the pavement looking apprehensive at this formidable list. 'Then this afternoon, Dickens and Smith...' She plunged into the shop pursued by Zenna, who was grimly resolving that, whatever else the day held, it was going to include a lengthy pause at Gunter's. A very lengthy one indeed.

At four o'clock that afternoon two very weary young ladies made their way up to Tallie's bedroom and collapsed onto the bed, scattering parcels and bandboxes on the floor as they did so. Behind them came the faint sounds of little Annie struggling up the stairs with still more packages.

'My feet!' Zenna moaned, pulling off her shoes and wriggling her toes with a gasp of relief.

Tallie levered herself up on her elbows from her position prone on the mattress and sighed happily. 'Mine too. Oh, thank you, Annie. Put them in the corner, please, and then please bring us some tea up.' She dragged the pillows up into a heap and sat back against them. 'A nice cup of tea and then all the fun of unwrapping everything.' She smiled at Zenna coaxingly. 'Admit it, Zenna, you did enjoy it a little bit, did you not?'

'Well...yes, I have to confess I did. Thank you very much for the gown and the slippers and gloves. It felt very good to dress up for once. But we do seem to have bought a vast amount of things—do you think you have almost everything you need now?'

'I should not think so for a minute,' Tallie replied, reflecting on the ladies' boudoirs she had glimpsed so frequently in her career as a milliner. 'Lady Parry would be very disappointed if she does not have the opportunity to supervise my shopping. No, this was just so that I did not feel too drab in the first few days. My old pelisse and walking dress are on their last prayers, all my stockings have been darned and both my pairs of gloves have got splits in the seams.'

She closed her eyes for a moment, letting the images of the day's extravagances swirl across her memory. 'It is fun to have a holiday and to be able to buy what one wants, but I am glad we have our business ventures to be working on, Zenna. I cannot feel comfortable with the thought of Society life. From what I have seen it is entirely composed of luxury and pleasure. I am sure I would soon become bored with nothing else to think of.'

Into the images of dress lengths and slippers, fans and feathers the picture of a tall, dark, elegant gentleman rose, quite unbidden. How did Lord Arndale spend his time? she wondered. In the company of actresses and opera dancers? At the card tables? At cock-fights and the prize-ring? She tried to imagine that coolly sardonic expression giving way to excitement, passion, anticipation—and failed. His lordship was undoubtedly a prime example of the indolent and aloof members of Society whose way of life she was about to sample. It would be satisfying to cause some emotion to cross those chiselled features or to provoke a response that was neither controlled nor temperate. A small smile caught at the corners of Tallie's lips. Yes, very satisfying indeed.

Two days later the indolent and aloof gentleman in question mounted the steps of the house in Upper Wimpole Street and found himself unexpectedly encountering almost the entire household.

Nick had spent a taxing morning with his steward, who had come up from the country estates with a formidable pile of problems and questions to be resolved, and later that afternoon he suspected he was going to have to have an equally long list of details to decide with Mr Dover before the final work could be completed on Miss Gower's will. That evening he fully intended leaving young William to his own devices, however dubious they sounded, and relaxing with a small group of friends over dinner, cards and several bottles of excellent brandy.

But he had been waylaid by his aunt and asked to call upon Miss Grey. 'You will tell her I will collect her in my carriage at ten on Wednesday morning, will you not, Nicholas dear? And if you can establish how many trunks she has, then Rainbird can organise the carrier.' She had stood on tiptoe to kiss his cheek. 'Thank you, dearest.' And she had rushed away in her usual whirlwind manner before he could enquire why a note would not serve the purpose just as well.

Now he was here, he might as well take the opportunity of smoothing over the friction from their last encounter. He could not really believe she had set her sights on young William Parry, but it had been bad tactics to let her see he was concerned. If she was the sort of woman who saw opposition as a challenge, she might attempt to attach the lad's interest simply as a game. And William was far too young to be breaking his heart over an older woman Nick decided, conveniently forgetting his own initiation into the arts of love at the age of seventeen by a beautiful, sophisticated lady more than ten years his senior.

The door was opened by a diminutive maid with a snub nose, freckles, an apron too large for her and an expression of alarm. 'Oh, sir! Miss Grey? Oh, yes, sir! I'll tell her you're here, sir, if you'll just wait in the front parlour, sir.'

She flung open the door to let him in, appeared to realise she should have asked his name to announce him, gave a scared squeak and shut the door again behind him. Nick found himself in a cosy, slightly shabby room with an indefinable air of comfort and femininity. The latter quality was enhanced by the presence on the sofa of an enchantingly pretty girl with large blue eyes and a mass of blonde curls. Tumbled in a pile by her side were undergarments of a most frivolous, intimate and dainty variety.

She bundled the lingerie under a cushion with what struck Nick as admirable quick-wittedness and got to her feet, placing a thimble and needle on the table beside her. 'I am sorry, sir,' she said, a faint blush colouring her cheeks. 'Annie is not yet trained as a downstairs maid and I am afraid she does not always remember to announce callers.'

'Nicholas Stangate. I called to see Miss Grey. May I presume to guess I am addressing Miss Amelie LeNoir? I apologise for disturbing you.' It would not be the slightest hardship to disturb Miss LeNoir, he reflected, watching the artless pleasure at his recognition, the lovely figure in a surprisingly modest afternoon dress, the parted lips and soft curves. No hardship at all.

'Oh, how did you guess? Your lordship,' she added hastily, bobbing a curtsy.

'You were described to me,' Nick said simply, enjoying the deepening of the flush of pleasure, the flutter of the long lashes. For a man who had always favoured dark-haired women, his life suddenly appeared to be full of blondes. It made an agreeable change.

'I…I had better go and find Tal…Miss Grey, my

lord. One simply cannot rely on Annie. Will you not sit down?' She gestured at the sofa, recalled her mending, hastily whisked it from under the cushion to under her arm and hurried out.

Nick grinned. The enchantingly fresh young woman who had just fluttered out was either an exceptional actress or that contradiction in terms, a chaste opera dancer, just as Talitha Grey had said. Instead of taking the proffered seat, he began to prowl around the room. It was a rare glimpse for a man into a feminine world that was not arranged for display or entertaining, but simply for a group of women to pass their daily lives in.

A neat stack of account books next to a spike impaling tradesmen's bills. A basket of laces, ribbons and artificial flowers by a sewing box and a large velvet pincushion studded with glass-headed pins. A pile of novels and some copies of fashion journals upon a shelf. A chessboard set out for the start of a game. He moved a pawn in an opening gambit and continued to look around. A quill stained with red ink lay beside an open exercise book.

Nick paused and flicked open a page of the lexicon next to the exercise book. Greek! The door behind him opened to reveal not Miss Grey, but her governess friend. 'Miss Scott, good afternoon. You have surprised me reading what I imagine must be your Greek lexicon.'

'Yes, my lord.' She stood there, regarding him from under level dark brows. He expected disapproval; instead, he found himself unable to interpret the assessing look in her eyes. 'I teach both Latin and Greek, besides the modern languages.'

'I had not realised you teach boys,' he remarked, more to make conversation than anything, and was surprised by the flash of irritation in her steady gaze.

'I do not. These days I teach only girls. Perhaps your lordship does not consider the female mind has the capacity for the ancient languages?'

'I had never given it any consideration,' he admitted. 'But I can see no useful purpose in it for a woman.'

'Beside the intellectual discipline, the improved understanding of modern tongues and of history and art?' she enquired frostily.

'Well, there is that, of course, but if a girl is to marry…'

'Not all of us do,' Miss Scott informed him. 'I see no reason why an unmarried lady should have her intellectual range diminished because of that. Nor why a married woman may not be educated.' Her expression softened slightly. 'No doubt you consider that a married woman has no need to use her intelligence on more than the ordering of the household? Not that housekeeping is as simple a task as most men appear to think it.'

Nick thought of his mother, smiling gently whenever any problem arose. 'Your papa will know what to do' was her inevitable response, and more recently, 'Whatever you say, Nicholas dear.' And his aunt, undoubtedly intelligent, vibrant, energetic—but quite content to place her business affairs entirely in his hands.

'There is no need for a lady to concern herself with difficult matters—' he began.

'But not all of us chose to be helpless pawns,' said another voice gently. Miss Grey walked into the room behind her friend. 'I believe you wish to see me, my lord?'

Nick took a step forward, found his foot entangled, glanced down and saw he was standing on a piece of fabric. He stooped to pick it up and found himself holding a garment he had no difficulty in recognising as a chemise. Neither young lady appeared prepared to help him out of his difficulty so he folded it neatly and placed it on the side-table. Keeping his face entirely bland, he looked up and found he had met his match in coolness in Miss Scott, whose expression showed not the slightest recognition that he had been handling a piece of intimate apparel. Miss Grey, on the other hand, appeared ready to give way to laughter. Her green eyes sparkled with amusement at his predicament and her lower lip was caught firmly between white teeth.

The thought of nipping that fullness between his own teeth struck him with a bolt of erotic heat. A flare of it must have shown in his eyes for instantly hers sobered, widened, and he wondered if she had read correctly the nature of his thoughts and was in tune with them. Then the moment of mutual awareness was gone and she was waving him towards the sofa.

'Will you take tea, my lord?'

'No, thank you. I have called simply with a message from Lady Parry.'

Talitha Grey answered the queries with a directness that reinforced his knowledge of her previously straitened circumstances. 'Trunks? Why, just the one, my lord, and a valise.'

'And several new bandboxes,' the governess added drily.

'Oh, yes. I was forgetting.' She turned to him, smiling slightly. 'I have been succumbing to the lure of shopping.'

'Indeed? In that case I am surprised you have had the time to attend to your new business venture.' He watched not Talitha but her friend and saw the look of surprise and speculation she directed at him. But to his disappointment the governess did not speak.

'Ventures, in the plural. Yes, when one has been accustomed to working for one's living, my lord, one can find plenty of time in the day for business. Shopping is hardly time-consuming.'

'I suspect you may modify your opinion on that after a short experience of my aunt's approach to the subject.'

Talitha merely smiled politely. It was intensely frustrating. Every time he spoke to her he had the impression that she was keeping a part of herself hidden from him and he only caught brief flashes of the real Talitha Grey. Now he had the question of her 'business interests' to add to the list for Tolliver to investigate.

It was not until Nick was halfway down the front steps that he caught himself wondering why he wanted to find out about that aspect of her life. She was being advised by Dover and by the bank; she was hardly going to do something imprudent. Nor was it his business if she did, as she had so frostily reminded him during that encounter in Gunter's.

He was not given to self-deception and he did not indulge in it now. Finding out about Miss Grey's 'secret' might have started out in his desire to protect his aunt. Now finding out everything about her had assumed an altogether different character. Nick Stangate smiled ruefully as he nodded to his groom and got up into his phaeton. This was becoming personal.

For Tallie, too, the encounters with Nick Stangate were beginning to feel very personal indeed. She felt gratitude, anger, fear and attraction in a disturbing mixture that was threatening to obsess her.

The degree to which she felt the various emotions he evoked varied wildly, depending on what he had just said to annoy or alarm her and also on those fleeting moments when their eyes met and locked and she felt as though a dentist's probe had touched a nerve. When it happened her heart beat rapidly, her breath caught and she felt a strange heated ache deep inside. Tallie told herself it was fear: fear at what he might find out about her, fear of exposure. But she was very much afraid that it was another raw, basic emotion and one that young ladies, especially respectable unmarried young ladies, were not supposed to feel.

She could only be grateful that for the first week of her stay with Lady Parry in Bruton Street she did not meet him once.

'Have you seen Nicholas lately?' Lady Parry enquired of her son at breakfast on the Wednesday after Tallie's arrival.

'Hmm?' William put down the paper he was idly conning and furrowed his brow in thought. 'Twice…no, three times. You know Nick, he just strolls in when you least expect him. Now, when was it? Oh, yes, he dropped in at Watier's when I was playing cards with Hemsley and some fellows on Saturday. And he arrived at Jackson's Saloon just in time to see me pop a terrific right over Jack's guard. That was Monday afternoon…'

'Is Jackson the famous bare-knuckle fighter?' Tallie enquired. 'And you managed to hit him? My goodness!'

'Lord, no.' William blushed at her praise, but hastened to set her right. 'No one lands a punch on the great Jackson unless he lets them. No, it was Jack Hemsley.'

'Oh, I see. Still, I am sure you must be very good to be admitted to Jackson's Saloon,' Tallie said encouragingly. 'Might I trouble you for the preserve? Thank you. And you saw Lord Arndale for a third time?'

'Er, yes. Last night.' William seemed disinclined to explain further, but Tallie, convinced she was beginning to see a pattern, persisted.

'And where was that? I do enjoy hearing about all these fashionable places. I can hardly wait until I am ready to be going about in Society,' she added artlessly.

'This wasn't the sort of place you would be going,' William said with a harassed glance at his mother. Lady Parry, however, had returned to her correspondence and was busily slitting envelopes with her butter-knife.

'Do tell,' Tallie encouraged quietly, giving William the sort of look designed to convince him he was an exciting rake.

'Well…it was a bit of a hell, if you must know. I was feeling rather uncomfortable actually.' William was blushing. 'Some of the young ladies there were…were…'

'Not ladies?' Tallie suggested. Bless the boy, he really was a decent young man.

'Exactly that.' He looked grateful for her tactful description. 'I wasn't sure how to leave, I mean, I'd been invited by one of the guests and it seemed rude just to walk away. And then Nick strolls in, looking bored to death, curls a lip and drawls that he's been looking for me all over and had I forgotten we were going to White's that evening? *White's!* As if I'd forget that!'

His eyes gleamed and Tallie recalled that the club

in question was the most exclusive in town and certainly one which a mere youth would not have the faintest hope of joining. The honour of being invited to spend an evening there by one of the members must have been overwhelming.

'So you went with him?' William was positively glowing. 'I imagine Mr Hemsley was a little put out.'

'Well, a bit. But you don't argue with Nick, you know.' It did not seem to occur to William that he had not told her he had been in the hell at the instigation of Jack Hemsley.

Tallie returned to her toast with a thoughtful expression. So, Nick Stangate was putting himself out to intervene every time William was in the company of the rakish Mr Hemsley. And he was managing to do so without his young cousin realising that he had a guardian angel at his heels. Very clever—and thoroughly admirable. She was sure that for a mature and experienced man about town, bear-leading an inexperienced youth must be a complete bore.

She took a bite of toast and wondered if Mr Hemsley was aware of just how closely his pursuit of a rich young lordling was being observed. She rather suspected he was, for he had not struck her as a

fool, however unpleasant his character. Lord Arndale had better watch his back and take care.

It was one of his most admirable characteristics,
she realised: taking care. He took care of William,
of his aunt—and of naked models in garrets. She
rather suspected that his irritating interference in
her life was part of that too. She had become family,
so she was going to be looked after whether she
liked it or not. With a little shiver Tallie decided
she liked it rather too much.

Tallie was soon able to test this new-found
charitable feeling. His lordship was waiting for her
that afternoon as she and Lady Parry came back
into the house.

Chapter Nine

'Nicholas dearest!' His aunt kissed him thoroughly, stood back to scan him from head to foot, flicked an invisible speck from his lapels and announced, 'I like that coat. Now, I must go and change before the orphanage committee meeting. Tallie, you need to rest. Nicholas, we have been indulging in an absolute orgy. Goodness, is that the time…?'

'Orgy?' Tallie made herself look at Nick, only to be met with one of his blandest, most infuriating expressions.

She raised an eyebrow. It was difficult, but she had been practising in front of the mirror and was almost satisfied with the effect. 'Of shopping, my lord.' Carefully sweeping the skirts of her newest afternoon dress to one side, she sank elegantly onto the sofa. 'Will you not sit down, my lord?'

'Certainly.' He took the chair she had indicated

and sat, legs crossed, one booted foot swinging gently, fingers steepled and just touching his lips.

Tallie tried not to look at his mouth and stared at his booted foot instead.

'Lobb's,' he said helpfully. 'That is a very fetching gown.'

'Thank you. Lady Parry's taste is excellent. I am much indebted to her guidance.'

'My lord.' Tallie stared at him. 'You forgot to say "my lord". Up to then you had managed to insert it in every sentence. You also forgot to raise that eyebrow again, although I can quite understand why—it is devilishly uncomfortable until one has the knack of it.'

Tallie glared at him, then her sense of humour got the better of her and she laughed. 'It is, is it not? You do it to such effect I thought it worth cultivating to depress pretension. But it gives me a headache if I practise for too long.'

'And what did I do that required depressing?' he enquired gently.

'Nothing,' Tallie admitted. 'I was practising, my lord.'

'There you go again! I have a perfectly good name, Tallie. Why not use it?'

Tallie. He had called her not just by her Christian name, but by the diminutive that only her friends used. It sounded different on his lips. She gave herself a little shake and said firmly, 'It would be quite inappropriate.'

'You call Lady Parry Aunt Kate, you call my cousin William. I did suggest to you once before that you adopt me as an honorary cousin.'

The idea of *adopting* anyone as large, sophisticated and self-reliant as Nicholas Stangate was a preposterous fancy. Tallie felt her lips quirk and saw an answering twist on his. 'Very well, Cousin Nicholas.'

'Thank you, Cousin Talitha.' So, she was Talitha now. She fought with the fantasy of hearing him whisper *Tallie* while he...while he...

'I am glad I caught you at home,' he was saying, reaching for a slim portfolio. 'Most of the house-agents are in the City and other areas where it is unsuitable for you and Miss Scott to be going unaccompanied. I have had my man of business assemble some particulars that should meet your requirements for both your projected schemes. If they are not to your liking he will find others. Meanwhile, if you or Miss Scott wish to view—' He broke off to get to his feet in response to Tallie positively leaping to hers. 'Cousin Talitha?'

'How did you find out?' she demanded. 'Who has

been spying on us? Or have you been worming it out of Zenna?'

'Miss Scott is the soul of discretion,' he said, sounding far too soothing. 'I would not dream of *worming* anything out of your friend behind your back.'

'But you are quite happy to set spies on me—behind my back?'

'Only to protect you,' he said, still so reasonably that Tallie wanted to hit him. 'It is your choice which properties you select.'

'After they have been edited and approved by you,' she said furiously, pacing back and forth on the fine Oriental rug. She used to be calm, she used to hide every feeling, she used to be self-contained—what was he doing to her?

'Cousin Talitha, young ladies do not conduct business on their own account.' He was standing relaxed by his chair, one hand resting on the back of it, his eyes hooded to hide the gleam that betrayed his appreciation of the sight she presented as she swept to and fro.

Tallie came to a halt in front of him, glaring up into his eyes. 'I am not a "young lady", I am an independent woman. I have had to earn my own living and I intend to carry on doing just that. I will be for ever grateful to Miss Gower for her wonderful legacy and to Lady Parry for the opportunity to experience the Season, but by this time next year I need to know what I am doing and how I am going to spend the rest of my life. And I need to prepare now.'

'But you will be spending the rest of your life as someone's wife,' he said, smiling at her. And that d…d…*damned* eyebrow was quirked at her as though she was an idiot.

'Really, my lord? I am twenty-five years old. I have been earning my living as a milliner. I have nothing to recommend me…' He opened his mouth. Tallie swept on, 'And before you say that I have my fortune to recommend me I must tell you, sir, that I would go back to hat-making for my livelihood rather than marry a man who wanted me for my money.'

'You think that your fortune is all that you have to recommend you?' Nick took her by the shoulders and turned her so that she was facing the great mirror that hung over the fireplace. 'Look at yourself.'

Tallie looked. Looking back at her was a young woman of slightly more than average height, dressed in a fashionable gown of soft spring green that clung to full breasts and skimmed over a slender figure. Her eyes, just a little darker than the gown, were wide and her lips full and slightly parted. Her colour was high, white cheeks flushed with rose.

Behind her a tall man held her with hands that rested firmly on each shoulder. In the glass their eyes met—hers wide and startled, his dark and hot as she had never seen them.

'If you would just let your hair free a little...' One hand left her shoulder to touch the pins that kept the gilt mass tight and disciplined.

With a gasp Tallie whirled round and found herself right against Nick's chest. 'No!'

'No?' He was not asking her about her hair. His voice was deep, dark, husky. His hands were on her shoulders again, pulling her inexorably against him. 'No?'

She should step back. She should say 'No'. She should...she should let him kiss her.

Tallie closed her eyes against the fire in his and stopped pulling back. The heat of him remembered from the studio seemed to burn her flesh through the fine muslin of her gown. The scent of him— male, exciting, overlain with a civilising veneer of sharp cologne—*that* she had not remembered.

Nor had she imagined how his mouth would feel when it came down on hers. How could she know what her first kiss would be like? She had not realised that his mouth would be both firm and soft, demanding yet tender. She had not dreamed that her lips, already parted in surprise, would open of their own accord under the pressure of his, that his tongue would slip caressingly, shockingly between them. And she had had not the slightest suspicion that a caress on the lips would make her breasts ache, would send strange, uncomfortable, wanton messages down—

Tallie jerked back gasping and instantly Nick released her. His eyes were dark, his breath was short, but the imperturbable mask of control was back. Then she made the error of dropping her eyes from his and became jarringly aware of just how unsuited for hiding the effects of male arousal the fashion of the day for tight trousers was.

It was probably impossible to blush more than she was already, Tallie thought wildly as she took refuge behind the chair. And she had thought Nicholas Stangate made her feel safe! She must have been insane. Insanely blind. 'My lord...'

'Cousin Nicholas.'

'That was hardly cousinly!' She could not look at him.

'Cousins may kiss. And adopted ones certainly may. I am sorry to have discomforted you, Cousin Talitha; it was just that you appeared to be quite blind to the effect you are undoubtedly going to have on a large proportion of the men who meet you. It is best that you are on your guard before some rake takes advantage of that enchanting modesty of yours. I thought a demonstration would be advisable.'

'Demonstration!' Now she did look at him, incredulity showing in both voice and expression.

'But of course. You are quite safe with me. I will go and leave you to rest as Aunt Kate advised. Good day, Cousin Talitha.'

Safe? *Safe?* She would be safer in a locked room with Jack Hemsley! At least she knew exactly what her reaction to any advance from him would be—a slapped face and a briskly raised knee would be a good start. But with Nicholas Stangate she also knew exactly what she wanted to happen, and she knew too he was the last man in London with whom it was safe to let her guard down. And to think that only a few days ago she had decided it would be satisfying to provoke a response from him that was neither controlled nor temperate!

Now it seemed she had fallen neatly into her own trap. He appeared capable of reining back his passion as it suited him. She was the one left palpitating with confused, humiliating desire.

Tallie was not left to brood on Nick Stangate for long. The next day Kate Parry finally announced herself satisfied with her preparation of her protégée for the start of the Season, but with one omission.

'Your hair, Tallie,' she announced, making her jump and almost drop the portfolio of properties Nick had left behind. Infuriatingly they all looked highly promising, both for the school and for the lodgings. Tallie had too much good sense not to use what had been laid out for her so efficiently, however she felt about the source of the information.

'My hair, Aunt Kate?' Tallie set down the portfolio and eyed Lady Parry cautiously.

'Yes, dear. Everything else is perfect. Your clothes and accessories are just as they should be, you have proved a quick study with your dancing lessons and I could not believe how rapidly you have soaked up all I had to tell you about Society and how to go on. That just leaves your hair.'

'But, ma'am, I like it like this. It is suitable.'

'It is certainly suitable for a hired companion. It is not at all suitable for a fashionable young lady. And definitely not for one who is going to make her come-out at the Duchess of Hastings's ball tomorrow night. Now, Mr Jordan is coming this afternoon to cut it for you.'

'Oh. I am very sorry, Aunt Kate, but I have arranged to take this portfolio of properties to Upper

Wimpole Street and discuss them with Zenna. I had not realised you had other plans.'

'Why not send a note round and ask her to come here? She might enjoy watching Mr Jordan at work.'

'Will he not object to an audience?'

'Tallie, he is going to be here as your employee; besides, he is bound to want to make a good impression on you by being as obliging as possible.'

'To me? But why?'

'Dearest, I keep trying to impress upon you that as the possessor of a fortune you are a very eligible *partie*. You are sure to take and it will do him good if you recommend him to other ladies.'

Tallie found this hard to believe, almost as hard as she found it to believe Nick telling her she would find herself the target of numerous amorous advances. But she could not bring herself to refuse whatever her kind friend wished her to do, so she obediently scribbled a note for Zenna and dispatched it with a footman.

To her surprise Zenna was not at all adverse to watching her having her hair styled, even tossing aside the portfolio of houses with a careless, 'I will look at it this evening.'

So Tallie submitted to the scissors so expertly wielded by Mr Jordan. She was prepared to dislike him, for she had never come across anyone quite so affected as the stick-thin coiffeur. She was convinced that he was wearing maquillage and his hands had certainly been manicured into an almost feminine softness.

However, from the moment he set those delicate hands on her hair he stopped mincing and became impressively professional. After an hour of brushing, pinning, snipping, curling and further snipping, he stepped back and gestured to the other ladies to admire the results. The response he got would have gratified the heart of even the most exacting artist.

'There,' said Lady Parry triumphantly. 'Now you are ready for your first ball.'

Nick Stangate accepted a glass of brandy from his cousin and leaned back in the chair by the fireside. 'Stop fidgeting at that neckcloth,' he advised as William peered in the mirror for the third time and prodded at the gold pin securing the crisp folds of palest lavender linen.

William came and took the chair opposite. 'How much longer can they be?' he enquired impatiently. Occasionally he squired his mother to dances, but he had never known her to take so long getting ready that the horses had to be sent back to the mews.

'As long as it takes for Aunt Kate to make her arrival at exactly the right moment,' Nick said lazily, swirling the amber liquid round and admiring the way the light hit it. 'She will wait until all the people she wants to impress are there and before it becomes too much of a squeeze.'

'But why?' William grumbled. 'She usually likes to get there early, all the better for a good gossip.'

'I think we are about to find out.' Nick got to his feet, forcing himself to do so slowly. He sauntered out into the hall with William at his heels and waited at the foot of the stairs, his head tilted so he could see the full sweep of polished mahogany treads.

His ears had caught the sound of bedroom doors shutting. He did not have long to wait. Faintly the sound of Lady Kate urging someone to go on in front of her reached the men in the hall, then a vision appeared.

Nick thought he had been prepared for what he would see. But he was not prepared for this. A tall slender figure in a dress of silver spider gauze over white crepe appeared to be floating down the stairs, one white-gloved hand resting lightly on the rail.

Huge green eyes, serious with the effort of maintaining both poise and a sweep of fragile skirts; full red lips slightly parted with nervousness and, crowning it all, a crown of gilt curls falling from a severely upswept mass of hair. As she got closer he realised that her face was pale and the soft tendrils of hair that had been teased loose around her temples were quivering slightly.

Tallie looked exquisite, terrified and, for the first time since he had known her, achingly vulnerable. There was no sign of the fierce independence, the anger when he crossed her, the aloof calm behind which she could so disconcertingly vanish along with her secrets.

Nick felt his entire body tighten, harden, racked with desire and that desire warred with a fierce protectiveness. He wanted to seize her in his arms, carry her to the nearest bed—or the floor, or the sofa—or take her here and now in the hallway. And he wanted to stop any man, himself included, who so much as laid a finger on her.

For once in his life Lord Arndale found words beyond him and it was his inexperienced cousin who knew exactly the right thing to say.

'Tallie, you look absolutely gorgeous. May I have a waltz?'

Nick felt more than saw Tallie's gaze sweep over him and past him to William. He saw her anxious face break into a soft smile of relief at the frank admiration and then she was past him in a soft cloud of silk gauze and jasmine perfume before he could find his own voice.

'Thank you, William. I would love that; here, please, can you write it on my card?' Nick watched as his cousin lifted the little folded card with its minute pencil that dangled from her wrist and carefully inscribed his name. He was aware of his aunt arriving at the foot of the stairs beside him and he turned abruptly to greet her as Tallie raised one hand to touch William's lapel. 'That neckcloth is the best yet,' she confided quietly.

Was Aunt Kate regarding him with covert amusement? People did not as a rule laugh at Nick Stangate. He narrowed his eyes at her, but she simply smiled and whispered wickedly, 'Close your mouth, dear,' before stepping to one side to allow room for her dresser who was carrying the ladies' cloaks.

It took some time to fit the four of them into the carriage without crushing skirts, knocking tall silk hats or mangling the magnificent plumes that were topping Lady Parry's coiffure, but it was achieved at last.

Nick hoped the forced closeness might break the ice a little with Tallie, for he had begun to realise that a good part of her nervousness as she came downstairs was because of their last encounter. He had been torn between kicking himself for letting that kiss happen, a fervent desire to do it again and a rather cooler interest in what it had taught him about her.

Whatever the secret she was guarding from him so carefully, it did not involve an entanglement with a man. There was no mistaking the innocent shock as his lips had met hers. That had been her first kiss and he felt a strange sense of privilege that it was he who had given it to her. Was that just a glimpse of a man's feelings when he took his bride's virginity? The thought shook him so much that he shifted in his seat abruptly, knocking William's elbow.

'Sorry. Cramp.' The thought of initiating Tallie into the arts of lovemaking was so powerfully erotic he could only be thankful for the dimly lit interior of the carriage. But it was the word 'bride' that really shook him. Marrying a milliner-come-lady, and one with presumably disreputable secrets, was not in his plans at all. He had no need of a bride with a fortune, he was eligible enough to have his pick of whatever Society beauties crossed his path and his intention was to find a well-bred young lady who would fit neatly into his life, produce his heirs, ornament his drawing room and generally make life agreeable.

Nick gritted his teeth, crossed his legs with care and reviewed his tactics. Discover exactly what that secret was. That was the first thing. Deal with it, if that were possible, cover it up if it were not. And if it was really bad, remove Miss Grey from his aunt's household and set her up with her school and her lodging-houses and whatever other schemes she had in mind. Safely out of Society, that was the best plan. It would be the most comfortable solution for everyone concerned. And in the meantime, make sure that no one made her a declaration. The thought of a lurking scandal being compounded by the girl having a romantic entanglement with a member of the *ton* was too much.

In consequence he emerged from the carriage looking so grim that rumours began to fly around the ballroom that Lord Arndale had suffered a crushing reversal on the 'Change, that his favourite racehorse had died or that he was about to be called out by an enraged husband.

A little thought caused these speculations to be dismissed. Arndale was too sharp to be burnt by his investments, his racing stable was too well stocked for him to suffer greatly by the loss of just one animal and he was well known to conduct his *amours* with the utmost discretion and a scrupulous avoidance of the charms of married ladies.

It was a mystery and one that gained savour by the fact that he did not appear to intend to dance and instead stationed himself at his aunt's side by a pillar against which he leaned, arms crossed, regarding the dance floor with brooding indifference.

'He is *so* romantic,' one impressionable young lady remarked languishingly to her brother. 'Just like Lord Byron.'

'Dash it all, Lizzie,' he replied, shocked. 'You can't compare Arndale to that poseur of a poet! Byron's dashed bad *ton*—and he's putting on weight.'

The object of their attentions was watching his cousin circle the dance floor with Tallie in his arms and was doing his level best not to scowl. They made a very fetching picture, both blond, both tall enough to be striking and both with a natural grace, which made up for the fact that William was still inclined to fall over his feet on occasion and Tallie had never danced in public before.

He had no real fear that Tallie was going to try and attach William whatever she said to tease him, so why he should feel so thoroughly out of sorts he could not imagine. He had a plan to deal with the chit and that should be the end of it.

Lady Parry had attracted her usual group of bosom friends around her and from the hum of conversation he could tell she had done her work well to prepare for Tallie's first appearance.

Ladies were sighing at the thought of the well-born girl forced by undeserved poverty to work with her needle and skilful fingers to earn an honest living. It was rapidly borne in on Nick that his inventive aunt had done more than sow a few seeds and let natural sympathy do the rest. She had been engaged on some major embroidery.

'How dreadful that a parent's well-intentioned plan should go so frightfully amiss,' one dowager was saying to another.

'Indeed,' the other lady responded, unaware of Nick's sharp ears bent in her direction. 'To have tied up Miss Grey's fortune until she was twenty-five in order to deter fortune hunters was very wise, but then to have omitted to provide her with the means of support until she reached that age...'

Nick swivelled slowly to meet his aunt's eyes and was met with a look of calm innocence that almost charmed a grin out of him. *'Baggage,'* he mouthed silently before turning to see where Tallie and William had got to. The music had ended and she ought to be on her way back to her chaperon.

There she was, talking with William in a knot of

attentive gentlemen. Nick caught William's eye and jerked his head slightly in a signal to steer her back, but he was too late. The music struck up again and Miss Grey was being led out onto the floor by Jack Hemsley.

Chapter Ten

Tallie knew perfectly well, even if William did not, that she should have made her way back to Lady Parry and allowed her chaperon to approve her partners. And she was certain she should not had agreed when Mr Hemsley had appeared at her elbow and had begged the privilege of the next dance. But the sight of him had so flustered her that she had not been able to decline gracefully.

It was a quadrille and Tallie quailed somewhat at the thought of the complexities of the steps. They joined a set with three other couples and at first Tallie was too focused on setting to the right partner at the right moment to pay much attention to Jack Hemsley.

But after the first repeat her confidence came back and she relaxed. Mr Hemsley was fortunately behaving himself impeccably and, if she had not known just how despicably he *could* behave to a defenceless woman, she would have felt perfectly comfortable in his company. It was obvious he had not the slightest idea he was dancing with the model for the 'Diana' picture and she even doubted he recalled the mousy milliner he had winked at in Lady Parry's drawing room.

She was quite certain, however, that he had garnered every scrap of gossip about her fortune and circumstances and this dance was the opening salvo in his campaign to woo the new heiress. It would be amusing to thank him coolly after the dance and to refuse another. She had no sooner resolved on this admirably sensible course of action than the parting lines of dancers gave her a view of Nick Stangate watching her across the floor.

His disapproval was as palpable as if he had spoken and she flushed angrily.

Did he think that after kissing her and lecturing her he was now going to try and exert some form of control over her in the ballroom? Well, it was time he was taught a lesson, Tallie fumed inwardly. She would show him she was not easily taken in by rakes and fortune hunters and could perfectly easily handle the likes of Jack Hemsley.

She pushed away the knowledge that she had been hurt that evening by his silence when she came downstairs. If she thought about it she would cry, which was ridiculous. She did not need Nick Stangate's approval or admiration. She knew she was looking very fine. Lady Parry had told her, William's open admiration told her, the expressions of the people she met told her.

Tallie tried not to refine too much on the look on Nick's face as she had walked tremulously down those endless stairs. She had expected him to be pleased at the transformation, to smile, to show some warmth and admiration. Instead his face had set into stone, his eyes had glittered coldly and he had not even managed to make some token remark.

Her thoughts must have shown on her face for, as the last notes of the dance echoed around the room and she rose from her curtsy, Jack Hemsley asked, 'Have I displeased you, Miss Grey? Do not say I am responsible for that frown.'

'Was I frowning? I do beg your pardon. It is just the…the noise and the heat. I am not accustomed to balls, you see.'

'Then you must have a glass of lemonade and some air, Miss Grey.' He was guiding her from the floor with practised smoothness, one hand just resting under her elbow, smiling and bowing as they made their way through the throng.

'I am all right, really, Mr Hemsley. If I could just

go back to Lady Parry.' It was difficult to know how to extricate herself without making a scene.

'In a moment, Miss Grey, you are quite flushed. I am sure there is a risk of you swooning if you return immediately to that crush and heat. Now just here…ah, yes.'

He pushed open a door and Tallie found herself in a little room, almost like a box at the theatre. It opened out onto a balcony overlooking the garden, although the windows were closed against the chill March night.

'I will just open this a crack, so, and if you sit here…' he patted a sofa encouragingly '…then you will not be in the draught, but you will have the benefit of the air.'

It all seemed very sensible, even innocuous. 'Thank you, sir.' Tallie sat down, suddenly aware of just how warm she was feeling. 'Perhaps if I was to drink some lemonade as you suggested, I will be able to go back in a moment.'

'Of course.' Instead of going out for the drink, he sat next to her and lifted her hand in his. 'Why, your pulse is racing my dear Miss Grey. I think I had better remain here for a moment just in case you feel faint. Put your head on my shoulder so…'

'Stop it!' Tallie struggled to stand up and found herself very effectively pinned against the upholstery. Mr Hemsley might affect the airs of a languid man of fashion, but the muscles under his coat were alarmingly hard as she pushed against them.

'Just one little kiss before we go back, my dear.'

Tallie freed a hand and swung it. It made satisfying contact with the side of his head, but left her gasping and clutching her wrist with the jarring pain. Hemsley's hands groped for her, found her hair and gripped in an effort to turn her face for a kiss.

Tallie wrenched back and felt pins and combs falling down. With a jerk of her knee she was free, on her feet, halfway to the door.

It opened and she found herself face to face with Nick, William at his back. She stopped dead, the carefully piled edifice of her coiffure broke free and hair cascaded down her back. Behind her Jack Hemsley swore, a sharp, vicious sound. In front of her she saw Nick pull William into the room and slam the door to behind him.

'Stop anyone coming in.'

William placed his back against the panels and stared at the scene. The sight of the shock and distress on his young face hurt Tallie more than anything else.

'You will name your seconds, Hemsley.' Nick sounded icily calm.

'Now look here, I know how this looks…'

'It looks as though you were assaulting Miss Grey.'

'Well, I wasn't. Thought she was going to faint—heat and so on. Brought her in here, opened the window, see. Wouldn't do a damn fool thing like that if I was going to tumble the girl now, would I?'

William straightened up from the door, his fists clenched. Nick put out a hand and stopped him. 'You will speak of Miss Grey with respect or I will not trouble with form and deal with you here and now.'

'You wouldn't do that—look, Nick old chap, it's all a misunderstanding, silly chit thought I was trying to—'

The blow landed with a satisfying thump right on the point of Hemsley's chin. Nick stepped forward, rubbing his balled fist in the other palm. 'Get up. I want to do that again.' He sounded as though he was asking the man to deal another hand of cards.

Tallie swirled round and stared at the wall. She didn't want to see what Nick was doing, didn't want to see the look on his face as he methodically began to take Jack Hemsley to pieces. And she did not want to see the disillusion on William's face as he realised what the man he thought was his friend was capable of with a young woman living in his house.

'Now get out. William, make sure he gets away from this room without anyone seeing him. And, Hemsley, don't even think of speaking of this, will you? Because if you do, I'll break your neck.'

Thank God, he hadn't killed him. Tallie wondered vaguely if she was going to be sick. Probably not, she concluded after a fierce struggle with her stomach. Was she alone? William had gone, and Hemsley. The room was quiet except for the sounds of music and talk and laughter penetrating the heavy door.

She put out a hand to the wall in front of her and just stood, head bowed, her hair shielding her face. Then she knew she was not alone. Someone moved behind her, so close she could feel his heat through her flimsy gown and hands turned her into the safety of soft linen, encircling arms, a strong comforting heartbeat.

'Nick.'

'What?' His breath stirred her hair. She felt a weight on the top of her head as though he had laid his cheek there.

'Just…Nick. I am sorry to have been so foolish, I really thought he was going to get me a glass of lemonade. He won't say anything, will he?'

'Not and expect to live, no. He is a coward and I am both a better shot and a better swordsman than he is.' There was a pause. 'Are you crying?'

'No,' lied Tallie, trying not to sniff. She felt so safe, so warm, so *cherished.*

'In that case, why is the front of my shirt becoming soggy?' Nick enquired.

Tallie felt his hand under her chin and her face was ruthlessly tipped up despite her efforts to resist. 'I have to tell you, Cousin Talitha, your nose is pink, but your eyes look absolutely enchanting swimming in tears. It is quite obvious that you did not pay the slightest attention to the warning I gave you the other day. I will just have to repeat it.'

This time the kiss was not so gentle, not so careful. Tallie found her lips parting under the onslaught of his, then gasped as his tongue invaded ruthlessly. Her body appeared to understand exactly what that intrusion meant, wanted more, was telling her to react in ways that were new and shamingly wanton in order to incite him.

She felt her own tongue darting to meet his, to caress, challenge his, flicker daringly into the heat of his mouth. Her body arched against him, soft against the answering hardness. Her breasts ached, her loins ached, she ached…

There was a knock on the door.

When William peered round, he found Tallie lying back against the sofa cushions looking flushed and Nick on one knee on the carpet gathering up hairpins.

'Has he gone?'

William nodded. 'I followed him. He went out through the back; no one saw him. I brought you a glass of lemonade, Tallie.'

Tallie forced a smile for him, her heart aching at the look of distress on his face. 'Thank you, William, I am quite all right, truly.'

'What can I do? Shall I fetch Mama and send for the carriage to come round to the back?'

'No.' Nick's voice was sharp. 'The ball has hardly started, Tallie cannot simply vanish like that. It will cause talk. Help me find all these pins and then go to the kitchens and ask for some rice powder.'

'Rice powder? I can't just—'

'You are Lord Parry and a guest. If you ask them for a bucket of earthworms, they'll give it to you. Tallie, how many pins were there?'

Tallie racked her brains. 'Twelve, I think, and two combs.'

'I can find ten, that will have to do. William, have you got a comb?'

Tallie found herself perched on the edge of the sofa while Nick combed, cursed and muttered through a mouthful of hairpins. Eventually she felt the weight of her hair lift and put up a tentative hand. 'Nick, it's wonderful! How did you learn how to do that?'

'I don't think I want to tell you,' he said. 'It would shock you. Well, Aunt Kate will be able to tell something has happened, but I don't think anyone else will suspect more than overenthusiastic participation in a country dance. Now, where's William?'

He appeared on the question, flushed and more than a little put out. 'They looked at me as though I was mad,' he muttered, handing over a large jar.

Nick grinned. 'I want to powder Tallie's nose, not bake a batch of whatever one cooks with the stuff, you young idiot. Oh well, it will give the housemaids something to speculate about in the morning when they find it.' He drew a handkerchief out of his pocket, dipped it in the jar and turned to Tallie. 'Sit still. There, that's better, now you look less like a white rabbit and more like an overheated young lady.'

Tallie dropped her eyes, too embarrassed to meet his amused gaze. He stood up and straightened his cuffs, then dabbed at his grazed knuckles with the powdered handkerchief. 'William, go and tell your mother that Tallie is all right and will be out in a moment.'

There was a long silence after the door closed. Tallie got carefully to her feet and smoothed down her gown. Surely the moment she stepped outside the door people would look at her and know that only a few minutes before she had been locked in Nick Stangate's heated embrace, kissing him back with all the fervour she could. Surely *wanton* was branded across her forehead?

'Tallie,' he said softly, one hand on the doorknob.

'Yes?'

'Will you not tell me your secret?'

Tallie's eyes flew to his face. Of all the things he might have said, this was furthest from her imaginings. 'No!' she blurted out. 'No! Was that why you kissed me? You thought you would confuse and befuddle me until I would tell you *anything*? No!' And she was through the door and into the corridor before he could stop her. Three hurried steps and she was on the threshold of the ballroom. Tallie ignored the footsteps behind her, took a deep breath, fixed a social smile on her burning lips and, with pounding heart, stepped calmly into the mêlée.

She made her way to Lady Parry's side and sat down with a careful smile on her face. After one startled glance her chaperon handed her a fan and said brightly for the benefit of their near neighbours, 'Talitha dear, how often did I warn you about the country dances? You look a sad romp.'

'Yes, Aunt Kate. I am sorry, Aunt Kate.' Tallie did her best to shrink back while around her amused chaperons tutted and smiled at her overenthusiasm.

She was rescued eventually by William asking her to accompany him to the supper room. He tucked her hand firmly under his elbow, treated her as though she was made of glass and scowled so forbiddingly at any man who came near that they ended up in sole possession of a table.

Tallie made herself nibble at a savoury patty and relax in the hope that William would relax too. It was rather like being escorted by a large, fierce dog. 'Where is Lord Arndale?'

'I'm not sure. I think he has left; he was certainly looking like thunder when you came out of that room. And he was pretty short with me when I tried to ask him what he was going to do next.'

'What…what did he say?'

'Didn't make sense.' William's brow furrowed. 'He said it was time to take some precautions and at least he now knew what he was dealing with. Does that make any sense to you?'

'No.' Tallie shook her head. 'None at all, unless… William, he wouldn't have gone after Mr Hemsley, would he?'

'What, to call him out after all? No, not without me. He'd need at least one second, and I'm the only one he can involve without risking talk.' William offered Tallie a plate of sweetmeats and, when she shook her head, stood up. 'Let's get back, shall we? Do you think we can have another waltz without all the old biddies shaking their heads over us?'

Tallie followed him, just relieved at the thought of being in a safe pair of arms and having something to think about other than Nick Stangate. All the contradictions were back, tearing her apart, making her unable to think about him coherently, let alone know how to deal with him.

He had saved her again, this time with his anger and his physical courage rather than his quick wits and self-restraint. And he had aroused in her feelings and longings that she could hardly comprehend, let alone control. And then he had struck at her with that question about her secret. He had tried to trick her into an answer when he must have known she was at her most vulnerable, must have known that he himself had contributed to that vulnerability.

Nick Stangate was ruthless and dangerous, and he had most cause to be when he thought something of his was threatened. If he found out the truth about her, he would see it as a direct threat to his family, never mind how forgiving Lady Kate was inclined to be about it. And now he knew how she reacted to being in his arms, he had a potent weapon she had to make certain he never again had the opportunity to use against her. *Never.*

Chapter Eleven

The household in Bruton Street received no visits from Lord Arndale during the week following the Duchess's ball. Which was not to say that he was not making himself very much felt.

Tallie heard from Zenna that she was receiving particulars of houses almost daily. Then there was a visit from a very helpful clerk who offered Miss Scott his escort to any properties she might wish to view.

'He brought Lord Arndale's card with him,' she explained on a fleeting visit to ask if she might borrow a maid to accompany her. Lady Parry had agreed immediately, explaining that she had a parlour maid with aspirations to become a ladies' maid. 'It will be useful practise for her to learn how to behave when out with a lady.'

William reported bumping into his cousin in various clubs and once as he emerged from a house near Pickering Place. 'Asked him what on earth he was doing there. He gave me one of his poker-faced looks and said he was calling on his agent. Rum sort of place for an agent if you ask me.'

But, disconcertingly, Nicholas appeared at every function Tallie attended. He did not ask her to dance or engage her in conversation, merely stopping long enough to give the appearance of normality before moving on to the card tables or another dancing partner.

Tallie moved rapidly from feeling relieved to being intrigued and then downright piqued—especially as she was beginning to enjoy a flattering amount of success with her come-out. The least Nicholas could do was to ask her to dance occasionally. When his parting shot at Lady Cressett's musical evening was, 'I am glad to see you are doing nothing indiscreet or unwise', Tallie was filled with an urge to do something quite outrageous out of sheer defiance.

Fortunately nothing occurred to her and the next afternoon she set off in the Parrys' carriage for a cosy evening in Upper Wimpole Street to discuss the lodging-house scheme with Mrs Blackstock.

She arrived early enough to spend some time with Millie before she set off for the Opera House and listened with interest to tales of backstage rivalries,

Millie's excellent progress in her singing and the flattering number of floral tributes she was receiving.

Tallie caught Zenna's eye. She had confided her experience with Jack Hemsley because she wanted to put Zenna on her guard if she had any further contact with him. Now she raised an eyebrow and nodded slightly in Millie's direction. Zenna shrugged and a few moments later took the opportunity to whisper, 'I have not seen him around, but it doesn't mean she isn't seeing him at the Opera House.'

'Probably hiding his bruises,' Tallie said grimly, remembering the sound of those blows thudding home on flesh and bone.

By seven o'clock Tallie and Mrs Blackstock found themselves alone. Zenna had been invited to visit the family of one of her ex-pupils and Millie had departed for the Opera House in a hackney carriage.

'I'll just spread out the details of the ones we thought most suitable,' Tallie suggested, picking up the sheaf of house particulars. 'If I move these things off the table… Is this not Millie's reticule?'

Tallie held it up and Mrs Blackstock looked anxious. 'Oh, dear, it is, she must have forgotten it. Is her purse inside?'

A quick glance found the stocking purse nestling within, along with Millie's house key.

'I had better take a cab and go to the theatre,' Mrs Blackstock said with a sigh. 'She could borrow the cab fare back from another girl, I suppose, but knowing Millie she won't think of it until she's outside the theatre on her way home.'

Tallie looked at the older woman's tired face and got to her feet. 'No, I'll go. I haven't seen the new production yet and it will be fun to do so from backstage.'

Mrs Blackstock accepted the offer with gratitude, but insisted on coming out with Tallie until she found a respectable-looking hackney carriage and made sure that Tallie had Millie's stocking purse tucked inside her own reticule.

It took some while for the cab to make its way through the crowded evening streets from Upper Wimpole Street to the point where the Opera House stood on the corner of Haymarket and Pall Mall. Tallie had never been backstage before, but she knew where to find the stage door and the elderly man on duty there let her in willingly enough when she asked for Millie and tipped him a silver coin.

Tallie had to push her way through shabby, crowded corridors half-blocked with scenery flats and overflowing wicker baskets. Faintly she could hear the orchestra tuning up ahead and small knots of people hurried past, careless of whom they pushed aside in their haste.

Searching for someone who was not in such a hurry, Tallie turned into a quieter passageway. A door opened in front of her and a man wearing nothing but skintight inexpressibles, an obvious wig of red hair and a scowl stepped out. Tallie blinked at this apparition, unsure whether to scream or give way to giggles.

'John!' the man bawled, breaking off to glare at Tallie. 'Where in the name of Heaven is my fool of a dresser?'

'I have no idea, sir,' she replied, tearing her gaze away from his naked torso. 'Where is the chorus changing room?'

'Boys or girls?' he demanded.

'Girls!' Tallie said indignantly.

'Never can tell,' he observed obscurely. 'Down there, turn left, down the stairs, follow the cackling. John, you idle bastard!'

With her hands clamped over her ears Tallie hastened down the corridor in the direction of his pointing hand. There was no denying that the noise betrayed the location of the dressing-room, and when Tallie peeped round the door she could quite see why.

At least two dozen girls in various stages of undress filled the room, which was overheated, glaringly lit and reeked of perspiration, cheap scent and face powder.

At the nearest makeshift dressing-table to the door a dark girl in a thin chemise was clutching a post while another in pink fleshings that left nothing to the imagination hauled on her stay laces. 'Tighter, you silly tart,' the first girl gasped when the second stopped heaving. 'Tighter or I'll never get into the costume.'

'Fall out of it more like,' her friend retorted with a chuckle. 'That'll be a crowd pleaser.'

'Excuse me,' Tallie ventured when they both subsided panting, 'is Amelie LeNoir in here?'

'Millie? Yes, over there. Here, luv, just stick your finger on that knot while I do the bow. Ta. Millie!' She raised a voice trained to be heard from the front row of the chorus to the back seats in the gods. 'Visitor!'

Tallie extracted her finger from the tangle of stay laces and hurried over to where Millie's startled face appeared round a rack of costumes.

'You forgot your purse,' she explained, plumping

down on a stool next to her friend. 'May I watch the performance from backstage?'

'Oh, thank you, Tallie,' Millie said warmly. 'Yes, of course, just take care you do not get in anyone's way—and you won't have to mind the language.'

Tallie settled down to absorb the atmosphere. Once her ears adjusted to the din and apparent chaos she began to pick out differences in costumes and to make some sense out of what was going on.

What had seemed to her first startled gaze to be Millie's state of near nudity was revealed as being a set of skin-toned fleshings over which a dress, apparently made of disparate pieces of fabric, was in fact held together by panels of pink net. It still revealed slender ankles and a quantity of Millie's well-turned calf.

Millie dusted her face with a vast powder puff and searched frantically through her cluttered table. 'Where's my lampblack? Jemmie!'

'Yes, miss?' A sharp-faced urchin appeared as though by magic.

'Where's my lampblack?'

'Suzy half-inched it,' the boy reported.

'Well, go and half-inch it back.'

'That's a boy!' Tallie gasped.

'Yes, I know. That's Jemmie. He's eight.'

'But you are all… I mean, half of you haven't got any clothes on and—'

'He's used to it,' Millie said calmly. 'Doesn't know any different. Thinks we're all his sisters in any case.'

A man stuck his head round the door. 'Overture and beginners! Shift your assets, you load of…' A chorus of abuse and thrown objects greeted this announcement and he ducked back through he door.

Tallie had a sudden vision of what Nick would say if he saw her now and had to suppress a laugh. He hoped she was being neither indiscreet nor unwise, did he? How would he categorise sitting in the middle of the opera-chorus dressing-room?

Millie was jamming a saucy hat on her head and picking up a beribboned shepherd's crook. 'Right. Here we go. I'm in the first scene with the other village girls.'

Tallie spent an exhilarating hour and a half being jostled, sworn at, deafened and shocked as she jammed herself into a corner of the wings and watched the performance. At last the final curtain came down and the cast rushed off, sweaty, exhausted and apparently ready to spend the rest of the night in a continuous party.

'Come on.' Millie caught Tallie's arm and dragged

her along. 'I need to get changed before they let any of them in.'

'Who?' Tallie found herself acting as an impromptu dresser, unhooking Millie's costume and handing her pieces of cotton waste dipped in goose grease to clean off the make-up.

'We get the lot: the bloods, the peep o'day boys, a few flats, some pinks of the *ton*,' Millie said calmly. 'I don't encourage them myself, of course, but most of the girls have got followers.'

'They are going to let them in here?' Tallie squeaked. 'Can we go before that happens?'

'If I really rush.' Millie stepped into her petticoats and reached for a walking dress hanging on a hook beside her. 'Normally I'm never finished before they come in. So long as I'm dressed properly I don't mind. I just get on and do my hair and things.'

Tallie fidgeted with impatience, unable to see anything she could help with to finish Millie's toilette. The last thing she had expected was to be found in here by a crowd of amorously inclined men—judging from the very half-hearted efforts some of the girls were making to get changed, any man coming here this evening was not going to want to be discussing the finer points of the script.

'Where are my shoes?' Millie demanded, dropping to her knees and scrabbling under the table. 'Oh bother, I've kicked one right through…' She scuttled under the table in pursuit of her missing slipper, leaving Tallie by herself as the door swung open to admit a crowd of men.

They were in a dangerously boisterous mood, already half-drunk, clutching champagne bottles and more than ready to enjoy whatever favours the chorus girls were minded to share with them. Tallie retreated behind a rack of dresses, only to freeze as a very familiar voice reached her from the other side of the wall of mirrors.

'Why, Miss LeNoir! Charmed to see you. I did so enjoy your performance tonight.' Hemsley. Tallie pressed herself back against the wall, then realised that she could not abandon Millie, who was obviously responding with flattered delight to his compliments.

'Your voice goes from strength to strength,' he was confiding. 'I think you are wasted in the chorus. I happen to know someone who manages performances at Drury Lane. I know he would hear you as a favour to me. Why don't you let me drive you home this evening so we can discuss it? You don't want to be here with this rabble—it is unsuitable for an *artiste* of your talent.'

'Oh, thank you, Mr Hemsley, but I cannot drive with you this evening;
 besides, should you be out when you have so obviously been injured? Whatever happened?'

Tallie tiptoed closer to the end of the makeshift wall of mirrors.

'Footpads, my dear, six of them at least. I had my cane, of course, and I flatter myself I have a good right hook, but even so, it took me some time to—' He broke off, his drawling voice choking on the words as Tallie appeared. She glanced around, but the rest of the men were gathered round a giggling group of girls by the door; they would not be overheard.

'Why, Mr Hemsley, what a dreadful mess those villains made of your face!' If she had not been present when it happened, she would never have believed that mass of bruises was the work of one man. 'How heroic of you to beat them off.'

'Do you know Mr Hemsley, then, Tallie?' Millie asked innocently, her face lighting up to discover two of her friends were acquainted.

'Yes, indeed,' Tallie said earnestly. 'You have been having a hard time, Mr Hemsley, have you not? Such ill fortune to be attacked by footpads immediately after Lord Arndale beat you so soundly for attempting to ravish me.'

'What!' Millie gasped, running to Tallie's side to put her arm around her. 'You…you beast!'

It was obvious that Millie trusted her friend's word absolutely. She stood by Tallie like a fierce little cat defending its kitten against a dog. 'Take one step nearer and I'll scratch your eyes out, you libertine!'

'My dear Miss LeNoir,' Hemsley was making the mistake of trying to bluster. 'It was simply a misunderstanding—'

'On your part,' a cold voice said. Three pairs of eyes turned to find Nicholas Stangate lounging negligently against a clothes rail. A semi-clad dancer ran over giggling and put her arms around him. 'Not now, darling,' he said absently, giving her a pat on her rounded little rump. 'Off you go like a good girl.'

Tallie made a serious effort to steady her voice, then observed, 'If you hit him here it will start a brawl.'

'I know. Tempting, isn't it? I feel like a little excitement…of some kind. But we don't want to upset the ladies, do we, Hemsley? Why don't you run along while I take them home?'

Hemsley stalked to the door with as much dignity as he could muster. Nick did not even trouble to watch him leave and missed the look of murderous hatred he shot back at Tallie. *I will make you sorry for this*, those eyes promised. She shivered. She had made an enemy, a very bad enemy, and so had Nick.

Tallie turned back to look apprehensively at Nick. What was he going to do? What, more importantly, was he going to say in front of Millie and a potential audience of drunken bucks?

'Do you have your cloaks, ladies? Then if you are ready to leave, Miss LeNoir?' He escorted them firmly out, a broad shoulder turned to the romp in the main part of the room that was rapidly becoming raucous.

Nick appeared to know the labyrinthine passageways backstage with remarkable accuracy. 'You have an excellent sense of direction, my lord,' Tallie remarked slyly. Her nerves were getting the better of her, she wanted to throw herself into his arms. Directing jibes seemed safer.

'Not at all,' he retorted smoothly, taking the wind out of her sails. 'I just happen to be very familiar with this theatre.'

Oh really, Tallie fumed, allowing herself to be steered towards the stage door. *And which opera dancers have you got under your protection, Cousin Nicholas?*

There was a closed carriage waiting, its sides black

with no arms visible. Millie settled back against the silk squabs with a sigh of pleasure and smiled prettily at Nick when he climbed in after them. He slid one of the shutters off an interior lantern and the inside of the carriage sprang into life.

'Thank you so much, my lord. I am very grateful to you. Tallie…Miss Grey was so brave to face up to Mr Hemsley like that. Why, I was quite taken in by him.' Her pretty face crumpled for a moment, then she regained her poise. 'I can see that I must be even more on my guard.'

Tallie leaned over to pat her arm and shot Nick a warning glance. Millie did not need any lectures on the dangers of her position.

He simply raised an eyebrow at her and said, 'Had you considered using your talents in any other way, Miss LeNoir?'

Millie smiled. 'I know I am not good enough to be a soloist. My voice is not strong enough.'

'For the stage perhaps you are right. But what about private parties, musical evenings, select gatherings of that sort? You would have to be very careful about what offers you accepted and you would need to employ a driver and a chaperon, but you could make an excellent living, I would judge, and be far less exposed to insult and unwanted attractions.'

Millie just stared at him, her eyes wide, then she

clapped her hands together in delight. 'Oh, yes! Oh, my lord, thank you—it would be just the thing.'

'I can make some recommendations to start you off,' Tallie offered. 'Soon you will make your own reputation. And, Millie, I had been wondering what present I could make you—may I employ a chaperon for your first year?'

They dropped an ecstatic Millie off at Wimpole Street. Nick waited until he saw the front door close behind her, then rapped on the roof of the carriage with his cane. As the wheels began to turn, he said, 'Well?'

'I had no idea he would be there,' Tallie said defensively. 'I had no idea they would let any men into the dressing-room at all. I only went because Millie forgot her purse.'

'I know. I went to collect you from Mrs Blackstock's and she told me where you were.'

'Oh. I thought…'

'You thought I had gone to the Opera House on much the same errand as Hemsley, did you not?'

'I did not know what to think, only that I was very glad to see you!' Now was not the time to throw his familiarity with backstage in his face. Tallie searched round for another means of attack. 'Collecting me alone in a closed carriage is somewhat unconventional is it not?'

'We are in a closed carriage now, as you can observe. You may also have noticed that I am able to restrain my carnal appetites. If you can refrain from lowering the window and crying "rape", I think we can brush through the experience without having to resort to wedlock.'

Tallie reviewed a number of possible responses to this, including throwing herself into his arms, slapping his face or insisting on him stopping the carriage and getting out. None of these would approach his own standard of infuriatingly cool indifference and she badly wanted to surprise him. 'Well, that *is* a relief,' she said warmly.

Tallie had intended to provoke him, but she was not prepared for his reaction. Nick tipped back his head and laughed. He laughed without any restraint, a genuine, uninhibited roar of amusement, crinkling his eyes shut, stretching the long tendons of his neck as he threw his head back, removing every trace of constraint and control from his face.

She stared, torn between fury at being laughed at and fascination at the transformation. The carriage slowed, then stopped outside the Bruton Street house. Nick mopped his streaming eyes and regarded Tallie with a grin.

'Tallie, you are *enchanting.*' He leaned forward and planted a brotherly kiss on her cheek as the groom came to open the carriage door for her. 'Now in with you or Aunt Kate will be worrying.'

The groom might be standing there pretending to be invisible with an expression of well-trained indifference on his face, but his presence effectively silenced any retort that Tallie might have made. Always supposing she was able to think of one.

'Goodnight, my lord,' she said with a chilly formality that provoked an equally formal half-bow, marred somewhat by the fact Nick's shoulders were still shaking. Tallie swept up to the front door without a backward glance and was relieved that Rainbird was already opening it.

'Good evening, Rainbird,' she said brightly. 'Is Lady Parry in?'

'She retired early, Miss Grey. May I get you anything?'

'No, thank you, Rainbird. I will retire too—could you send my maid up?'

The minute she was in her room Tallie regretted that last request. Now she had to act with calm and dignity while Susan helped her undress, unpinned her hair, put away her jewellery. What she wanted to do was find another cushion and beat the stuffing out of it.

Instead she sat in her wrapper while Susan plied the hairbrush and calmed herself by mentally listing all Nicholas Stangate's numerous faults. *He is cool, he is manipulative, he is domineering, overbearing and suspicious, he kisses innocent young women, he makes me lose my temper and my self-control.* That was a satisfyingly long list.

Tallie bit her lip and decided in all fairness she should catalogue the few—very few—virtues Nick possessed. *He loves his aunt and looks after William with a great deal of tact. He rescued me from Jack Hemsley twice. He behaved with chivalry when he found me in the attic. He is highly intelligent. He has a sense of humour. He looks... He is very handsome. When he kisses me I want to...I want him never to stop. He makes me lose my temper because...because...*

Her thoughts stumbled to a halt. 'Thank you, Susan, that will do. I do not require you any further tonight.'

The fire flickered and crackled in the grate, hypnotically drawing her eye. Tallie gazed at the flames and let her mind go free. Why did Nick crack right through her painfully acquired poise, her calm common sense?

'Because I love him,' she said out loud to the room. *'Because I love him.'*

Chapter Twelve

The following morning Tallie found she had no idea what to do about her moment of self-revelation the night before. She had felt strangely calm afterwards and had simply gone to bed and slept. So far as she was aware she had not dreamed.

The odd calm persisted, but underneath she was disturbed. It was as though she was sleepwalking into danger, watching herself do so and yet unable to wake herself up. Something had to be done about it, of course, she quite realised that. Nick was certainly not in love with her and, even if he were, she was a most unsuitable wife for him.

The odd feeling persisted despite an expedition with Lady Parry to Ackerman's Repository. Although Tallie already possessed every gown she could ever imagine she would need, Lady Parry wished to get ahead of what she called 'the others' by procuring all the latest fashion plates now, so that a refreshed wardrobe could be paraded halfway through the Season.

'I am certain you will be receiving some offers soon, Tallie dear,' she remarked complacently as they embarked in the barouche for the Strand.

Tallie was staring absently at a thin individual in an overlarge greatcoat and battered beaver who was lounging against the railings near the house. He looked oddly familiar. She focused on Lady Parry. 'Offers, ma'am?'

'Of marriage. You are not sickening for something, are you, Talitha?'

'No, no…I beg your pardon. Who would offer for me?' Several gentlemen had appeared to enjoy her company, that was true. There were a number who always sought her out to dance, several who took her driving and more than one who had introduced the subjects of their family, country estates and interests in life into the conversation in a way that she supposed she should have recognised as being somewhat pointed.

Lady Parry rolled her eyes. 'Making all due allowance for modesty and inexperience—*honestly*, Tallie! Let me list a few—Mr Runcorn, Sir Jasper Knight, Dr Philpott, Lord Ashwell, the Reverend Mr Laxton…'

'Truly?' Tallie gazed at her incredulously. 'But…I

had not considered marrying any of them. I simply had not thought of them in that way.'

Lady Parry shook her head at this folly. 'I will lay any odds you like that at least three of them come up to scratch by the end of the week, so you had better decide what you want to say to them.'

'No.'

'No? You want me to speak to them first? They will not necessarily approach me, as they know you are of age and I am not your guardian.'

'I mean, no, I do not want to marry any of them.' *I want to marry an infuriating man who does not trust me, laughs at me—and for whom I am entirely ineligible as a wife.*

'Oh well, the Season is young yet,' Kate said philosophically, gathering up her reticule and fur as the carriage began to slow down in the Strand. 'You are suffering a little from tiredness and nerves, I have no doubt. We must buy some more hats—I find that is always such a tonic.'

Nicholas Stangate awoke feeling decidedly cheerful, a sensation that lasted through a leisurely bath, a careful shave, an excellent breakfast consumed in the comfort of his bedchamber before dressing and two cups of coffee.

It was at the point where the second cup was

making its stimulating effects felt that he woke up enough to consider just why he was feeling this good. A moment's reflection was enough to produce a vertical line between his brows and a decided diminution in his feeling of *joie de vivre.*

Miss Talitha Grey was proving a serious worry. She might be enchanting to observe on her alarming progress through Society. She might be delicious to kiss and charming company for his aunt… But he was now convinced that if Aunt Kate thought she knew Tallie's dark secret, she was deceiving herself. One blinding flash of revelation at the Duchess of Hastings's ball left him suspecting a far more unusual and scandalous secret than any he had imagined. And if he were correct, it could prove both dangerous for Tallie and, at the very least, could cast a blight over Lady Parry's position as a leading member of Society.

If she had only failed to 'take'! But Tallie had been an instant success and, if he was not much mistaken, would soon be receiving any number of offers. Had he known it, his list of likely candidates was the same as his aunt's, but Nick regarded it with considerably less favour.

Knight was a dull dog, Runcorn had a tendency to gamble, the Reverend Laxton was a prosy bore, Dr Philpott was only looking for a wife with money before retreating back to Oxford and his books and Ashwell was…Ashwell was probably perfect for her.

A title, a modest fortune, a nice little estate, bright, pleasant, responsible. Perfect. Nick kicked a boot across the room and contemplated a newly wedded baron storming into Lady Parry's house to demand why she had allowed him to unwittingly marry a woman with a shameful secret. It had to be stopped.

His aunt was delighted to see him arrive at the dancing-and-card party she was holding that evening, fluttering forward to kiss him on both cheeks. He looked down at her with a smile. 'You are very fine this evening, my love.' She put her head on one side and smiled back. 'What are you up to? You look positively smug.'

'Nicholas!' She rapped his wrist with her fan, then cast a swift glance round and whispered, 'I think Tallie is receiving her first declaration.'

'What? Who?'

'Lord Ashwell.' Lady Parry was positively glowing with pride. 'For him to come up to scratch so early is a triumph. A much, much better match than I could have hoped for. He is perfect.'

'Perfect,' Nick agreed. 'And where is this romantic interlude taking place?'

'The conservatory, I believe. He was steering her in that direction just five minutes ago with considerable aplomb.'

We will see about that, Nick thought grimly. With a smile for his aunt he surrendered his place by her side to General Hepton and strode off in the direction of the conservatory.

So early in the evening it was deserted except for one couple virtually concealed behind a large potted palm. Nick advanced cat-like until he could see Lord Ashwell on one knee holding Tallie's hand, his head bowed as he made his declaration.

Tallie looked up and Nick saw her eyes widen and her chin go up at the sight of him. 'Go away,' she mouthed silently over her suitor's head. If he strode forward now she would know it was no accident that he had stumbled into the middle of the declaration, but a deliberate attempt to break it up.

Inwardly cursing, he forced a look of surprised apology onto his face, mouthed 'I'm sorry' and silently backed away out of the conservatory and into the reception room it opened onto.

The minutes seemed to drag by. Nick scooped a glass of champagne off a passing tray, agreed vaguely to make up a hand for whist later and bent an apparently attentive ear to the involved story concerning a bet on a curricle race being recounted by Lord Beddenton.

Lord Ashwell emerged from the conservatory so discreetly that Nick almost missed him, but he did not miss the droop of his lordship's shoulders, nor the lack of a smile on his face. He allowed him to get well clear into the room where the dancing was taking place, excused himself to Beddenton, snared another glass of champagne and made his way into the conservatory.

Tallie was still sitting where he had seen her before, playing with her fan. She tapped it, let its folds pour open, then flicked it closed, only to open it again. He watched her calm face, her air of concentration, wondering at the reserve behind which she could hide her feelings. Hide them most of the time, he corrected himself. Since he had known her she had appeared more transparent, more open. It seemed that either he was learning to read her moods or in some way he provoked her into revealing them.

How long had he been standing there watching her? He realised he had no idea. Long enough to have closed his eyes and repeated faithfully what she was wearing, from the tortoiseshell combs in her high-piled hair to the amber silk slippers just peeping from beneath an over-gown of golden brown lace with a pale yellow under-dress. The mix of golds brought a flash of recollection: a picture of masses of golden-gilt hair, shot through with deeper tones, waving over the bared shoulders and back of that naked goddess in the garret. Heat washed through him as he fought for control.

He must have moved. Tallie's head came up and she looked directly at him, her face expressionless. She raised one eyebrow smoothly. It seemed she had perfected the trick of it. 'Good evening, Cousin Nicholas.'

'Good evening. I apologise for blundering in just now.'

A faint sceptical smile. 'I doubt if you ever blunder anywhere, my lord.'

'You rejected him then.' He made it a statement.

'You asked him?' Her voice sharpened.

'I saw his face.' Nick strolled forward and took a cast-iron seat at right angles to her. The embossed ferns made an uncomfortable perch.

'I was sorry to hurt his feelings,' Tallie said. 'But I doubt they were deeply engaged. Thank you, no champagne.' He put down the glass.

'You think him insincere?' Nick let his surprise show in his voice.

'No. Not at all. I am sure he likes me very well and honestly believes that we would make a good match.'

'Then what is there to dislike?' It was suddenly important to know. 'He has breeding, a fortune, intelligence. He is kind…'

'Is that what you look for in marriage?' She swung round suddenly. It took an effort of will not to lean back away from her vehemence. 'Breeding, money, intelligence? *Kindness?*'

'Why, yes, they all seem admirable qualities.' Why was he on the defensive? Why was it his feelings that were the focus of attention now? She had just defined exactly what he had always felt he needed in a wife.

'You would settle for so little?' Tallie sounded genuinely curious.

'Little? It seems to me all one could want.' Suddenly he was not so certain. Her intensity seemed to slash open a hole in his philosophy. A void that ached. 'What do you look for?'

'Love, of course.' She stood, brushing against a jasmine in a pot and releasing a cloud of perfume from its early flowers, forced by the heat. 'I look for nothing more. I would settle for nothing less.'

'You could end up a spinster,' Nick said harshly, getting to his feet.

'Better that than compromise,' Tallie said calmly. 'Better that than mediocrity. And it is all I have ever expected, in any case.'

Something inside Tallie, some separate part of her that seemed to be watching the rest of her from a distance, registered surprise that she could regard Nicholas Stangate with such an appearance of calm. She was, after all, confronting the man she had only just realised she loved.

Tallie wondered if she had angered him, or even perhaps hurt him by attacking his views on what he would consider a suitable marriage. His grey eyes glittered like the interior of a newly split flint and there was colour on his high cheekbones.

'May I escort you back to the dancing, or were you expecting any other gentlemen?'

'No, not just now, thank you. I will have to go out and see if there are any I can lure in here,' she retorted, feeling the colour rise in her own cheeks. 'Aunt Kate tells me there are at least two more from whom I should expect a declaration within the next few days.'

A dark brow rose. 'Tut, tut, Tallie, a lady does not boast of her conquests.'

Tallie stood up in a swirl of tawny silk and lace. 'A *gentleman* would not provoke her into doing so.' She took a step forward, but Nick did not yield ground to her and she found herself standing almost on his toes.

His eyes dropped from the challenge in hers to linger appreciatively on the white slope of her breast and shoulders revealed by the low neckline of the gown. The single heavy diamond pendant lying where the valley between her breasts began was moving in tune with her heightened breathing.

'That is a very fine stone. Have your admirers been showering you with diamonds?'

'Aunt Kate has kindly lent it to me, as she has all the jewellery I wear. I possess none of my own.'

'We must hope your admirers will make you some suitable presents.'

'I have told you: I do not wish to be on such terms with any of them that gifts of jewellery would be eligible.' It was becoming difficult to breath. The conservatory was really quite stuffy and the scent of the jasmine so close was positively overpowering.

'Look how it reflects the light.' He appeared to be taking no notice of what she said. He was still watching the many-faceted stone and the scintillation of light as it moved. 'Is it your heart that is making it jump and tremble so, Tallie?'

Before she could reply he raised his right hand and laid it gently, palm to skin against the curve of her breast between her collarbone and the neckline of her dress. Tallie started and stepped back, but his other hand came round to gather her to him and she was trapped, one palm at her breast, the other flat on her shoulder blade. 'Your heart is beating like a drum.'

Tallie made herself stand still, certain he was about to kiss her, telling herself that when he did he would have to move his hand and she could slip under it and away, knowing that she would do no such thing.

But instead of bending his head to take her lips Nick continued to hold her eyes with his while the thumb of the hand lying on her breast began to move slowly, insidiously stroking the skin just under the edge of her gown. She gasped, tried to make her legs move, but all that happened was that her eyes fluttered closed as the skilful caress slipped under the neckline.

She had been doubtful about the gown: the edge of the fabric was only an inch above the aureole of her nipples, but once she had tried it on she was reassured that the cut and fit were so good that there was absolutely no need to fear that sudden movement or bending would cause the gown to gape or shift embarrassingly.

But neither she nor the dressmaker had planned

for seductive fingers. The ball of Nick's thumb found the puckered skin, then the bud of the nipple, and began to tease it. Tallie moaned deep in her throat, arching into his hand. Her breasts felt heavy, swollen. The sensation seemed to shaft through her. Her lips opened.

There was the sound of footsteps, a man's voice said playfully, 'Now where are you hiding, Miss Grey?' and then broke off abruptly. 'I do apologise, er…I will…' It was Sir Jasper Knight.

As the sound of hasty retreat faded, Tallie felt Nick's hand lift from her breast and his other hand release her. She opened her eyes slowly, knowing that anger on her part was completely unjustified. She could have stopped him at any time—but how could she face him now?

In the event he made it extremely easy for her. 'Oh well,' he said lightly, 'that's the second one routed.'

Tallie set her lips, drew back her hand and slapped Nick across the face with all the force she could muster. He made no move to avoid the blow, which rocked him back on his heels.

There was a long, difficult silence. Nick regarded her with eyes that held an uncomfortable mixture of rueful apology and still smouldering desire. His left cheek bore the mark of her hand as graphically as if she had drawn it. Tallie knew she must be scarlet. Her lips felt swollen, although his had not touched them. Her nipples pressed against the silk lining of her gown, a humiliating reminder of her own arousal.

'Drink this.' Nick held out the neglected champagne glass. 'Then you had better go out—I suspect I show more evidence of this encounter than you do.'

Tallie gulped the wine desperately. There was a fountain in the corner: she dipped her handkerchief in it and dabbed her cheeks and temples.

'Tallie! Tallie dear, are you still here?' It was Lady Parry.

'Oh, God!' Nick swung round on his heel, but she was between him and the door. He stepped behind the potted palm as his aunt emerged into sight.

'There you are, dear. Whatever is going on? I saw Lord Ashwell come out looking most disconsolate, and then in came Sir Jasper—and came straight out again.'

'I did tell you that I did not want to marry either of them, did I not, Aunt Kate?' Tallie said, keeping her voice light as she stepped towards Lady Parry. She took her chaperon's arm and steered her firmly back towards the reception rooms. 'I just feel rather flustered. The encounters were rather difficult, you understand.' She did not look back. It felt as though Nick's eyes were burning through the back of her gown.

The next morning Tallie awaited Nick's arrival in Bruton Street with a sort of paralysed calm. She was quite certain he would come, for it would take a sang-froid even beyond what she believed he possessed to pretend that that encounter in the conservatory had not taken place.

He arrived at ten-thirty, which gave her time both to perfect what she was going to say and to develop a fine flock of butterflies in her stomach. Was he really going to believe that it was simply unmaidenly physical attraction that made her react the way she did in his arms or could he have any suspicion of the way she felt about him?

He arrived looking immaculate in cream pantaloons, Hessian boots and a tailcoat of darkest blue. He also looked infuriatingly cool and calm, not even a touch of colour staining his cheekbones as he was ushered by Rainbird into the drawing room. Tallie had no fear that the butler would hasten off to find her a chaperon; Lord Arndale was regarded as a son of the house.

He regarded her from a strategic position by the fireplace, one boot on the fender, a hand on the mantelshelf. She had not asked him to sit down which she now realised was a tactical error—he had the advantage of height.

'Good morning, Cousin Nicholas,' she said composedly.

'Good morning, Talitha.' So far, so good. 'Last night we—'

Tallie smiled and interrupted him. 'Last night we succumbed to a rather unfortunate physical attraction. I am sure it will not happen again.'

She was interested to see that he had not expected any such reaction from her. 'Are you? Well, I'll be damned.'

'Very likely, Cousin Nicholas, but I would be obliged if you would moderate your language.'

He ignored this crushing reproof. 'Physical attraction? Is that what you call it?'

'What would you call it?' Tallie asked. This was dangerous ground indeed.

'The same, but I hardly expected an unmarried girl to do so.' His expression was grim.

'Indeed?' Tallie got up and stalked towards the door. 'Well, my lord, I am not a girl, I am five and twenty, and I prefer the truth without hypocrisy. I have doubtless acted very imprudently, shockingly and in a downright unmaidenly manner. However, it was an interesting experience, which we can now forget all about.' She smiled sweetly and opened the door. 'It was most intriguing to see what all the fuss is about.' Nick took a long stride towards her, a noise alarmingly like a mastiff growling emanating from his throat.

Tallie, who was beginning to think she had gone somewhat too far in her efforts to disabuse him of the slightest suspicion of how she truly felt, was relieved to see Lady Parry in the hall.

'Ah, there you are, dear, I was looking for you. Nicholas! Excellent, would you care to accompany us to Mr Harland's studio?'

Chapter Thirteen

Mr Harland's studio. Tallie felt the blood drain out of her face and wondered wildly if she was going to faint. Then she saw Nick watching her speculatively and she rallied herself. 'Mr Harland, ma'am?'

'Yes, I have decided to have my portrait taken after all and I need to call to arrange terms and so forth. Do you mind accompanying me?'

'Oh,' Tallie managed feebly. 'No, no, of course not.'

'I am sorry, Aunt Kate,' Nick said, gathering up his hat and gloves from the hall chest. 'I had only dropped in for a minute. I have a business appointment now, otherwise I would be delighted to accompany you.'

Tallie's anger that he had considered 'only a minute' sufficient to discuss yesterday's encounter allowed her to put on her outdoor clothing and join Lady Parry in the carriage without refining too much upon where they were going. But once the carriage started her thoughts began to spin.

She had written to Mr Harland, apologising for having to cease her sittings and had received back such a carefully worded reply that she was reassured about his continuing discretion. Absence, and Kate's revelation that she knew all about her sittings, had lulled her still further.

Now she realised how dangerously she had let her guard down, even if Lady Parry knew her secret. What if Nick had been able to oblige his aunt and accompany them and saw something that linked Tallie and the naked Diana in his mind? Even a slight suspicion would be enough to spell disgrace.

The journey to Panton Square passed quickly, too quickly for Tallie, who was desperately trying to regain her composure. She held furs and muff for Lady Parry as she was handed down by the coachman, then descended herself. As she did so some instinct made her glance back to where the tiny square opened out into Coventry Street. A hackney had drawn up and a man was paying his fare—a thin man in an overlarge greatcoat. She shook her head, convinced she was imagining things. When she looked back both man and cab had gone.

The sound of the door opening behind her recalled her to the immediate problem and Tallie followed

Lady Parry into the hallway of Mr Harland's house. Peter the colourman was standing holding the door, his best green baize apron in place, his scanty grey hair carefully brushed. On 'portrait days' he was always well turned out to greet clients. On the days when Tallie had posed for the classical works he had hurried back to his workshop, oil-stained apron flapping, knife or pestle in hand.

He helped Lady Parry with her things, then saw Tallie behind her. 'Miss Grey! This is a pleasure, miss. You'll be glad to know I've managed to get a nice consignment of mummy in at long last.'

'Good morning, Peter. I am pleased to hear that—supplies were getting very difficult, were they not?' Peter had sometimes allowed her to look round his workshop and had explained the contents of the jars and twists of paper that filled each shelf and spilled from every drawer.

'Mummy?' Lady Parry, always ready to be interested in something new, paused with one hand on the baluster.

'Yes, my lady. I'll show you.' The colourman vanished into his sanctum and emerged with a box, which he opened carefully. Inside were a number of fragile sheets of a flaking substance the colour of dried tobacco and a gnarled object which looked exactly like part of a human finger.

'Whatever is it?' Lady Parry asked, extending an elegantly gloved forefinger to prod it.

'I rather think it is a…a human finger.' Tallie swallowed. It had been fascinating to hear how artists ground up the remains dug from the hot Egyptian sands to use as a brown pigment. It was considerably less appealing to see it in the…flesh. She swallowed again. That had been an unfortunate thought.

'Oh, my goodness! The poor creature! What do you want it for?' Lady Parry withdrew her own finger sharply.

'It was only a part of a heathen, my lady, and been dead since the Flood, I daresay.' Peter shut his precious box carefully. 'It makes a wonderful deep brown pigment; nothing quite matches it. But the cost, ma'am, that is terrible. Lucky those rogues who broke in last night didn't think to come down here—why, I've got lapis and gold leaf—'

'You had burglars? What happened?' Tallie asked, concerned. 'I do hope no one was hurt.'

'Nothing like that, I am glad to say.' It was Mr Harland, alerted by the voices, coming down to greet his new client. 'Good day, Lady Parry, this is an honour. Miss Grey, how very nice to see you again.' Tallie smiled despite herself. Frederick Harland might be vague, inconsiderate and distracted when painting, and he might profess to despise his portrait work, but he did know how to charm his lady clients with every attention.

He was ushering them up to his public studio and reception room, a world away from the dusty draughty attic where his great canvases would be set up and where Tallie was used to shivering in flimsy draperies.

'Was anything taken?' she asked as he drew up chairs for them next to a series of empty display easels.

'No—a very strange thing, that.' The artist frowned. 'They rummaged through the canvases—fortunately damaged nothing—and that was all.'

'Possibly they were disturbed,' Lady Parry suggested. 'Or they thought you might hide your valuables amongst them.'

'You are most likely correct, ma'am. Now, as I understand you have decided upon a portrait and are most graciously entrusting me with the task. I think the first thing we must decide is the size and style of the work. I will show you some examples...'

He proceeded to prop canvases on the easels. First a head and shoulders of a formidable lady with grey hair. 'Lady Agatha Mornington. I am about to begin varnishing this one.' Tallie started nervously; this was Jack Hemsley's aunt. Next, a three-quarters length of a young lady holding a child. Then a full-length canvas of a graceful figure in a clinging gown, one hand lightly resting on a classical pillar. It was a preparatory sketch only, but well detailed, and the face that smiled serenely back at the viewer was Tallie's.

'Ah, there is that delightful portrait I saw last time I was here,' Lady Parry said with pleasure.

'Yes, my lady. As you had already seen it, I thought there was no harm in producing it again, and I expect Miss Grey will be amused to see it once more. I will just fetch my notebook,' Mr Harland said and left the room.

'That…that is the picture of me you saw?' Tallie asked, hideous apprehension beginning to ball in her stomach. 'The one I sat for because Lady Smythe was expecting?'

'Yes, of course, dear. Were there any others? I do think it is nice that Mr Harland bothered to draw your face, even though in the finished work it is Lady Smythe, of course.'

'And that is the…costume you thought shocking?' The ball of apprehension was turning into lead shot in the pit of her stomach.

'It looks as though the petticoats have been dampened,' Kate said severely. 'One can see every line of your figure. And what is holding the bodice up—if one can call it a bodice—goodness only knows. Still, everyone knows Penelope Smythe thinks of herself as a dasher, and it must have hit her hard to have lost her figure, however temporary that state of affairs was.'

Tallie sank back in her chair aghast. So Lady Parry had not seen one of the shocking classical nudes, only this portrait. She should have trusted her instincts that her kind patroness was being too tolerant. Now what was she going to do?

Mr Harland had returned and he and Lady Parry were deep in discussion on the relative merits of head and shoulders and full length—three-quarters having been rapidly dismissed as neither one thing nor another. Eventually full length was decided upon, with a draped background. Tallie found it quite impossible to do more than keep an expression of interest on her face and then follow Lady Parry downstairs when her business was concluded.

Her head was spinning and she was conscious only of an overwhelming desire to throw herself on Nick Stangate's chest and confess all. As this was dangerous insanity she stood on the pavement in the light mizzle which had just begun to fall and tried to drag air into her tightened lungs. Then she saw the man.

'Tallie? What is it? You have gone quite pale.'

Lady Parry hurried her into the carriage and began to rummage in her reticule.

'I think I...we...are being followed,' Tallie blurted out.

'*What?* By whom?'

'A man—he has just ducked back into an alley-way down there. I saw him getting out of a hackney behind us when we arrived here, and I saw him lurking outside the house when we went to Acker-man's the other day. And I am sure he has been around before—I thought him familiar then.' Tallie broke off and tried to speak calmly. 'I am sorry, Aunt Kate, I am probably imagining things.'

'Perhaps, perhaps not. There are any number of dangerous characters around,' Kate Parry said grimly. 'I will speak to Nicholas about it.'

'Oh, no! He will think me over-imaginative to worry about such things.'

'Well, *I* am worried, and he had better not suggest that I am over-imaginative,' Lady Parry retorted with a twinkle. 'And in any case Nicholas uses en-quiry agents from time to time, he will know all about how to deal with this.'

An unpleasant thought crept into Tallie's mind. She knew Nick had had her investigated before she had joined his aunt. And he knew she still hid a secret from him. Was this man his, following her to discover that secret? If that was the case, then today he had been closer than he knew.

Nick was waiting for them when they returned to Bruton Street. They found him sprawled in an armchair with a careless elegance that took away Tallie's breath. He tossed aside the portfolio of papers he was reading and got to his feet as they entered the room. Tallie realised she had never been so conscious of how long his legs were nor of how easily he moved.

'A successful meeting?' he asked with a smile, which faded as he took in the anxiety on his aunt's face. 'What is wrong?'

'I think we had better talk about it over luncheon, Nicholas. Talitha and I will be down in a moment; will you be so kind as to tell Rainbird we will wait upon ourselves.'

Shortly after, Tallie sat down apprehensively and passed cold meats to Lady Parry at her side. She took a slice of bread and began to cut it into thin fingers.

'Aunt Kate?' Nick took a slice of beef, but did not start to eat. 'What has occurred?'

'Just a foolish idea of mine,' Tallie said defensively. 'The more I think about it, the more—'

'Talitha believes she, or perhaps we, are being followed.'

Nick's brows drew together sharply. 'By whom?'

'A thin man in a greatcoat and beaver hat.'

'I am sure it is just a coincidence,' Tallie murmured. His grey eyes turned to her face and he raised one brow.

'And how often has this coincidence struck you?'

'Four times,' she admitted. 'At least three I am certain of. I am sure I had seen him before—perhaps once, perhaps more—which is why I noticed him the next time.'

'Did he approach you? Try to speak to you?'

Tallie shook her head and Lady Parry added, 'I am certain he has some criminal intent. Perhaps he is trying to find a pattern to our comings and goings so he can break into the house. After all, look at poor Mr Harland.'

For a second the mask of calm enquiry that Nick was wearing cracked. His head turned sharply to his aunt. 'Harland? What has happened to him?'

'The house was broken into,' Lady Parry explained. 'It is dreadful how lawless the streets of London are becoming.'

'And what was taken?'

'Nothing apparently. They just searched amongst the canvases.'

'Interesting.' He said it almost to himself. 'Now that *is* interesting.'

'What shall we do about the man in the beaver hat, Nicholas dear?'

'Go nowhere without two of the larger footmen in attendance and tell the coachman to carry a blunderbuss. I will speak to Rainbird. I would not worry, Aunt Kate—if this man has any sinister intent, he will soon see you are well protected and shift his interest elsewhere.'

Lady Parry appeared to find this sufficient reassurance and began to talk cheerfully of her planned portrait. Tallie was not so sure. She made herself eat her bread and butter and sip a little from her glass while watching Nick from under her lowered lashes. She could tell he was thinking furiously, despite the flow of inconsequential talk he was maintaining in response to his aunt.

When they rose from the table he intercepted her. 'Tallie, I would like to speak to you if I may.'

She cast a hunted look at the dining-room door closing behind Lady Parry. She knew she should reprove him for using her pet name, but the sound of it on his lips was seductively sweet.

'I promise I am not going to kiss you,' he said infuriatingly. She narrowed her eyes in suspicion and he added, 'Or do anything else to take advantage of—what did you call it?—oh, yes, our unfortunate mutual physical attraction.'

'Good.' Tallie edged around the table. Despite his assurances she still felt safer with a width of shining mahogany between them. Quite whether it was Nicholas or herself that she was nervous of she was not prepared to examine. 'What do you want to talk about?'

'Will you reconsider telling me about your secret? The one you believe my aunt knows all about. Only I do not believe she does.'

'No, you are correct. She does not. I honestly believed it when I told you that, but I was wrong.' It was a relief to tell him some of the truth if not all.

'Tell me.' He sat down opposite her.

Feeling a little more secure, Tallie sat too. Her legs were shaking. 'Why?'

'Because I think it would be safer if you did.'

It was very tempting. Tallie stared into the grey eyes, but they did not hold the reassurance she was looking for. It would not take very much to make her blurt it all out—she could quite understand why people confessed to crimes when questioned. But the inimical gaze regarding her belonged to the man who did not trust her, did not approve of her friends, who wanted her out of his family's house and lives. The fact that she loved him did not make it any easier, it simply made the thought of the expression on his face when he discovered the truth harder to bear.

'No.' He looked a question and she said angrily, 'Why should I? You make it quite clear you do not trust me. You disapprove of my friends, you wish me gone from here. Why should I hand you a weapon against me?'

'Is this a war, then?' He raised a long-fingered hand and rubbed a hand over his face. It was an uncharacteristically weary gesture.

'It feels like one.' Tallie wanted to go round and stand behind his chair, massage his shoulders, gently rub his temples until that tiredness ebbed away and he relaxed. She clasped her hands tightly in her lap.

'I did not approve of your friends. I was wrong. I apologise. Miss Scott is an intelligent and principled woman. Miss LeNoir is a talented and virtuous one, and Mrs Blackstock seems eminently respectable.'

'Thank you,' Tallie said stiffly.

'If I do not trust you, it is your judgement I mistrust, not your motives. As for your presence in this house—' He broke off, pushed his hand through his hair and got to his feet, turning as he rose so that she could not see his face. 'It is my aunt's house, it is up to her who resides here. She enjoys your company very much. I believe she is proud of your success.'

'Why, thank you.'

'I try and fight fair,' he said ruefully.

Tallie almost fell for it. Then she caught herself. *Fight fair?* With enquiry agents investigating her? Fight fair when he had discovered that if he took her in his arms she trembled and responded to him with an utterly shameless ardour?

'Thank you,' she said again. 'But unfortunately I trust your motives as little as you trust my judgement, so I am afraid we are at a stalemate.'

'You will not tell me? Is it so very dreadful? You were prepared to speak of it to my aunt, and presumably would have done so if she had not said something that convinced you she already knew.'

'What I might discuss with another woman— and one who is my patroness—is quite different from what I might discuss with a man,' Tallie said, casting down her eyes in what she hoped might be mistaken for maidenly confusion. She glanced up through her lashes and saw Nick was regarding her with amusement.

'A very nice try, Tallie; however, I am not at all convinced by the shrinking maiden who is too shy to reveal her horrid secret to a man.'

'I most certainly am—' Tallie broke off, suddenly aware of the large hole her tongue was digging her.

'A shrinking maiden? Hmm. I am prepared to believe one part of that description, but not the other.' Only her determination not to give him any further cause for amusement stopped Tallie from an indignant retort. She glared instead. 'You realise you are effectively challenging me to discover the truth for myself?' he added.

'You could simply mind your own business.'

'But I am enjoying myself, Tallie,' Nick said, turning towards the door. 'You are proving an irresistible puzzle.' With a mocking bow he let himself out, closing the door gently behind him.

Tallie took an angry turn down the length of the room and back. Infuriating man! In an effort to stop thinking about Nick Stangate, she turned her thoughts to his aunt. She should tell Lady Parry the truth about her sittings. It was one thing to be innocently deceiving her, but now she knew Lady Parry did not know the true state of affairs she could not, in all conscience, continue the deception.

Best to do it now, confess while she was feeling determined. Tallie marched over to the door, flung it open and walked into a scene of chaos.

Chapter Fourteen

It was a testament to the quality and thickness of the doors that Tallie had not heard the uproar from the dining room.

A young woman in modest, travel-stained but respectable clothing was weeping unrestrainedly on a hall chair despite the housekeeper's efforts to calm her and wave smelling salts under her nose. William was standing back with the unmistakable air of panic of a man trapped by feminine emotion while his mother was alternating between anxious glances at the hysterical girl and attempts to con a letter she was holding. Lord Arndale, driving coat half-buttoned and hat and gloves in his hand, appeared to have given up trying to get out of the front door and was giving instructions to a footman who turned and hurried off towards the back stairs with unmistakable relief.

Rainbird, emanating disapproval of such a scene

in the front hall, was trying to usher the entire party into the drawing room, but for once was being ignored by both family and staff alike.

Tallie decided she could either retire again, add to the chaos or attempt to be useful. With a sigh she stepped into the breach and touched Lady Parry on the arm. 'I think she might calm down a little, ma'am, if there were not so many people. Shall I try and take her into the morning room?'

'Oh, would you, Talitha dear? She just cries more when she sees me.'

Tallie was by now making out the tenor of the young woman's plaint, which appeared to alternate between bitter self-recrimination that she should have so let Lady Parry down and inexplicable references to 'that monkey being the last straw'.

'What is her name?'

'Miss Clarke. Maria Clarke.'

'Come along, Miss Clarke…Maria. There's a good girl. You come and sit down in a nice quiet room. No, Lady Parry is not at all angry…yes, this way. Mrs Mills, could you have some tea sent up, please?'

It took half an hour to calm the young woman and at the end of it Tallie was no wiser. However, Miss

Clarke was red-eyed but subdued and had been sent off with the housekeeper to lie down and rest.

Feeling as if she had just emerged from Bedlam, Tallie emerged and found the butler surveying the quiet hall with austere satisfaction. 'Where is her ladyship, Rainbird?'

'Packing, Miss Grey.'

'Packing? Is something wrong?'

'I could not venture to say, Miss Grey. However, Miss Clarke, the young lady who was so afflicted, is the companion to her ladyship's elder sister, the Dowager Marchioness of Palgrave.'

'I see.' Tallie saw nothing at all clearly, although it appeared that some domestic disaster must have struck the Dowager's household. Could it possibly involve monkeys, or was that simply hysteria? 'I do not believe I have met the Dowager,' she began cautiously.

'Her ladyship lives much retired.' Rainbird hesitated and unbent further, dropping his voice in case any menial should overhear his indiscretion. 'Her ladyship is considered…eccentric.'

Oh, dear, the monkey was probably real in that case. Tallie recalled hair-raising stories of Princess Caroline's menagerie. 'I had better see if there is anything I can do to assist Lady Parry. Have their lordships gone out?'

'Lord Arndale has gone to arrange her ladyship's carriage and outriders, Miss Grey. Lord Parry is, I believe, with her ladyship.'

As Tallie climbed the stairs she could hear William sounding plaintively defensive. 'Of course I will escort you, Mama, I would not dream of doing anything else, but can I not put up at the Palgrave Arms when we get there?'

'No, you cannot, William,' his mother was saying briskly. 'Goodness knows what we are going to find: monkeys could be the least of it. Remember last time?'

'Surely not another zebra?'

'Anything is possible with your Aunt Georgiana. At least she has got past the stage of unfortunate infatuations with pretty young men… Tallie dear, thank you so much for settling Miss Clarke. I must say I had not thought her the hysterical type, and after six months I was hoping she would prove ideal.' Lady Parry heaved a sigh and sat down on the bed. 'William, go and tell your valet to pack for at least four days. It took that long last time—and you are *not* putting up at the Arms.

'Tallie, my love, I am very sorry about this, but I am afraid I am going to have to go down to Sussex and see what can be done about my sister, Lady Palgrave.'

'Is she unwell, ma'am?' Tallie sat on the bed too.

'My sister, to be plain about it, is very strange—only, being a Dowager Marchioness, she is called eccentric. As a girl she was given to harmless but unconventional enthusiasms and regrettably her marriage proved unhappy, which only served to drive her further towards unsuitable obsessions. Her husband's death has left her without any restraining influence and with a fortune large enough to indulge whatever fancy enters her head.

'Her house is a menagerie of the most unlikely creatures, although fortunately now they are from the animal kingdom. There was a time when she was entertaining one unsuitable young man after another. All in pursuit of her money, of course—and I probably should not be telling an unmarried girl about it.

'Anyway…' she sighed again '…she swings between relative normality, when all that is required of her companion is to humour her, and really wild excesses. Apparently she has acquired a number of monkeys—quite large ones, according to the housekeeper's letter—and has established them in the guest bedrooms. I shall have to go and see what can be done to restore some sort of order.'

'Will Lord Arndale accompany you? I imagine he would cope very well with this sort of crisis.'

'And so he would. Unfortunately my sister has a *tendresse* for him and is given to the most embarrassing displays of, er…affection.'

'Goodness,' Tallie said blankly, trying not to giggle at the thought of Nick being pursued around an animal-infested mansion by a middle-aged lady with amorous intent. 'I had better go and pack.'

'No, dear, it is very sweet of you, but I could not possibly inflict that household on you. You will be quite all right here with Mrs Mills and Rainbird and if you want to go to any parties while I am away, I will drop a line to Lady Cawston and Mrs Bridlington—their girls are usually invited to all the events you are. Or you could stay with your friends at Upper Wimpole Street if you do not feel quite comfortable here while I am out of town.'

'I will be perfectly easy here with Mrs Mills, I assure you, Aunt Kate. In any case, Mrs Blackstone and Millie and Zenobia are going to Putney for a few days. Zenna has found details of a house that sounds exactly right for the school and Mrs Blackstock has a cousin living nearby, so they are all having a little holiday. They went off this morning.'

'Are you sure you will be all right?' Lady Parry regarded Tallie distractedly. 'It hardly seems fair, but I could not possibly take you with me—one never knows *what* one might find.'

'Dear Aunt Kate, I will be perfectly fine, I assure you, and I promise I will send a note round to Jane Cawston or Sally and Lydia Bridlington if I wish to go out in the evening. Although I would not be sorry for a little holiday from parties myself. I will have a quiet evening or two and will doubtless be all the better for it.'

'If you are certain, dear.' Lady Parry smiled with relief. 'I intend leaving as soon as possible. It will mean a late arrival, but the roads are good and there is a full moon tonight. As my sister rarely retires before three in the morning, I have no fear of arriving and finding the house in darkness.'

In a remarkably short time—a circumstance that Tallie had no difficulty attributing to Nick Stangate's forceful methods of organisation—Lady Parry's cavalcade set off. Tallie stood on the front step to wave goodbye to her ladyship's travelling carriage, Lord Parry driving his curricle and Nick astride one of his raking hunters.

He reined back at the kerbside, obviously desiring a final word, and Tallie came down to stand by the big horse.

'I will stay overnight at the Palgrave Arms, just in case the situation is beyond my aunt's capabilities to resolve, and will return tomorrow. If you need to speak to me, send word to Brook Street and I will come and take you for a drive.'

'Will you not call?' Tallie asked, puzzled. Nick was such a regular visitor to Bruton Street that it seemed strange that he would not come there directly on returning from Sussex.

'Given that you are alone in the house save for the servants, I do not think that you should be receiving gentlemen visitors.' He touched his whip to his hat and gathered up his reins, then hesitated. 'If there should be any problem while I am away… if you should feel in any way alarmed by this man who may be following you…send to Mr Gregory Tolliver, Pickering Place, off St James's Street.'

'Who is he?' Tallie asked, remembering William mentioning meeting Nick leaving 'his agent's' house in that same location. How frank was Nick going to be with her?

'He is in my employ and will know what to do,' he said curtly, then unexpectedly leaned down and touched her cheek with his gloved hand before spurring the horse into a canter after the retreating carriages.

Thoughtfully Tallie climbed the steps and went into the house. So, Nick's agent—presumably the same man whom he had used to make his enquiries into her background—would 'know what to do' about the mysterious man. Which meant that Nick was confiding in him and was taking it seriously. A slight tremor of anxiety was replaced by one of irritation. Why could he not confide in her and tell her what he thought was afoot?

She answered her own question. *Because he does not trust you, Tallie*, she thought grimly. *You will not confide in him, so neither will he in you. Stalemate.*

The next morning Tallie was enjoying the novel sensation of having nothing to do, nowhere she was expected to be and no one to please but herself and was employing the holiday by trimming a promenade hat of Lady Parry's from last season. It was restful to be able to employ her old skills again, to concentrate closely on what her hands were doing rather than having to think or talk.

There was a knock at the door, which she ignored, then looked up in surprise when Rainbird brought a letter in. She was rather enjoying the solitude and regarded him with well-concealed irritation when the butler proffered the salver.

'The man is waiting for a reply, Miss Grey.'

Tallie turned the folded sheet over in her hands, then recognised the handwriting: Mr Harland.

Her hands froze, but her heart seemed to turn in

their stead. Why should the artist be writing to her? Slitting the wafer seal with her sewing scissors, she found that his letter was lengthy enough to occupy two closely written sheets.

The artist had penned it in an obvious state of excitement to inform Tallie that he had sold all six of the large classical canvases in which she featured.

With an internal sensation of having eaten far too much ice cream, Tallie read on. *Please do not suppose that there is the slightest danger of the works being seen by London Society*, Mr Harland had written, obviously anticipating Tallie's anxieties. *The gentleman concerned tells me he is buying them to decorate his private rooms in his castle in the far north of Scotland. He has lately returned from the Mediterranean lands and wishes to have a tangible reminder of the classical landscape.*

Tallie blinked at the closely written sheet. It seemed likely enough, she supposed—but how had this Scottish patron heard of Frederick Harland, and particularly how did he know he had classical scenes for sale?

She opened the door and looked into the hall. As she hoped, it was Peter who had brought the letter and who was sitting patiently on one of the hard shield-back hall chairs, hat on knee, waiting for the expected answer.

'Peter? Could you come in here, please?' With the door safely shut on Rainbird, Tallie asked, 'Have you any idea how this gentleman who is buying Mr Harland's classical canvases came to hear that he had them available?'

'Why, yes, Miss Grey—he said he made enquiries for a painter of classical scenes at the Royal Academy. You know, Mr Harland talks a great deal about his ambitions for that style of art, even if he does not exhibit.'

'Oh.' That seemed plausible, but Tallie was still uneasy.

Peter appeared to understand. 'He is genuine, Miss Grey, I'm sure of that. Gentleman with a strong Scottish accent and his skin deeply tanned by the sun—he's been in the south, all right.'

Tallie turned back to the letter. The artist must want some sort of response from her, otherwise Peter would not be waiting.

As you know, none of the canvases is entirely complete and the purchaser—who does not wish to be named—requires to take them back with him in two weeks' time. In most cases the outstanding work is architectural or landscape and I have every expectation of completing these before he leaves. However, the last canvas, the 'Diana' scene, requires one more sitting from the live figure. While fully appreciating your reluctance to be further involved with my work, might I hope that you will oblige me on this one final occasion? To think that six major pieces of mine will be hung together in a fitting setting is a matter of such importance to me it gives me the hope that you may find yourself able to oblige me.

Tallie dropped the pages onto the sofa and stared blankly at Peter. 'Do you know what is in the letter?'

'Yes, Miss Grey. Mr Harland wishes you to sit for him one last time.'

Tallie's immediate reaction was simply to say 'no', but then the recollection of how grateful she had been for the money Mr Harland paid her, the gentlemanly manner in which he had always treated her and his intense belief and pride in his classical paintings made her hesitate.

'I do not know when I can sit for him, though,' she said. 'Lady Parry is away, but when she returns she will expect me to accompany her. It would be difficult to explain why I wished to spend several hours at the studio.' She bit her lip. 'I suppose this afternoon…?'

'Mr Harland is painting a portrait this afternoon and the gentleman in question will be attending the studio.'

'Oh, dear. Then I cannot say, for I do not know

when Lady Parry will return—it could even be to-morrow.'

'Would this evening be convenient, Miss Grey?' Peter asked hopefully.

'But the light—surely that would be impossible?'

'Mr Harland has invested in some of the new oil lamps, Miss Grey—why, it is almost as light as day with those all lit up.'

Tallie bit her lip. It seemed that both circumstances and her own conscience were conspiring together.

'Shall I tell Mr Harland a time?' the colourman pressed.

'Eight o'clock?' Tallie suggested faintly. She could have an early dinner and take a hackney. Rainbird would suppose her to be going to Upper Wimpole Street, for she had not mentioned to him that the household was away.

In the event it proved almost too easy to evade difficult questions, for Rainbird had not been in the hall when she asked a footman to call her a hackney carriage. She remarked carelessly that she was going to meet friends and the sight of her evening dress and opera cloak was obviously sufficiently usual for the young man not to make the sort of more probing enquiry that the butler in his more privileged position would have had no hesitation in making.

Tallie checked nervously up and down Bruton Street but could see no one lurking suspiciously in the evening drizzle and she sat back against the squabs feeling slightly reassured. It appeared that her mysterious follower had gone—or she had re-fined too much upon a series of coincidences.

As they neared Panton Square, however, she discovered that her stomach was a mass of but-terflies. Somehow there was all the difference in the world in sitting for Mr Harland when it was a routine matter of earning her living. Now—with no excuse other than a sense of obligation that she was certain any respectable lady would tell her was misplaced—she was creeping out alone in a cab, dressed up to deceive the servants and feeling thor-oughly uneasy about the entire enterprise.

The hackney turned into Panton Square. *Too late to go back now*, she told herself firmly, paying the driver. She would insist that Peter found her a cab for the return journey before she left the house, she decided, glancing up nervously from returning her purse to her reticule as another cab drew up a little further down. But the short, middle-aged man who climbed down bore no resemblance to her sinister follower and she watched in relief as he opened an area gate and vanished down the steps after a word with the driver.

Once she was inside a sense of familiarity took over from the nervousness and she climbed the stairs to the attic studio, feeling calmer. The artist had the large canvas already set up and his palette set and was busily adjusting the bright new lamps around the model's podium and the old blue screen.

'My dear Miss Grey, I cannot thank you enough,' he exclaimed, bustling forward to shake her hand. 'I understand how difficult it is for you now, but to be able to complete the canvases…to know that they will be fittingly hung, even if it is in remote and private rooms, not in a gallery…I cannot begin to explain…'

'I quite understand,' Tallie assured him. 'I will just go and change.'

'I have set up screens, in the corner.' Harland gestured to a set of old Spanish leather folding screens from which hung a length of white linen. 'With the new lamps it is so much warmer up here, I thought it would be more convenient.'

Tallie found the screened area contained a chair, a mirror and a clothes stand and began to undress. She had chosen the evening gown for its ease of removal and was soon draped in the linen and unpinning her hair. The gold filet hung from the mirror and within a few minutes Diana stared back at herself in the fly-spotted glass. Forcing herself to be practical, Tallie flicked her hair into the style of the portrait, gathered the linen around her as modestly as she could and went to stand on her mark.

After the first few, strange, minutes it simply became ordinary and familiar again. The attic still creaked, mice still scuffled in the corners and the familiar drafts penetrated even the warmth created by the powerful spermaceti lamps. The artist paced and muttered behind her, once hurrying down to twitch the hem of the linen drape, again to adjust the angle of the lights.

After an hour he observed, 'Splendid! Splendid. Now, Miss Grey, if you would like to take ten minutes to rest, then I believe another half-hour will see all complete.'

Tallie swathed the drape around her and turned, flexing her shoulders gratefully. 'How are the other canvases progressing, Mr Harland? Are you—?'

She broke off at the sound of thunderous knocking on the street door and froze, gazing at the artist in wild surmise. What was happening? It seemed just like that terrifying afternoon when Jack Hemsley and his friends had invaded the studio.

Harland threw open the attic door and once again, just like that nightmare day, Peter's voice rose up the stairwell. 'No, sir! You cannot go up there! Mr Harland is occupied.'

Tallie grabbed his arm. 'Who is it? Are you expecting anyone?'

'No! Get back inside, I will go down...'

But the sound of footsteps was clear on the stairs. Someone with a long stride was taking the stairs at the run. Frantic, Tallie spun round and began to flee across the dusty floor towards the only hiding place, the closet.

But she was only halfway there when the attic door crashed open behind her. She turned again, clutching the illusory protection of the linen drape around her and stared wild-eyed at the doorway where a man was thrusting the protesting artist aside with a peremptory hand.

Mr Harland staggered back and, trembling, Tallie braced herself for humiliation, disgrace and the ruin of her reputation.

Chapter Fifteen

His lungs heaving from the effort of taking four precipitous flights of stairs at the run, Nick Stangate stood in the doorway and regarded the goddess standing at bay in front of him. In the strong light she seemed bathed in a strange sunlight that gave her an ancient magic all her own and his breath caught in awe. Then he saw her wide, frightened eyes, the way her breasts rose and fell with her breathing, the courage that made her stay there, facing him down despite her terror.

He strode forward and seized her arm, forcing himself to ignore her nakedness, her nearness, holding her despite her frantic efforts to wrench herself away. 'Tallie, stop it! Listen to me, there isn't much time, Hemsley and a pack of his friends are on my heels—this is a trap.'

He saw Tallie turn her eyes on the artist, only for him to shake his head in furious denial at the accusation on her face. 'Good God, no, Miss Grey, I had no idea. Mr Laidlaw's offer seemed perfectly genuine—*he* seemed perfectly—'

'Later,' Nick snapped. 'Laidlaw *is* genuine. He's Hemsley's cousin, just back from Greece, and he must have seemed the ideal tool for his purposes. Harland, where are the back stairs?' The terrified girl was struggling in his grip, he tightened it, one part of his mind recoiling at the thought of hurting her soft flesh, the other ruthlessly aware that he was going to have to force her to obey him for her own protection.

'There are none,' the artist wailed, then gave a startled exclamation as the knocker thudded again. He ran towards the door, calling 'Peter! Do not open it!'

'Too late,' Nick said grimly, 'they're in.'

Tallie tugged at his hand. 'Let me go, I must get dressed at least.'

'No time. Harland, can you hide her clothes, her reticule?'

'Yes, my lord.' He was already hurrying towards the screen. 'I have trunks full of old clothes, hangings for props…'

'Nick!'

'Quiet.' He dragged her towards the window, thrust it up and peered out into the darkness. The street seemed miles below; the attic of Harland's house was a clear storey above the other houses surrounding it.

'Thank Heavens for small mercies: there's a ledge.' It was narrow, shining with dampness, maybe crumbling, but it stretched across the width of the house just below the window line. He closed his mind to the possible dangers, focusing on the immediate one. 'Harland, close this after us—hurry, man!'

The artist thrust Tallie's evening cloak into a mass of multicoloured hangings, tossed her reticule and shoes on top of a bookcase and hurried towards them.

Nick began to climb out of the window, keeping a grip with one hand on Tallie. 'Come on.'

'I…I cannot. I can't stand heights…I…'

The sound of approaching voices was getting closer. 'Harland, get out there and hold them up as long as possible. I'll try and shut the window after us. Do nothing to draw attention to it.'

As the artist ran for the door, Nick forced himself to stillness, pulled Tallie close and folded his arms round her. She was quivering against him, her soft warm skin achingly vulnerable under his hands. He pushed up her chin and put all his power into his voice and his eyes.

'We are going out there and I will keep you safe. I will not let you fall. I will not let them find you. Do you believe me, Tallie?'

'Ye-yes.' He saw the terrified green eyes focus, her lips tighten. He could almost feel the effort of will it was taking her to control her fear. 'I believe you, Nick.'

He released her and ducked under the raised sash and out onto the sill. The drizzle had stopped, but everything he touched had a grimy, sooty dampness. He tugged at the cornice above his head, found it firm. He craned back, wondering if he could get them up on top of the cornice where the attic roof met the gutters, but there were no handholds. He reached in to Tallie with his free hand. 'Come on, out onto the ledge, face out and inch along to your right. There is a downpipe—hold that with your right hand and the edge of the window reveal with your left.'

'Don't let me go!' The panic was back in her voice.

'Just while I close the window. You can do it, Tallie, come on, show me.'

With a little gasp she took his hand and climbed out, her naked limbs flashing white in the darkness. Then she was standing, groping with her free hand.

'I have got the pipe.' She swallowed audibly.

'Here is the window reveal.' He guided her hand to it. 'Now, hold on.'

Her fingertips seemed to cling to his for a fraction of a second, then she released his hand and he saw her fingers tighten on the rough brick. Nick shoved down the window, stepped across and flattened himself against her, his back to the drop, his hands gripping the same handholds above hers.

The sound of the door banging open and loud voices in the studio reached them clearly. Against his chest he could feel Tallie's breathing. Rapid, frightened. Then she whispered, 'It is all right, Nick. I won't panic, I will not let you down.'

The trust in her voice was so absolute it almost unmanned him as nothing else could have done. For a moment he closed his eyes, let his forehead rest against the wet brick. He found his voice and whispered, 'I know you won't, my brave darling. But I'm afraid we have to move: if anyone opens the window, they'll see us.'

Tallie wondered if she had heard him aright. It was difficult to think, let alone to hear properly. The blood seemed to be roaring in her ears, the sound of Nick's heart was loud where her face was pressed against him; on the other side of the window shouts and catcalls marked the hunt in progress.

Below them, four storeys down, was the street, below that the spiked railings and the further drop to the unyielding flags of the area courtyard. Her naked back pressed against rough brick, her skin was crawling with cold and terror. But he had called her *my brave darling*. The poor little flickering flame of courage that had helped her get out onto the ledge burned stronger, then the rest of his words came into focus. *Move?* He wanted them to *move*?

She heard herself say, 'Yes, Nick', and, as nightmares do, this one shifted into new horrors.

He was edging carefully along the ledge, nudging her feet along inside his, his body arched out to give her room. He seemed to be holding on to something above their heads, she could feel the tension in his arms as they rose past her face. At first all she was aware of in their infinitely slow progress was pain; the bricks grazing her buttocks and shoulders, the grit on the ledge digging into her feet, Nick's body ruthlessly pushing her on, so hard against her that she could hardly breathe.

Then the cold began to numb the pain and fear took over. Under her bare feet she could feel how crumbly the ledge felt; pressed against him so tightly she was utterly aware of the strain on Nick's body and arms, the gasp of pain as he arched himself out to enable her to slide around the downpipe.

Once, twice, his foot slipped and the jerk as he took the weight on straining arms froze her with terror.

It seemed endless, this nightmare; perhaps she would spend eternity on this ledge, her back raw, her feet frozen, crushed against the man she loved until even his strength gave out and he fell, leaving her alone as he plunged to his death far below.

He stopped suddenly; she felt his hand outstretched, groping into air. 'The corner,' he whispered. 'The ledge goes around and continues down the side of the building. If we go round, we will be out of sight.'

There was a moment where his body left hers, the damp night air striking icy on the one part of her that had been warm, then he was swinging her around the corner as behind them the window creaked upwards and loud voices echoed out.

'Not out here, not unless she's jumped.' The voice was unfamiliar, drunken, utterly uncaring.

'The bitch. How the hell did she escape?' That was Hemsley.

Faintly from inside the room she heard the indignant artist. 'Gentlemen, you have made a mistake. Someone dropped off a note for their mistress earlier, then left again. No one is here...'

'I am going to make Jack Hemsley sorry he was ever born,' Nick said close to her ear. Under any other circumstances his tone might have been considered politely conversational.

Tallie shivered. 'You are going to call him out?' she whispered back.

'Eventually.' Nick lingered over the syllables as though savouring them. His tone changed. 'Thank goodness for that, the moon's out.'

It was intermittent, still partly obscured by the clearing rain clouds, but Nick seemed pleased, which as far as Tallie was concerned was all that mattered now. She was keeping upright by sheer will-power and the strength of his body and she was so cold that she could feel nothing else at all.

Nick moved as though to turn his body and she gave a little cry.

'Shh. It is all right. The roof next door is lower than this one and almost flat, just a few more inches and we will be over it and can get down.'

How would that help? Tallie wondered hazily. *How could you get off a roof?*

'I'm going to let you go for a moment, Tallie,' Nick said firmly. 'Just stay still, leaning back. It will only be for a second.'

Before she had a chance to protest he was gone. Terrified, her eyes tight shut, Tallie flattened herself against the wall and waited for the sickening thud from far below. When he spoke, his voice coming from the level of her ankles, she was so shocked that she lost her balance and tumbled straight off the ledge and into his arms.

'Shh, it's all right, my darling, I have you, we're quite safe, off that ledge now.'

Tallie made a huge effort and opened her eyes. She was cradled in Nick's arms as he walked across the flat leads of a house. She was also stark naked. The linen drape had vanished and her white skin was luminous in the moonlight. 'Oh!' Tallie tried to wriggle free, but Nick held her tightly.

'As soon as we are in the house you can have my coat, I promise. No one can see us, we are still too high up. Can you stand for a moment?'

Without waiting for an answer he set her on her feet, steadying her with one hand while he bent to tug at a trapdoor let into the roof. 'Damnation, it is bolted.' He tugged a knife from his boot top and attacked the edge of the trap. The wood splintered with a sound like gunshot and the flap hinged open. 'Sit down while I investigate—there can't be anyone sleeping up here or they'd have appeared by now.' He swung himself into the hole and vanished.

Tallie sank down onto the cold leads and peered into the blackness below. She was shivering uncontrollably now and it was very hard to focus and to think straight. Nick's voice came up to her in a clear whisper. 'Sit on the edge and drop, I'll catch you.'

Beyond caring what she was falling into, Tallie did as she was told and was caught neatly and swung to the ground. Nick had already stripped off his coat and began pushing her arms into it like a nurse dressing a clumsy child. It was blissfully warm from his body, but the cold went so deep her very bones seemed frozen and the shivering did not stop.

Nick forced the door with as much ruthlessness as he had opened the hatch and led her out onto a landing. Peering over the balustrade, she could see the staircase descending into darkness.

'Either all in bed, which seems unlikely, or out,' he whispered. 'Come on.' Tallie took a faltering step and felt her legs go. The next moment she was caught up in Nick's arms again and he was descending the stairs, step by cautious step.

When they reached the hallway she was vaguely conscious of him fumbling with the door lock, then they were out on the street and Nick was striding rapidly out of Panton Square, across Coventry Street and into the narrow mews entrance of Coventry Court. *Goodness knows what this looks like*, Tallie thought hazily, but no one raised an outcry.

Nick whistled and a carriage emerged from the shadows.

'All right, my lord?'

'All right, Roberts. Drive us to Upper Wimpole Street, fast as you can.'

'No one there,' Tallie mumbled against Nick's chest. 'All gone…Putney.'

He lifted her onto the seat. 'What did you say?'

Tallie made herself focus. 'No one at Upper Wimpole Street. Gone away on a visit.'

'Hell.' The carriage door closed and she was vaguely aware of Nick in low-voiced conversation with the coachman. It all seemed a long way away. She wasn't even very cold any more, just numb and dizzy and very sleepy…

She was so warm, so blissfully warm. Tallie lay with her eyes closed, letting her sore and aching body relax into the softness of the mattress. Over her there was the comforting feel of linen sheets, the reassuring weight of bedcovers. She nestled her head into the goose-down pillow and sighed gently, letting the memory of why she had so much wanted to be warm, why she seemed to be bruised all over, come seeping back into her half-conscious mind.

The studio, Jack Hemsley—and Nick appearing just in time to save her. So strong, so reassuring, and he had called her *my darling*. Tallie drifted back to sleep, dreaming of Nick, dreaming of his arms around her, the steady beat of his heart against hers, his strength and his courage as he got them both safe along that ledge and to freedom.

When she surfaced again the early morning sunlight was flickering on her closed lids. She was still deliciously warm, wherever she was. This was definitely not her bed, although that was not an alarming thought. She allowed the idea to penetrate her waking consciousness and with the realisation came the awareness that while she might be warm all over, it was her back, her buttocks, her thighs that were warmest. And they were warmest because she was curled up against another naked human being. And the weight over her waist was not the bedcovers, but an arm.

Tallie's eyes snapped open onto closed green brocade bed curtains. Whoever she was curled up against was lying very still; their breathing was hardly audible. Tallie made herself relax and concentrate on what she could feel.

A long arm, still now but promising strength. A long body. A *male* body. Tallie might never have seen a naked man in the flesh, but she had seen enough drawings of classical nudes in Mr Harland's studio to have a fairly clear understanding of the male anatomy. And the scent of him. Nick.

Before she could give herself time to think, Tallie levered herself up on the elbow she was lying on and twisted round to face the man behind her. It was a confused and tangled manoeuvre. Somehow she ended up with both his arms around her and her uppermost leg over both of his.

It brought them so close together that she had to tilt her head back to focus on his eyes. Those grey eyes with their long black lashes. They held hers and she could not pull her gaze away. Fascinated, she saw his pupils widen, the dark flecks expand until his whole gaze was almost blackly intent on her.

He did not speak; she seemed to have lost the power to. His breath feathered her lips and she felt them part as though welcoming a kiss. Her tongue touched her sensitive upper lip and she saw the awareness of it in his eyes, knew from the change in the breath caressing her mouth that his lips had parted in response.

Nick's arms held her to him, encircling her but not moving. She was conscious of every point where the pads of his fingers rested lightly on her sore, grazed shoulders and the small of her back. The heat and the gentle pressure stung, but it stung with the reminder that she was alive, able to feel pain and pleasure; alive and with her reputation intact only because of the man who was holding her in his arms.

The embrace brought them breast to breast, just close enough for her nipples to brush the crisp hair on his chest. The sensation was incredible. Their breathing was enough to generate a teasing friction that tormented her nipples into hard peaks of arousal, made her breasts ache and grow heavy, made her want to arch into him, beg him to take her in his hands and caress her.

Waves of heat flooded through her, down to where her leg lay over his, her soft smooth skin of her inner thigh against his hard muscle. To the place where she was left in absolutely no doubt of just how aroused he was. She saw reflected in his eyes her own shock and excitement, realised just what an effort of self-control was keeping him still. If she in her inexperience throbbed with the need to move against him, draw him to her, surrender herself to him, how was he fighting the instinct to crush her under him, take her, make her his?

Her eyes stayed locked with his, despite the languorous feeling of surrender that seemed to drag at her eyelids. His breathing was harder, faster, the breath on her parted lips like fierce kisses, demanding, promising. Their breathing quickened. She was aware of the infinitesimal movement of his fingers as he widened his already spread fingers on her back and all the time she was aware of the heat and arousal and sheer overwhelming masculinity of his need for her.

Only his stillness and his silence kept her from moving, arching into him, urgent, begging for his caresses. Perhaps her own stillness was strengthening his resolve, perhaps in itself it was an incitement. Tallie did not know, could not read the dark grey eyes, hazed with passion. Passion for her.

Was that what it was? Only passion? Could he love her? Tallie tried to speak with her eyes, tried to fight the clamorous messages her body wanted to send him and replace them with a message of love, of trust.

She tried to free her mind, fight all her instincts that had taught her to guard her feelings, hide her innermost emotions in case she was hurt, exposed. The heat in his eyes was still there, but something else as well, something she had not seen before, something she could not read.

Tallie found she had a voice after all. Her lips moved but only the faintest whisper emerged. 'Nick.'

It broke the spell of his control. He moved, his

breath hot on her mouth. His lips touched hers, his hands tightened on her back. Tallie gasped and arched towards him as though bonds had been re-leased.

'Tallie.' His voice was ragged, hoarse, the voice of a man who has reached the end of his tether.

Chapter Sixteen

Nick brought his mouth down on Tallie's, felt the sweetness as her lips parted under his, the instinctive yielding trust to follow wherever he took her. A silent shout of triumph and possessiveness rose in him, overwhelming, extraordinary, beyond anything he had felt with any other woman.

The knock on the door, as discreet as only the most highly trained valet could produce, was like a cannon shot in his intensely sensitised state. Nick froze, the erotic dream he had been immersed in giving way to broad daylight and the appalled realisation that, despite his firm resolve, he was in his bed making love to an innocent virgin who had every right to expect his protection and his respect.

Wrenching his eyes away from Tallie's face, seeing the softness of sensuality being replaced with a sharp edge of awareness and alarm, he threw back the bedcovers and stalked towards the door.

The soft gasp from the bed made him glance down and realise just what a betraying state of arousal he was in.

Nick seized his dressing-gown, praying that after the first startled glance Tallie had closed her eyes. With the bed curtains partly drawn, she was at least sheltered from the door, he thought grimly, dragging the garment closed and tying the cord.

He yanked the door open to find no one outside, but a tray left on the table. He lifted it and brought it inside, flicking open the folded note as he put it down.

I apologise for waking your lordship but, as you intimated last night a desire to make an early visit to Bruton Street this morning, I thought it advisable. Matthews.

His valet was the only one of his household, other than Roberts the coachman, who had any idea that he had brought a woman home with him last night. With his usual tact Matthews had placed only one cup and plate on the tray, but the jug of chocolate was larger than usual and, instead of the single roll he would normally consume with it, there was a selection of sweet pastries. Matthews never showed the slightest inclination to judge his master, whatever queer starts he got up to. He was fiercely protective of his reputation amongst the other servants and would doubtless swear blind they were all hallucinating if they came in this minute and saw who was in his bed.

There was silence behind the bed curtains. Nick stood regarding them, suddenly conscious of the ache of passion denied competing with the appalling stiffness that racked his shoulder and arm muscles. He grimaced and flexed his arms, welcoming the distraction from his other discomfort while he pondered on what to do now and just what a mess he had got himself into.

The clock stood at quarter past seven. There was time to plan Tallie's return to Bruton Street with some care. He opened the clothes press and found a thin silk dressing-gown he used when travelling and extended an arm around the curtains.

'Thank you.'

At least she was still speaking to him. Nick cleared his throat. 'If you draw the curtain when you are ready, I have some breakfast here for you.' Again, a polite acknowledgment. 'Then we need to discuss what to do next.'

That was greeted by silence. Just how long did it take to put on a dressing-gown? But instead of pulling back the curtain Tallie emerged from the far side of the bed, the gown wrapped tightly around her, her bare feet shuffling so as not to trip over the trailing hem. She pushed back the weight of her hair with both hands, an action that caused her breasts to lift and thrust against the thin silk. Nick closed his eyes and turned abruptly to pour chocolate, wishing he kept a bottle of brandy in his bedroom.

Behind him Tallie cleared her throat and then asked in a voice of determined calm, 'What happened last night?'

She watched Nick turn, his eyes on the cup of chocolate, apparently intent on not spilling it. He set it on a table in the window embrasure and pulled out a chair for her. Tallie stayed standing, wondering if the pounding in her blood was ever going to calm down, or if the throbbing ache in places she had hardly been aware of before was ever going to subside.

Nick added the plate of pastries to the table and said abruptly, 'Please sit down. If you don't, I can't.'

She went to sit where he indicated and pulled the cup towards her, suddenly both hungry and thirsty. The sweet warmth sank into her stomach and she sighed and sat back, sitting up again with a sharp gasp as her lacerated skin hit the wood.

'Your back is badly grazed,' Nick said shortly. 'I put basillicum powder on it; I do not think it will scar.'

'Thank you.' He was obviously not going to make this easy for her. 'What did happen last night? I need to know.'

'How much do you remember? My carriage was waiting, but when you told me Mrs Blackstock and the rest of the Upper Wimpole Street household was away I had to think where else to take you. I could hardly return you to Bruton Street to a houseful of servants, stark naked.' Tallie closed her eyes momentarily at the thought. 'And you were freezing cold to the bone, scarcely conscious. I did not trust anyone else to look after you, so I brought you here, warmed you up the only way I could think of. I did not intend to stay after you had got warm, but I must have dropped off to sleep. I am sorry.'

Tallie bent her head over her plate and crumbled a roll. 'It was not your fault, you must have been exhausted. But…' This was so difficult! 'I must know—did anything…happen? I mean, once I was here…'

Nick moved abruptly and stood up. 'You mean, was I not content with waiting until you woke up to force myself on you? Did I ravish you while you were unconscious?'

As soon as he spoke Tallie knew how insulting her suspicions had been. 'No, of course not! I just thought…everything is so muddled. I thought perhaps we had…and I had forgotten. And you did not force yourself on me.' She seized the cup and took a long gulp to hide her burning face.

To her amazement Nick laughed. She stared at him, forgetting how embarrassing it was to meet his eyes, uncertain whether he was mocking her. But no, it was genuine amusement. He came and sat opposite her again, leaned across and took her hand in his. 'Tallie, my dear, you may have been in a poor way last night, but I do flatter myself that when I make love to a lady she does at least recall the experience the next morning.'

'Yes, of course,' she said hastily. Doubtless he had made love to scores of ladies, none of them as insultingly gauche as she was being. 'And I am sure I would be aware, I mean I would feel…' Her voice trailed away and she took a desperate bite of roll. Probably it was impossible to blush any redder than she was now, not without bursting into flames.

Nick appeared to pull himself together, which, she reflected bitterly, was a good thing because just at the moment the self-sufficient, practical, sensible Miss Talitha Grey would be unable to deal with a kitten who had stolen her knitting wool, let alone the tangle she seemed to have got herself into.

'I had no intention of being in the bed when you woke,' he said firmly. 'I apologise for my reactions when you did—the result of only that moment waking up myself, which is, of course, an explanation, not an excuse. I should have been able to control myself.'

'You appeared to be making a very good job of self-control,' Tallie observed. It seemed that one passed some kind of barrier of embarrassment beyond which it was impossible to feel any more humiliated or shy than one already did.

'Not good enough. There are things we must discuss, but not now.'

'Oh, yes,' said Tallie eagerly, wondering why Nick seemed so taken aback by her response. 'How did Mr Hemsley know I was going to be at the studio and how did you know that he knew?'

He relaxed. 'I will tell you about that later. Now, the next thing is to find you some clothes, I can hardly take you back to Bruton Street dressed like that.'

'You could go back to Mr Harland's studio and ask him to give you my clothes back.'

'No, the place might be watched still. I will write and ask him to make a parcel of the whole lot and send them back to Bruton Street. Beside anything else, you will want your reticule back.'

'That is a good idea,' Tallie agreed. 'In any case, I could hardly arrive home in the morning wearing the gown I left in the evening before.' A thought struck her. 'My goodness! What will the staff be thinking has happened to me? I must send a note at once to say I am safe.'

'No need. I called on my way back here with you and simply told Rainbird that you had decided to spend the night with your friend and had desired me to pass on the message as I was passing. He immediately assumed it was Miss Scott to whom I referred.'

'That was very deceitful,' Tallie observed, secretly admiring his cool thinking.

'Indeed it was,' Nick said penitently with a poorly suppressed smile. 'I should have told him that you were in my carriage without a stitch of clothing on and I was about to take you to my bed.'

'It is a lowering and sobering thought,' Tallie observed gloomily, 'that I have sunk so far into immodest behaviour that I can find that even moderately amusing.'

'Indeed it is. I suggest that you write a note to the housekeeper, saying that as you had not intended to stay the night you did not take a valise with you and asking her to pack one with a change of clothes and a walking dress. Naturally you wrote this last night and I, being a heedless and careless man who had consumed one too many glasses of brandy, forgot to deliver it. I will therefore appear, willing to atone for my fault by delivering the valise personally and not troubling Rainbird to send a footman with it.'

Tallie smiled her agreement and finished her roll. Then she realised that there was only the one cup and refilled it, pushing it across the table to Nick. They ate and drank in silence, he staring rather blankly at the bookcase on the far wall, she marvelling that it was possible to be lying in a man's arms in the throes of passion one minute and calmly sitting eating breakfast with him the next.

Presumably marriage was like this. That was a dangerous thought. Tallie let her gaze stray across to Nick. Those long fingers idly playing with the sugar tongs were marked with cuts and grazes from last night's adventure. They were also the fingers that had splayed on her back, pressing her into his embrace.

The expressive mouth, now rather immobile and straight, had curved in amusement just now, had compressed in anger and determination in the studio last night, and in bed had caressed her lips with a tender, demanding expertise that made her tremble to recall.

And as for the glimpse of him as he strode from the bed to answer the knock at the door—that image was overwhelming. Clothed she could appreciate his fitness, his strength, his elegance. Naked he was magnificent. And frightening.

The frightening male animal suddenly put down his cup, ran his hand through his hair and stood up with a grin that banished all her heated imaginings. 'Right, now you get back on the bed and pull the curtains round. I will ring for water, have a shave, get dressed and go to Bruton Street. While I am away you can wash; I'll tell Matthews to bring up plenty of water. He'll make sure you are not disturbed.'

'Is it not rather early?'

'The sooner I get you out of here the happier I will be. Rainbird will be confronted by a man with a hangover who woke at six with a crashing headache and a bad conscience for not delivering your note. I will be on my way to my club for the hair of the dog.'

Tallie duly retreated into her hiding place and sat curled up against the pillows while Nick washed and shaved. It was all very interesting. It seemed he sang quietly to himself while washing, in a very pleasant tenor. The song he began with proved highly improper, a fact that appeared to dawn on him by the second verse, which was abruptly cut off and replaced by something unexceptional.

He also shaved himself. Tallie listened to the sound of the razor being stropped, the soap being whisked up into a lather, the rather strangled hum the song deteriorated into as he shaved, the swish of water as he rinsed the razor.

Matthews came back from the dressing-room at the end of this ritual for an earnest discussion on that morning's clothes and was disappointed by the decision over which waistcoat his lordship was determined to wear, and mollified by a compliment on the state of his Hessians.

'I'm off now,' Nick said eventually. 'Matthews will look after you, and mind you don't set foot outside this door.'

It closed behind him and Matthews remarked, 'There is fresh hot water in the ewer, madam, and I have taken the liberty of replacing his lordship's soap with something more to a lady's taste. The towels are on the chair. Is there anything further madam requires? I suggest it would be unwise to ring. I will return to the dressing-room in thirty minutes and tap on the door. If there is anything you require, I will then be able to fetch it for you.'

Tallie scrambled off the bed and pounced on the hot water and soft towels with delight. Her feet were black; goodness knows what the laundry maids would think of the state of Nick's bed linen. She pulled off the robe and tried to look at the state of her back in the glass. It looked dreadful and felt worse with the grazes stiffening as they healed, but it probably looked worse than it really was. No lasting damage had been done.

No damage except to her heart. If she thought herself in love with Nicholas Stangate before, now she was convinced of it. He was courageous, strong, intelligent, amusing. And the touch of his fingers turned her bones to water. But all those things were just the parts that made up the man. He was more than the sum of them, and she loved him.

And it seemed that he cared enough about her to rescue her from the difficulties she had got herself into, despite discovering in the process that her secret was every bit as scandalous as he had always suspected.

Tallie allowed herself to dream a little, then applied some chilly common sense. She was his aunt's protégée—of course he was going to look after her to spare Lady Parry worry and embarrassment and to protect the family name.

She got dressed again in the robe and wandered round the room, studying how Nick lived in his most private space. She did not open any drawers or cupboards, but studied the pictures on the walls, the books on the shelves, the careless litter of banknotes, invitations, seals and fobs on the dressing-table.

It was a comfortable, masculine, unplanned and very personal room. Some of the books and pictures looked as though they were old family possessions, presumably from his country seat. Others were newer. She kept coming back to an oil painting over the fireplace. It was a landscape that did not seem quite finished at first; then, as she stared at it, began to make perfect sense. It was disturbing and she went close to peer at the signature. Turner. It meant nothing and she resolved to ask Mr Harland if he knew of him.

By the time Nick returned she was curled up in a chair, her bare feet peeping out from under the robe, a book of travel memoirs by a member of the East India Company open on her lap.

He closed the door behind him and leaned back against the panels, regarding her with a slight smile on his lips.

'What is it?' Tallie asked, suddenly defensive.

'I was just thinking what a charming scene to come home to this is.' He strolled over and looked to see what she was reading. 'Interesting account, that.'

'Mmm. I would love to travel, but as I cannot, I enjoy well-written descriptions.'

'Why can't you travel?' Nick enquired, bringing over the portmanteau he had put down by the door.

'Are those my clothes? Thank you so much. Why can't I travel? Well, it is not something single young ladies can do, is it?'

Nick shrugged. 'Doubtless your husband will indulge you, even if it is only to Italy and not as far as India.'

Tallie stopped, her hands on the buckle of the portmanteau. 'Husband? You have more confidence in my acquiring one than I have! Now let me see— how do you think I should go about explaining that I have modelled naked for an artist or have scrambled around the rooftops of London in a state of nature? And at what point during the proposal does one introduce the subject?'

Nick opened the dressing-room door and paused on the threshold. 'I'll be in here, knock when you are ready. You know, Talitha, you are so intelligent and so practical and independent that sometimes I forget just how young you are and just how sheltered your life has been.'

What on earth did he mean by that? Tallie blinked at the closed door, then shrugged, regretted carelessly moving her sore shoulders and began to pull garments from the bag. Both of them were in rather an odd mood this morning, which was hardly surprising considering what had happened last night, to say nothing of what had almost occurred when they woke. Doubtless Nick would be back to his habitual cool, infuriating, distrustful state by the end of the day and she could maintain a safe and comfortable distance from him.

Indeed, when she tapped on the door and he emerged from the dressing-room the mask was firmly back in place and Tallie wondered if she had dreamed those intense, burning eyes, the flashes of deep amusement, the unguarded sharing of thoughts.

He carried her empty portmanteau downstairs, his other hand lightly under her elbow. The hall was empty: presumably when Lord Arndale told his servants he wanted privacy, that was what he got. He lifted a long cloak from the hall table and swept it round Tallie's shoulders, pulled up the hood and ordered, 'Keep your head down.'

Outside his carriage was waiting, blinds drawn, and she was inside and it was driving off before she could catch her breath.

'Now,' Nick observed, dropping onto the seat opposite her. 'The trick is to drop you off at Aunt Kate's front door and be away before anyone inside realises you have not got down from a hackney carriage.'

This manoeuvre was carried out with apparent success and Rainbird opened the door to Tallie without any appearance that her arrival after an unplanned night away was anything out of the ordinary.

'Good morning, Miss Grey.'

'Good morning, Rai...' Tallie was overcome by an enormous yawn. 'Oh, I do beg your pardon, Rainbird! I am afraid I was up far too late last night, and you know how it is when you sleep in a different bed.' She stifled another jaw-cracking yawn with difficulty. 'Would you be good enough to ring for my maid? I think I will go and lie down.'

Tallie had just enough wits about her to remember the state of her back as she was about to be helped out of her gown and to dismiss the girl as soon as she had unhooked the bodice. Her grazes smarted as she lay down, but within seconds the familiarity of her own bed lulled her and she fell into a deep, dreamless sleep.

Chapter Seventeen

Tallie awoke with a start to a bustle on the landing and the unexpected sound of Lady Parry's voice. She tumbled out of bed and dragged on her dressing-gown before peeping round the door.

She was not imagining things. Lady Parry was just untying her bonnet strings and talking to her maid while the footmen carried her portmanteau into her room. She caught sight of Tallie's tousled head and sleepy eyes and hurried across.

'My dear! Are you not well?'

Tallie allowed herself to be bustled back into her room. 'I am quite well, Aunt Kate. It was just that I had a very tiring evening last night and found myself yawning my head off this morning, so I thought the best thing to do was to go to bed and catch up on my sleep.' Sooner or later she was going to have to confess the whole ghastly business, but she needed to be awake first.

'My goodness! What have you been up to while I have been away?' Lady Parry asked archly, her eyebrows rising at Tallie's answering blush.

'Oh, it is a long story, ma'am! I will tell you all about it later. But how is it that you are back so soon? How did you find Lady Palgrave?'

Lady Parry made an ambiguous noise, waved her hands vaguely and subsided into a chair, gesturing Tallie to sit down opposite her. 'Really, in some ways it was better than I could have hoped, which is why I am back so soon. She was already out of sympathy with the monkeys, which had quite wrecked the Blue Bedroom, were attempting to eat the wallpaper in the Chinese suite, of which she is very fond, and had bitten her favourite footman. So she had got rid of them.'

Something in Kate's voice suggested that this was not quite such good news. 'How, ma'am?'

'By the simple expedient of opening the windows and letting them go. Two have already been shot by the gamekeepers on neighbouring estates and a delegation of villagers and the vicar arrived as we did, to complain about the remaining two, which had taken up residence in the church. The vicar was talking darkly about reconsecration—I let poor William deal with that.'

'How?' Tallie asked fascinated, forgetting her own troubles.

'He commandeered a basket of peaches from my sister's succession houses, drove up to the village, had the church doors opened and placed a trail of fruit from the porch to the lych gate. The curate proved to be a crack shot, apparently.'

'Poor things,' Tallie observed compassionately. 'It was not their fault; I am sure they were only acting according to their natures.'

'I quite agree,' Lady Parry said. 'I remonstrated with Georgiana and put it to her that she should not interfere with God's dumb creation. At least pretty poets can be expected to look after themselves. She did appear chastened and somewhat sobered, so I deemed it safe to come home. William was becoming somewhat restive.' She stood up. 'I must go and change. Are you ready to get up, Tallie? We can have a late luncheon. William has gone to find Nicholas, doubtless for some sympathy.'

Tallie agreed with as much enthusiasm as she could muster. Her stomach seemed to contain a cold ball of lead, but she knew she must tell Lady Parry all about her connection with Mr Harland as soon as possible.

As she walked downstairs, schooling her face into an appearance of calm, the front door opened to admit both William and his cousin. Thankfully they did not see her for Tallie stopped dead three steps down and had to stay there for a full minute while she regained her composure. Nick here already! He was obviously not going to waste a moment in telling his aunt what a cuckoo she had been harbouring in the nest.

When she finally made her entry into the dining room, William greeted her with enthusiasm and proceeded to regale his audience with tales of the horrendous experiences he had had to endure. This kept everyone harmlessly occupied for the duration of the meal.

When the footmen came in to draw the covers Nick remarked, 'I have some matters I need to discuss with you, Aunt Kate. William, could you do me a favour? You know that new bay gelding I bought at Tatt's last week? I am not sure it is fully sound. You have a good feel for that kind of thing—could you take him out for me this afternoon, give me your opinion?'

He could not have offered a more tantalising bait. Glowing with pleasure at the compliment to his judgement, William made his excuses to his mother and hurried off to change.

Lady Parry was less easy to gull. She led the way

into her writing room and sat down, regarding the two of them with a quizzical eye. 'Well?'

'I have a confession—'

'Aunt, there is something I have to explain—'

They broke off, then Nick said, 'If you start, Tallie, I will join in as we get to my part in events.' She stared at him, suddenly overcome with nerves and he smiled reassuringly. 'We had best get it over with, do you not think?'

Tallie nodded dumbly and took a moment to order her thoughts. 'You recall, ma'am, that I came to you and said there was something I felt I should tell you about? A reason why I should not have accepted your offer to sponsor me?'

Lady Parry nodded. 'Yes. You were concerned that you had sat for Mr Harland.'

'Indeed, I had sat for him, ma'am. But not just to assist with portraits he was undertaking. When you said you knew all about it, I thought you really knew what I had been doing.'

'Which was?'

Tallie took a deep breath. 'Posing naked, or only lightly draped, for classical scenes.'

Lady Parry gasped, her eyes widened and she stared back at Tallie, apparently bereft of words for once.

'Extremely tasteful compositions,' Nick interjected as neither woman appeared capable of speech. 'And Mr Harland, as I am sure you will realise, has always behaved with the utmost respect and propriety towards Tallie.'

'Propriety?' Lady Parry moaned faintly. Then her gaze sharpened. 'And how do you know about this, Nicholas?'

'I visited the studio with Jack Hemsley. He wanted to make arrangements to have his aunt's portrait painted. William was with us and some other young cub.'

'I was posing for a scene as Diana the Huntress,' Tallie added. 'When he realised that Mr Harland was painting from a model, Mr Hemsley forced his way in. Ni...Lord Arndale tried to stop him—'

'But failed,' Nick finished grimly. 'It turned into a hunt.'

'Not William, surely?' Lady Parry asked, obviously appalled.

'It was not real for the two youngsters,' Nick explained gently. 'They had no understanding that they were searching for someone real, someone who would be frightened. If William had found Tallie, he would have protected her, I am sure of it.'

'I hid in a cupboard,' Tallie pushed on, her voice wavering, desperate to get the tale told. 'I lost my drape running away, the key fell out of the door—

all I could do was turn my back on it, hide my face and wait.'

'I saw the drape and managed to divert the others. Luckily I saw the key and was able to give it to Tallie so she could lock herself in.'

'You were wonderful!' Tallie said vehemently, suddenly finding her voice again. 'You saved me and you acted with such…such consideration, such tact. If that awful man had found me I do not know what I should have done. And I have never thanked you for it, even this morning…'

Her voice tailed off as she saw Lady Parry's expression. 'I am afraid there is more, ma'am.'

'I presume you did not recognise Talitha?' Lady Parry asked Nick.

'No, Aunt. I did not know her then, of course, and her hair was down. I never saw her face.'

His aunt closed her eyes fleetingly, apparently considering just what he had seen. 'Go on,' she said grimly.

'I bumped, quite literally, into Lord Arndale when I was delivering your hats the next day. I recognised his voice, but I do not think he knew me.' Tallie looked questioningly at Nick, who shook his head.

'I must have been blind, especially as I cannot deny that my experiences of the day before were more than somewhat on my mind.' Tallie bowed her head, blushing.

'Someone in bare feet with their hair down is going to look different from when they are wearing shoes and have their hair up,' Lady Parry conceded in a calm voice that Tallie found more worrying than a storm of anger would have been. 'No wonder you were so upset when you arrived at the house, Talitha.'

Without thinking, Tallie nodded agreement. 'It is very difficult, feeling so desperately grateful to someone when you cannot thank them and at the same time being extremely angry with them.' She caught Nick's eye and warmed at the flash of understanding she saw in them.

'Indeed. Well, let me see if I understand how the situation stood when you joined my household, Talitha. You knew who saved you at the studio and also believed that I knew about your... unconventional employment. You, Nicholas, had no idea that Talitha was the model you saw?'

'You are correct, although I knew that Tallie had a secret that she had managed to conceal from my enquiry agent and also that she intended to tell you about it, for she informed me of that when I challenged her.'

'So, when did you discover the truth?'

'At Tallie's first ball. Jack Hemsley managed to lure her into a retiring room and attempted to kiss her. Tallie put up a spirited resistance and her hair came down—at which point William and I found them. As soon as I saw her from the back, I knew.'

Tallie stifled a gasp. He had known for *weeks* who she was?

'And my son?'

'He was too busy being furious and disillusioned with Hemsley—one good outcome of the situation—to make the connection between a glimpse of a picture weeks before and the lady living under his roof and his protection and now the subject of insult.'

'And do you think Mr Hemsley recognised Tallie?'

'I think he must have done; I cannot account for what happened afterwards otherwise. He was too afraid of what I would do if he talked. Then Tallie gave him added reason to hate her by interfering in his attempt to seduce her friend Miss Blackstock.

'You had been the cause of his humiliation twice,' he said to Tallie. 'And he had reason to dislike me too. He had guessed I was instrumental in foiling his attempts to fleece William—' he ignored his aunt's indignant gasp '—and now I had witnessed his rout at the hands of you and Miss Blackstock.

But he was still too wary of me to do anything direct.' Nick got up and began to pace slowly up and down the room.

'I became concerned. He had reason now to want revenge on both of us. Together we had humiliated him and been the cause of separating him from William in whom he had invested many months of patient grooming before settling down to fleece him.'

'I never liked the man!' Lady Parry burst out, her carefully maintained composure vanishing. 'I tried to for William's sake and because his aunt, Agatha Mornington, always speaks so fondly of him. And she is not someone easily taken in.'

'She has been this time,' Tallie said. 'He has taken a post-obit loan out against her life.'

'Undutiful creature! What a revolting thing to do, to leech onto the fortune of one's relative in that manner. And doubtless he will be investing much time and trouble in ensuring she remembers him generously in her will.'

'Hence the portrait,' Tallie reminded her.

'A post-obit.' Nick regarded Tallie thoughtfully. 'Are you sure?'

'Mr Harland thinks so.'

'Well, well, that *is* a useful piece of information.'

Nick's grim smile boded Jack Hemsley no good whatsoever.

'So then what happened?' Lady Parry demanded. 'Do come and sit down, Nicholas, you are making me positively jumpy and you are usually so restful to have about.'

He threw himself into an armchair, crossed his legs, and regarded his aunt. 'I set a man to follow Hemsley. And when I heard that Tallie thought she was being followed, I set a man to follow her as well. You were quite right,' he added, turning to look at her. 'Hemsley's man.'

'And Hemsley organised the burglary at the studio!' Tallie gasped, suddenly making the connection. 'All he wanted was another look at the pictures to make sure it was me, and to confirm that they still needed some work doing on them. Then he had someone go and pretend they were interested in buying classical scenes…'

'His perfectly genuine cousin Oliver Laidlaw, just returned from Greece and on his way back to Scotland.' Nick grimaced. 'He took some finding, Hemsley was keeping him close.'

'And in all innocence Mr Harland asked me to pose one last time to finish the paintings.' She looked ruefully across to Lady Parry. 'I had realised by then that you had no idea what I had been doing after all. I was going to tell you when you came back, but meanwhile I went to the studio yesterday evening to help Mr Harland.'

'Hemsley's watcher told him you had stepped into the trap and that I was out of town. Mine too reported to me what was afoot.'

'And you were able to rescue Tallie in time?' Lady Parry asked anxiously. Tallie noticed with relief that she was once again using the affectionate diminutive.

'Just,' Nick said. 'I got there only moments ahead of Hemsley and a pack of his friends, all drunk and primed for fun.' He hesitated. 'We had to leave by the window.'

There was a silence. Then Lady Parry said carefully, 'Wearing what, my dear?'

'Nothing, ma'am.' Seeing the older woman go pale, Tallie added, 'It was a narrow ledge, and it was raining and we were high above the rest of the houses. Lord Arndale was wonderful—if he had hesitated for a second they would have found me. As it was, it must have been very difficult for him to get me down safely.'

Nick made an impatient gesture with one hand. The bruises and grazes stood out starkly and he clasped both hands together out of sight. 'She was frozen,' he said directly to his aunt. 'Mrs Blackstock's household were all out of town. I could not bring her here with only the servants and not a stitch on. I took her home with me and made sure she was warm and unhurt.'

Into the silence that followed this confession Tallie said, 'I returned this morning properly dressed. The staff think I was with the Blackstocks.'

Lady Parry did not seem either as angry or as shocked as Tallie had imagined she would be. Perhaps her patroness was just stunned, which would be understandable. Tallie discovered that she had a throbbing headache, which seemed to have appeared out of nowhere.

'May I be excused, ma'am?' she ventured. 'I would like to go and take a little sal volatile. I find I have a headache coming on. I will be back directly.'

'Of course, dear. There is no need to hurry back. And, Tallie…' Lady Parry smiled at her '…please call me Aunt Kate again. I feel a hundred when you both call me "ma'am" so stiffly.'

Nick relaxed at the twinkle in his aunt's eye. So, they were not in such deep disgrace as he feared; he was glad for Tallie's sake. He got to his feet and smiled reassuringly at her as he opened the door to let her out. She blushed and dropped her gaze sharply.

Nick turned back to his aunt. She knew exactly what must follow from last night's adventures, even if Miss Talitha Grey appeared not to have worked out the consequences. How would she react when she realised? Not that it made any difference—she was as committed as he had been from the moment they had stepped out onto that nightmare of a ledge last night.

He began to pace again, filling in more detail than he had done in front of Tallie, outlining the decisions he had reached after a morning's hard and serious thinking.

Upstairs Tallie poured a few drops of sal volatile into a glass of water and tossed it back with a grimace. The thought of lying down on her bed was very attractive, but she could not just run away and leave Nick downstairs, doubtless on the receiving end of a lecture from his aunt. Once Lady Parry had recovered sufficiently from the shock of their revelations to react, she could not believe they were not both going to be thoroughly in disgrace and Nick did not deserve anything except her grateful thanks.

Rainbird was just closing the front door as Tallie reached the hall again and he placed an envelope on a salver before handing it to her. 'This has just arrived for you, Miss Grey.'

Recognising Zenna's handwriting, Tallie tore open the wrapper without ceremony and scanned the contents.

...absolutely perfect, Tallie dearest! I have taken the liberty of sending the details direct to your attorney, but naturally I could not say anything to commit us without your personal approval. Do, please come and see—I could not bear to lose such a perfect house...

Tallie glanced rapidly through the closely written pages. It was unlike Zenna to wax so enthusiastic, she must indeed have found the ideal home for her long-dreamed-of school. She was walking slowly towards the writing room as she read and stopped outside the partly open door to shuffle the pages back together before entering.

Inside Lady Parry was speaking and the words froze Tallie where she stood. '...not at all what you planned. A suitable débutante this Season—I believe that is what you said when we last discussed your marriage.'

Nick appeared to be moving around. His voice became louder, then unintelligible as Tallie strained to hear, unaware that Zenna's letter was crushed in her hands.

'Of course, about time as you keep telling me… set up my nursery…perfectly suitable…I had thought Lord Rushingly's eldest, perhaps. Invite her to Heronsholt in the summer, make up a house party…'

'Well, you have not had the opportunity yet to fix her interest,' Lady Parry observed, sounding a little concerned. 'Unless I have missed something?'

'…too distracted by this business, which is a mercy as it turns out…'

'I rather think she has not realised this all means she must marry you,' Lady Parry observed.

Who? Tallie shook her head, puzzled, confused and with a growing knot of dread tightening inside her. *Who?*

'Tallie?' Nick's voice was so close by the door that she jumped and dropped the letter. 'I do not think it has occurred to her for a moment just how compromised she is or what the consequences of that are.'

Tallie was on her knees, scrabbling to pick up the scattered sheets as Lady Parry said, 'Certainly, one could not imagine for a moment that the poor child would intend to make such a match.'

'She is not so ineligible,' Nick said coolly. 'Her birth is perfectly respectable, her fortune, now, is more than comfortable.'

'Of course not, and she is a dear child. But not what one would expect for an Arndale of Heronsholt.'

Tallie stayed on her knees, transfixed, waiting for Nick's reply.

'Needs must, Aunt Kate. There is really no choice in the matter.'

Tallie stood up, her knees shaking. Until that moment she had not realised that all she wanted in the world was Nicholas Stangate. Now, and for ever. Yes, she had admitted to herself that she loved him, desired him, admired him. The word 'marriage' had never entered her thoughts; somehow, while he was a part of her everyday life, that had not been a consideration.

'You fool,' she whispered to herself, backing away down the hall. Her mind churned. *How else could you have him? Be his mistress? Why, when the world is full of skilled courtesans, should he bother with you?* Hope answered her, desperate. *He is attracted to you. He kisses you, takes you to his bed. He risks danger for you.*

Tallie reached the foot of the stairs. Mercifully neither Rainbird nor any of the footmen were in sight. Her clear-sighted common sense trod firmly on her optimism. *Of course he kissed you, of course he took you into his bed. He is a man, is he not? You stood naked before him. What did you expect him to think, to do? And he is a gentleman. Of course he would protect you. He would have protected Zenna or Millie if he had found them in such straits.*

The writing-room door opened and Lady Parry emerged. Tallie whisked round and under the stairs just in time to avoid being seen. But she was careless as she stepped out again once her patroness's footsteps had died away.

'Tallie. May I speak with you, please?'

It was Nick.

Chapter Eighteen

'Tallie,' Nick repeated, 'if your headache is not too bad, I would like to speak with you.'

'Of course,' Tallie replied composedly. It was easy to seem calm. She felt as though she had just stepped off a cliff: it was a very long way down, time would pass until she hit the ground, nothing much mattered in the meantime.

Nick held the door for her and she stepped into the writing room again, sank gracefully into a chair and waited, her eyes unseeing on Zenna's letter between her clasped hands.

'I hope you managed to have a little rest since you got home,' he began politely. 'It was hard to have to explain everything to Aunt Kate so soon after it happened, but I think it was for the best.'

'Thank you, yes. I feel quite restored, and I am sure you are correct.' Tallie took a deep breath. 'It seems to me that I have never expressed my sense of obligation to you for the way in which you have acted towards me, both before you knew who I was, and since.'

She was not watching him, so she could not tell whether the abrupt movement he made away from her chair was surprise, or simply embarrassment at her words.

'Thank you. But I do not look for thanks for acting in a way that any gentleman would consider appropriate under the circumstances.' His voice sounded as stilted as the words. Tallie began to pinch the letter into tiny, perfect pleats.

'I doubt that many gentlemen would have the initiative to put in place such a careful screen of watchers and informants, nor would many men have the courage to go out onto that ledge as you did.' She was managing, somehow, to keep her voice as calm and level as his.

'I did what seemed necessary at the time, including the breaking and entering. Which reminds me, I really must send a note to that householder to warn him that his attic is now unsecured.'

Despite everything, a little snort of amusement escaped Tallie and she looked up. 'I hope you do not mean to sign it?'

He smiled in return. 'No, I think that would be taking honesty a little too far. I will include some money for repairs, but I do not intend to add my seal.'

Nick came and sat opposite her, crossed his legs, steepled his fingers and regarded her over the top of them. 'My agent has collected your clothes from Mr Harland and has ensured that the canvases have been removed and stored securely. Hemsley will not be able to find any evidence to connect you with that studio now, however hard he tries.'

'Well, that is a relief,' Tallie said briskly, setting her hands on the arms of the chair and beginning to rise. 'Thank you for setting my mind at rest. How very efficient your agent is.'

'Please, do not go. Surely you did not think that was all I wished to speak of?'

His eyes were steady on her face and Tallie schooled her expression carefully to one of mild puzzlement. 'Why, yes. Was it not?'

'No. Tallie, you realise that after last night you have been completely compromised?'

'But no one saw me,' she protested. 'Except Mr Harland, who does not count, and your coachman, who I am sure will be totally discreet.'

'I am referring, not to our rooftop escapades, which by some miracle we did scrape through unseen, but to the fact that you spent last night in my bed. With me.'

'You put me there,' Tallie pointed out. 'And nothing happened.'

That maddening eyebrow lifted as he lowered his hands. Tallie saw his mouth was twisted into a wry smile and found herself hopelessly distracted by the subtle changes of expression those flexible, sensual lips could evoke.

'Your definition of "nothing" is an interesting one,' Nick observed evenly. 'For myself, I retain a very vivid recollection of how your body felt in my arms and how it felt to kiss you.'

Tallie flushed, but held his gaze. If he could recall how her body felt, she was certain she was branded scarlet at every point his naked frame had touched hers. 'You have kissed me before. Jack Hemsley kissed me, come to that. No one suggested I had been compromised as the result.'

'There is all the difference in the world between a few kisses and being in a man's bed. Face it, Tallie, you are *ruined*.'

What was it she had said to him, days…weeks ago? That this struggle of wills between them felt like a war? What was happening now felt like a duel.

She took a moment to calm her breathing, then asked politely, 'In what sense ruined? For what am I now unfit? I am physically exactly the same. I have perhaps acquired a little more knowledge of certain matters that I did not have before, but those can stay shut up in my mind. So, please define ruined, Cousin Nicholas.'

Suddenly his control snapped. Nick brought both hands down hard on the arms of his chair and was on his feet in a fluid movement, which gave her a glimpse of what a lethal swordsman he would be.

'Damn it, Tallie. For marriage, of course.'

It took an effort of will not to press back into the illusory safety of the high-backed chair. Mentally Tallie rallied, raised her guard and riposted, 'Why? No one else knows. I am still a virgin. And in any case, I have never had any intention of marrying, so the entire matter is academic.' She saw him begin to open his mouth and added tartly, 'And kindly do not swear again.'

'Swear?' Nick's eyes narrowed dangerously. 'Of course not. I apologise. What I will do next, if you persist in this ridiculous pretence that nothing of any consequence occurred last night, is to put you over my knee and—'

'Inflict violence upon me?' Tallie enquired sweetly. Her mind and consciousness seemed to be existing on two levels. On top there was a dangerous enjoyment in sparring with Nick, provoking him, seeing how she could strike sparks from his temper. Underneath something was shrivelling, dying. The man she loved was telling her that his actions had made her unfit for marriage to anyone else. It could only be a matter of moments before he explained that—as any gentleman must—he would therefore marry her himself.

Nick stood glaring at her. 'No, of course I would not hurt you. It is just that you are so—'

'Irritating? I must be, to make you lose your prized self-possession, your *froideur.*'

He stilled, his eyes narrowed, regarding her. 'Is that what you think I prize? Self-control? Coldness?'

'Is it not? I heard it in your voice before I even saw you. Calm, controlled, slightly aloof, just a very little amused at the caperings and emotionalism of us lesser mortals. You need to know everything, be in command. No surprises for Lord Arndale. No messy emotion or ill-bred displays of temper.' Now even the fencing was no longer amusing. All she wanted was to hold him off, perhaps hurt him a little, just a very little to counterbalance the pain inside her.

It seemed she had succeeded. The grey eyes were like black flint, the sensual, mobile mouth a hard line. Tallie expected a stinging rebuttal. What she got were hands on her shoulders pulling her hard into a crushing, furious embrace. She struggled, stamped one slippered foot futilely onto leather boots, lifted a hand to strike out and found both captured and pinioned neatly between their two bodies, ducked her face away from the angry purpose in his and found that with his free hand he had grasped her chin and was forcing it up.

'Now *this*, Miss Grey, is a display of messy emotion and ill-bred temper,' he ground out before bringing his mouth down hard on hers.

Tallie struggled furiously, her lips a tight line against the onslaught of his anger and her own desperate desire to yield to him, open to him, let him do what he would with her. She closed her eyes, felt the heat beginning to flood through her, felt her legs begin to tremble and suddenly she was no longer struggling.

She had no idea whether he had sensed her capitulation or had merely decided the demonstration of mastery was sufficient. Tallie found herself released as rapidly as he had seized her and sat down. By some miracle the chair was behind her. Furious with herself for her weakness and with him for exploiting it, she dashed the angry tears from her eyes and glared back at him.

Furious grey eyes glared back. 'Now, Miss Grey, as we have both comprehensively insulted and offended the other, might I suggest we return to discussing what we came in here to resolve?'

'What *you*, my lord, came in here to resolve. As I thought I had made clear, there is absolutely nothing I wish to speak about, other than to reiterate my gratitude for your actions yesterday. They were, if nothing else since has been, the actions of a gentleman. No, that is unfair.' She held up a hand to silence him and continued in a manner of frigid politeness, which she could see was inciting him to even greater depths of anger. 'I must also be grateful for the manner in which you assisted me in telling Lady Parry a story that must have been very shocking for her.'

'I do not want you to be fair, Tallie, I do not want your gratitude, what I want is—' He broke off, one clenched fist poised to thump the table as the door opened.

'That horse is as sound as a bell. I cannot imagine why you thought—' William stood in the doorway, whip in one hand, hat in the other, regarding the two of them with some confusion. 'I beg your pardon. Have I interrupted? I could hear voices and I thought you would want your mind set at rest about the animal.'

'Not at all, Cousin William,' Tallie said warmly. 'I am delighted to see you. Do, please, come in and tell Cousin Nicholas all about his horse. I must go and write a letter.' His arrival had only put off the painful declaration she was certain Nick was going to make her sooner or later, but, although she reproved herself for being a coward, she could only be glad of the respite.

'We were just discussing Jack Hemsley's latest activities,' Nick said smoothly, ignoring Tallie's horrified expression. He moved across and placed a hand on her shoulder. Without an unseemly struggle she was effectively trapped. 'Cousin Tallie thwarted his attempts to seduce a friend of hers and it appears that two blows to his pride by one young lady was more than he could stomach. Added to that, it seems he realised that to attack the young lady living under my aunt's roof would be to attack me—and I have been acting in such a way recently that his dislike of me has grown inordinately. He hatched a plot to ruin Tallie, which fortunately misfired last night. I have been considering what to do about him.'

Tallie sank back into the chair and considered giving herself up to strong hysterics. Nick was blandly ignoring the furious looks she was shooting him while William was reacting with predictable indignation. 'What to do? How can you even hesitate? Why, I will call him out, the bast—blackguard. Cousin Tallie is a guest under my roof, my mother's companion. This is outrageous!' He took an agitated turn around the room and swung round to face them. 'What did he do?'

'I really would prefer not to discuss it,' Tallie interjected hastily. If she had not been feeling so flustered she might have been amused at the confusion into which she had thrown William, who blushed and began to stutter at the thought he had embarrassed her. 'And, please, I could not bear it if either of you call him out. What if you were to be wounded?'

William looked hurt, Nick merely raised an eyebrow and remarked, 'Unlikely. No, we need to avoid any hint of scandal in dealing with Hemsley— Tallie's position in this household is too well known not to arouse suspicions if one of us openly challenges him. I have a better idea—one that I can thank you for, Tallie. Financial ruin is going to be a much more effective punishment for Jack than an uncomfortable dawn meeting on the Heath. Is Aunt Kate downstairs, William?'

'In the front salon,' he replied. 'I thought it was odd; she is usually in here at this time of day.'

Tallie glared at Nicholas through narrowed eyes. So, Lady Parry had tactfully removed herself while he made a declaration, had she? It was regrettable that she had to disappoint her kind patroness, but she was not going to marry Nicholas Stangate to satisfy anyone's ideas of what was the right and proper thing for a compromised young lady to do.

'Then let us consult her.' Nick opened the door for Tallie and steered them both in the direction of the front of the house. 'If my memory serves me right, we will have the perfect opportunity for our retribution tonight.'

Lady Parry looked up with a smile that rapidly faded as she took in Tallie's tight lips, Nick's expressionless face and William's pink-cheeked indignation.

'We have just been telling William that Jack Hemsley has attempted to ruin Tallie.'

'Oh, dear.' Lady Parry fluttered a white hand and lay back against the sofa cushions. 'This is all very…distressing. You will not say anything, William dear, will you?'

'Of course not.' Her son looked indignant. 'Don't know what happened anyway, so I can't say anything. I just want to put a bullet in the man. Damn it, when I think I believed him my friend!'

'Language, dearest! You are not going to call him out, are you, Nicholas?'

'No. There is too much risk it would draw attention to Tallie.' Nick pulled over a chair and sat down. 'Am I right in thinking it is Lady Agatha Mornington's dress ball tonight?'

'Oh my goodness, yes, it is! I had quite forgotten, what with all the excitement of having to go down to Sussex and then poor Tallie's adventures. Were you thinking that Mr Hemsley would be sure to be there in attendance on his aunt and it would therefore be embarrassing for Tallie to see him?'

'Not at all. I was wondering if you felt rather too tired after your journey to go, that was all.' Nick sat twisting his signet ring round his finger with a vaguely abstracted air. Tallie eyed him cautiously. He was plotting, she was sure of it.

His aunt was even more certain. 'Out with it, Nicholas. What do you have in mind?'

'A punishment for Jack Hemsley that will ensure he is hurt where it will do him most damage—in his pocket and in his reputation. And it will ensure he will not dare to return to town for a good long while. If he can afford to, that is. But I am going to need all three of you to pull it off.'

Lady Parry sat up sharply, eyes sparkling. 'Wonderful! I have been wanting to box that young man's ears ever since I heard of his ungentlemanly behaviour.'

Nick turned to look at Tallie, who found that her hands were clenched into fists in her lap. The thought of turning the tables on Jack Hemsley was powerfully attractive. 'Tallie? Do you feel you can cope?'

'With anything,' she affirmed with emphasis. 'What do you want us to do?'

At ten that evening Nick smiled at his troops as their carriage drew up at the steps of the Morningtons' town house. In the light from the flickering flambeaux their faces were curiously intent and dramatic. 'All ready? Are you sure you know what to do? We cannot know the layout of the ballroom in advance, so we will have to improvise if necessary.'

'We will cope,' Lady Parry declared. 'After all, there are only so many ways one can arrange the room and Lady Mornington is not one to be endlessly seeking for variety and novelty. But poor Agatha! I do dislike being the one who reveals the depths of infamy her wretched nephew has sunk to.'

'Think how she is being deceived now, though,' Tallie comforted. 'And you did say she had some very pleasant nephews and nieces on the other side of the family from whom she has been estranged because she so favours Jack. How much better it will be if she has their loyal support and not that of a money-seeking rake.'

'I would not put anything past him,' William added grimly. 'If the moneylenders get impatient at having to wait too long for that post-obit to be repaid, goodness knows what he might do to get his hands on her fortune.'

Lady Parry gasped, but Nick said repressively, 'Your Gothic imaginings are frightening the ladies, William. Now, if we are all ready, let us draw the first covert.'

With butterflies in her stomach Tallie followed her patroness up the double staircase to the wide landing outside the ballroom. They had deliberately timed their arrival for when the receiving line would have ended and their hostess would be found inside with her guests. Kate stepped into the hot, noisy throng, nodding and bowing to friends. With her hand under Tallie's elbow, she steered her firmly past the young gentlemen who stopped to request a dance.

'A little later, Lord Dimsdale, we are on an errand at present… Good evening, Mr Hubbert, I am sure Miss Grey will give you a dance later, but just now we really must find our hostess for a few words.'

Tallie craned to see the other side of the room. Nick's dark head could be glimpsed in the gaps between sets of the country dance, which was boisterously under way. He was making steady progress up the room and suddenly Tallie saw his objective at the same time as Jack Hemsley saw Nick.

He turned abruptly on his heel and headed deeper into the onlookers towards the head of the room. 'Gone away,' she whispered to Lady Parry. 'Nick has successfully flushed him out of cover.'

'Good. Ah, there is poor Agatha Mornington.'

'And there is William, dodging into the retiring room and out of the other door to get ahead of Mr Hemsley.'

'This is very exciting... Good evening, General! Yes, indeed, *what* a crush.' Kate bowed graciously to the military man and bore down on their hostess, a formidable matron whom Tallie recognised from her portrait at Mr Harland's studio. 'Agatha! What a delightful dance! Have you met my dear young friend Miss Grey? Talitha, make your curtsy to Lady Mornington.'

Tallie bobbed neatly and shook hands, finding herself under a sharp and intelligent scrutiny. How had such a lady been taken in by her scamp of a nephew? she wondered. Presumably she was not the first doting aunt to be deceived by charm and address, and doubtless not the last.

Kate, with one rapid glance across the ballroom

to where her son was converging with Jack Hemsley from one direction and Nick Stangate from another, turned slightly and began to stroll towards the head of the ballroom. Just a few steps away a small sitting-out area had been contrived with chairs and divided into two by a screen of potted palms.

'Agatha, my dear, I wonder if you can spare us a moment,' she said earnestly. 'Miss Grey has a favour to ask you.'

'Oh, please, Lady Parry,' Tallie interjected, obedient to her script. 'I would not want to trouble Lady Mornington by asking her about dogs when she must want to be talking to her guests.'

'Dogs? Are you interested in dogs, my dear?'

'Oh, yes, ma'am, and I was thinking particularly of buying a pug. Lady Parry says no one knows more about them than you and perhaps you could advise me where the best place to obtain one would be?'

She had been dubious when Lady Parry had told her that a discussion about pugs would be guaranteed to divert Lady Mornington whatever the circumstances, but it seemed that she had been quite correct. Tallie found herself seated and being comprehensively lectured and questioned.

'Well, yes, ma'am, I do enjoy walking…' There was Nick a few yards away. He had halted and was standing with his back turned, apparently deep in conversation with another man. That escape route had been stopped then; Jack Hemsley would not care to pass so close to Nick.

'I had no idea they would need so much exercise.' Lady Mornington was waxing lyrical about the boundless energy of pugs and the need for long walks whatever the weather. 'How very invigorating. I had rather imagined them to be lap dogs.'

Through the potted palms she could just glimpse William's blond head, then she heard him. 'Jack! I should have known I would see you here.' He sounded wary, but not unfriendly.

Hemsley's slightly deeper voice carried even more clearly and Lady Mornington turned her head slightly and smiled, obviously recognising her favourite nephew. 'Parry, old chap. Er...'

'Oh, look, I think I overreacted the other week at the ball, you know...' William was doing an admirable imitation of a callow youth in the throes of hero worship. 'I mean, I'm sure things weren't what they seemed... Thing is, I don't want to fall out with you...'

'Don't give it another thought. Tell you what, come to the prizefight in Bedford with me next week—we'll make up a party, what do you say?' There was relief and suppressed triumph in the affected voice and Tallie bit the inside of her lip in an effort to keep focused on Lady Mornington while watching Kate Parry out of the corner of her eye.

Lady Parry, who was dressed in an unusual shade of deep salmon to ensure she was visible, shifted her position and Tallie saw her nod. William must have glimpsed his mother through the palms and seen her signal, for his voice became a little louder and Tallie, hearing her cue, dropped her fan and dance card. With a murmur of apology she fell to her knees and began to hunt round under her chair, cutting off Lady Mornington in mid-sentence.

'That's a damn nice new curricle you've got, Jack,' she heard William say enthusiastically. 'More benefits of that post-obit loan you took out on your Aunt Mornington? Or has the old lady coughed up some more of the readies, seeing what a handsome portrait you commissioned of her?'

Tallie glanced up. Lady Mornington had frozen where she sat, her eyes riveted on the screen of palms. 'Wish I had your knack of turning old ladies up sweet,' William persisted loudly. 'What's the trick to it?'

Go on, Tallie willed Jack Hemsley. *Go on, boast about how clever you are.*

Chapter Nineteen

Jack Hemsley did not disappoint Tallie.

'Trick, old chap? Nothing to it. Old trouts like her will lap up any amount of honey, you can't pour too much on, trust me. Flatter her dreadful hats, take her driving in the park so she can wave to her ghastly friends, pet her God-awful pugs—they've all got something like that, if it isn't pugs it's a parrot—you can't fail. A bit of sharp work with the other relatives to put them out of favour and there you are—favourite nephew and all the dibs in tune.'

Lady Mornington surged to her feet. 'Excuse me, my dear,' she said with awful calm to Tallie, who was still crouched by her chair making a business out of picking up her fan. A terrible figure in puce, she stepped round the screen of palms. Kate pulled Tallie upright and the two of them followed apprehensively after her.

The scene that greeted them might have been

a tableau from a melodrama. Lady Mornington, bosom visibly quivering with indignation, confronted her white-faced nephew who was pinned between his outraged relative, William—who was inconsiderately standing fast at his back—and an interested crowd of onlookers who, realising something was afoot, had turned to watch. Prominent amongst them was Nick and the man he had been talking to: the Honourable Ferdie Marsh, the worst gossip in London Society.

'Despicable boy!' Lady Mornington hissed, the plumes on her coiffure shaking. 'Lying, toadying, deceitful wretch! This is how you repay my kindness, this is how you serve your cousins, poisoning my mind against them! I shall change my will tomorrow morning, not one penny shall you get from me. In fact...' her eyes narrowed, regarding his pinched and furious face '...in fact, I will not risk leaving it to tomorrow. The Lord Chief Justice is here tonight—I am sure he will be only too pleased to draw up a codicil for me here and now.'

She swept round, magnificent in her fury, and her eyes fell on Tallie. 'And you, dear child, can help me find him. Are you acquainted with his lordship? Tall man, always looks different without his wig, I find...' She swept Tallie off without a backward glance. 'You shall have one of Esmeralda's puppies from the new litter. You are a good child and I am sure will look after it excellently well.'

'Tha-thank you, ma'am,' Tallie faltered, taken aback by this powerful self-control. 'Ma'am…I am so very sorry about what just…' She did not know whether to feel guilty or not. It was horrible for Lady Mornington to have Hemsley's character exposed before an audience, but perhaps it was much worse that she should be estranged from her honest relatives because of the greed of one unpleasant nephew.

Lady Mornington gave her a sharp look. 'I have been a foolish old woman,' she said briskly. 'Serves me right. His father, my younger brother, was just the same—should have realised the bloodline would breed true.'

'Is that the Lord Chief Justice over there, ma'am?' Tallie asked hastily.

'Indeed it is, you have sharp eyes. Now, off you go, back to Kate Parry and have a good time, child. I,' she added with a note of grim amusement in her voice, 'I intend to.'

Tallie hurried back, seeing William energetically dancing a boulanger with a pretty redhead and finding Kate just accepting a glass of lemonade from her nephew.

'Well done,' Nick said appreciatively. 'That was an

entirely successful ambush. One cannot but admire Lady Mornington—did you notice the insinuation that she had to change her will immediately or she might not live to see the next day?'

'*Everyone* is talking about it,' Kate Parry said, fanning herself vigorously. 'And it is losing nothing in the telling, I can assure you. Tallie—is Agatha much upset?'

'Very cross with herself, I think,' Tallie said. 'And resolving to make amends with her other nephews and nieces. But I do not think she is sad, or greatly distressed.' She looked at Nick. 'Where is Mr Hemsley? Did he see us?'

'He has gone. Even someone with Jack's brass neck could not brazen it out in front of an entire ballroom full of people sniggering at him. There is no need to worry—he saw William and me and I am sure he has wit enough to know that we set out to entrap him, but I do not think he realises the part you and Aunt Kate played.'

'I am not frightened of him,' Tallie said scornfully, then caught Nicholas's eye and added ruefully, 'Not while I have you and William to look after me at any rate. I have to admit, I am not a match for someone like that without help.'

Nick bowed ironically. 'That is gracious, Tallie. May I solicit the next dance?'

It seemed they were on ordinary speaking terms again, and at least he could not launch into embarrassing lectures on how ruined she was or, even worse, make a declaration in the middle of Lady Mornington's dress ball.

'Thank you, Lord Arndale,' Tallie said politely, allowing him to lead her out onto the dance floor. 'What is it? I have lost track of the dance programme with so much excitement.'

'A waltz,' he replied, catching her efficiently around the waist with one hand and capturing her right hand with the other. 'You have to admit, my timing is perfect.'

'Perfect,' Tallie agreed hollowly as the music struck up and she was swept into the dance. *Perfect.* The last thing she needed was to be held in Nick's arms as the sensuous, exciting music took them. It was hard enough being with him and fighting to keep the yearning out of her voice, the love out of her eyes, without being so close to him that she could feel his warmth, smell the clean, sharp, indefinable maleness of him.

She needed to concentrate on thwarting any attempt to make her an offer, or, if she failed in that, to refuse him convincingly. As it was she could feel him gathering her tighter into his arms and could make no effort to draw away. Another couple brushed against her skirts and Tallie found herself touching his body, then he had released her again and all she was conscious of was the pounding of her heart and the glitter of his grey eyes when she looked up at him.

The music drew to a crescendo and stopped. Couples stepped apart, clapping politely and beginning to stroll off the floor, but Tallie found herself steered ruthlessly through the onlookers fringing the dance floor and into a deserted retiring room.

'My lord! What on earth are you about! Please return me to Lady Parry at once—she will concerned to know where I have gone.' Tallie tried to convince herself that the breathless catch in her voice was simply natural agitation and not the effect of being masterfully carried off in the midst of a crowded ballroom.

'You may return to her side the minute we have had this much-overdue conversation,' Nick said patiently, moving round to lean broad shoulders against the door panels.

Tallie eyed the only other exit from the room, a narrow window.

'And we are one floor above pavement level and, if I am not mistaken, that window will overlook the area, which adds another floor to the drop. If you feel you have overcome your fear of heights do, by all means, feel free to leave.'

Tallie glared. 'I have no intention of scrambling out of a window to escape you, my lord. You have only to remove your shoulders from that door and I will walk out.' Provided she could stay angry with him, it was easier to cope. Tallie stamped her foot. 'Will you please open that door, my lord!'

'Only if you stop calling me "my lord" every sentence…'

'Very well then, Nicholas, please—'

'And if you agree to marry me,' he finished.

It was not unexpected. She had been trying to avoid him putting that very question all day, but that did not make it any better. Every fibre of her being was screaming *yes*! Tallie raised both eyebrows haughtily. 'You will excuse me, *my lord*, if I find the warmth and sincerity of your offer less than compelling. I am, naturally, conscious of the honour you do me in making such a proposal; however, I must decline.'

'Tallie.' It was a warning growl.

'My lord?'

'I suppose you would like me to come and kneel down, clasp my hands to my heart and beg you to do me the honour?'

'That would certainly be an improvement,' she

agreed, casting her eyes downwards so that he could not see the sudden resolution in them.

'Very well.' Nick straightened up, took two long strides forward and fell on one knee in front of her. He placed one hand on his heart and said, 'Miss Grey, may I solicit—'

Tallie whirled away and made a dash for the door. Her fingers were closing around the handle when he took her by the shoulders, spun her round and trapped her against the panels, one hand on either side of her head. It had been a mistake to forget just how good his reflexes were and just how fast he could move.

Now what are you going to do? she asked herself. *If he kisses you, you are done for and you know it.*

'Tallie. As we were discussing this morning when William interrupted us, I have thoroughly compromised you. There is only one outcome from that. You must marry me.' He sounded as though he were keeping the lid upon his patience with some effort.

'And as I explained to *you*, you may have compromised me, but nothing *happened*. No one else besides ourselves and Lady Parry knows about it. I *have* to do nothing whatsoever, and if you tell me that your honour is at stake or some such masculine nonsense, I give you fair warning, I will kick you.'

Frustrated grey eyes stared into hers. 'Why will

you not say yes? I am hardly ineligible. You know you may acquit me of fortune hunting. Is there someone else?'

'No, there is not.' Where the breath to keep talking was coming from Tallie had no idea. She was not conscious of breathing at all and her heart was banging so hard she thought it must be visible through the fine gauze of her bodice. 'I do not wish to make a loveless marriage, it is as simple as that.'

'But—' Nick broke off, for once silenced. Then he said with a hint of a smile, 'I had rather thought that when I kissed you you were not averse to the caress. In fact, when I have held you in my arms you reacted with warmth.'

'I am aware that ladies are not supposed to enjoy such things,' Tallie retorted, wondering if the guardian spirit of Modest Behaviour was about to strike her down where she stood. 'But I can see that is nonsense, some tale put about to shelter innocent girls. After all, if married ladies did not enjoy it, why would they have affairs? I must confess that I find being kissed by you very…pleasant, and being in your arms is positively stimulating. However,' she hurried on as both Nick's eyebrows rose alarmingly, 'that does not mean I want to marry you. Naturally I realise that now we have had this discussion you are not going to kiss me any more—and that is a pity because I do enjoy it and I would certainly not trust any other gentleman of my acquaintance in that way.'

'Well, that is frank speaking indeed.' The familiar cool expression was back on his face and she could not tell whether he was shocked, angry or even, just possibly, amused.

'I am afraid so.' Tallie tried to look penitent. 'I did feel ashamed of myself and then I realised that it is foolish to deny one's natural, er…appetites. Of course, one should not indulge them any more than one should drink too much wine or eat too much rich food, and one realises in the case of ladies that the penalties are somewhat more extreme.' Now, surely, she had shocked him sufficiently to put an end to any desire to marry her. She was certainly shocking herself.

'But within marriage you could indulge those appetites completely,' Nick observed. 'You know, Tallie, you are not managing to shock me, which is what I believe you are trying to do. Amuse me, exasperate me and try my patience, certainly. But I am hard to shock and quite alarmingly patient when I want to be. And I do not believe your assumption of the mantle of a loose woman remotely convincing. Now, be a good girl and say "yes" and we can go out and tell Aunt Kate and all will be easy.'

'No.'

'Tallie, you have failed to convince me you do not wish to marry me because you are a wanton…'

'Not a *wanton*,' she protested. 'Or at least, only with you. I like you kissing me, I have to admit it, but I would not have said so if you had not produced that as a clinching argument as to why we should marry. But liking kissing someone is absolutely no reason to think they would be the right person to marry. How many women have you kissed?'

'Me?' He removed his hands and straightened up, although he did not move back. 'I have no idea.'

'Did you enjoy kissing them?'

'On the whole, yes. Tallie, what *has* this to do with our marriage?'

'And how many of them have you married?'

'None of them!'

'Precisely my point,' Tallie said triumphantly. 'Just because you enjoy kissing someone, it does not mean you want to marry them. So that, my lord, is not a good argument. How else do you intend to convince me?'

'You enjoy sparring with me, do you not, Tallie?' He had his hands on his hips now, head on one side as he regarded her thoughtfully. His lips quirked and she fought the urge to either smile back or stand on tiptoe and kiss the corner of his mouth. She was proving a puzzle to him, a problem, and Tallie sensed that she was also becoming a challenge, almost an intellectual conundrum to be solved.

'Yes,' she admitted. *And how much fun it would be to be married to him, to stimulate that sharp brain and tease that flashing sense of humour.*

'You will not win, you know,' he observed.

'That is not gentlemanly of you.' Tallie tried a pout for effect. The only reaction that produced was a grin of sheer devilment.

'Are you a gamester?'

'No…no, I do not think so. I have never been tempted by games of chance.'

'Well, let me tempt you with a bet upon a certainty. I wager you will agree to marry me within two weeks of today.'

That seemed safe enough, she was not going to agree, whatever wiles he used. 'Marry you within two weeks or simply agree to do so?'

'Agree, I think. I see no point in setting myself any harder a task than I have to.'

'And if you win?' she asked.

'You marry me.'

'And if you lose?'

'What would you like?' He stepped back and smiled again at the innocent calculation her face betrayed.

'My own phaeton and a team of match bays.'

'Very well.'

Tallie gasped. 'Seriously? I never thought you would agree.'

'I have absolutely no intention of losing, so I can afford to be generous. Of course, if you want such a rig, you only have to marry me and you can have one anyway.'

'You are absolutely the most infuriating man I have *ever* come across.' Tallie reached behind her for the doorknob. 'Now, are you going to let me out of here?'

'Once we have sealed the bet,' he said and took her in his arms. His mouth silenced her protests and he made not the slightest attempt to restrain her, simply allowing the drugging, languorous, sensual slide of his mouth over hers and the insidious caress of his fingers on her throat and shoulder to hold her to him.

Tallie moaned softly and let her body mould to his for a long, shuddering moment. Her lips parted and his tongue slid between them, so gently, so subtly that before she knew what she was doing her own tongue had begun to caress his in turn. He left her mouth and began to nibble the taut tendons of her neck. The blood was roaring in her ears so loudly that she hardly heard the question at first, then he repeated it, murmuring it as his lips teased and tormented the soft skin behind the curl of her ear.

'Marry me, Tallie.'

Tell me you love me, Nick, say it. Then I will marry you. Tell me...

'You stir my blood, Tallie. Marry me.'

Not enough. Oh, I want you too...but it is not enough.

'No.' Tallie pushed him away with both palms flat on his chest. 'No, and I am not going to kiss you again.'

Nick stepped back, his own hands raised in the fencer's gesture of surrender. 'I promise not to try—for tonight at least.'

Tallie caught a glimpse of herself in the mirror that hung on the opposite wall. 'Oh, for goodness' sake, just look at me!'

'I am,' Nick drawled. 'You look delightfully tousled and it provokes the most terrible desire in me to tousle you even more.'

'Well, you can't,' she retorted crisply, more to suppress her own longing to be back in his arms than out of any real fear that he would snatch her into them. She smoothed her hair, rescued some pins that were hanging on by their very tips, fastened the roses, which her maid had tucked into the knot at the nape of her neck, back with their comb and surveyed herself critically, managing not to catch Nick's amused eye as he watched her. 'It will have to do. Now, how are we going to get out of here unseen?'

'Through the window?'

'You certainly deserve to!' Tallie peeped round the edge of the door and saw with relief that a particularly noisy and energetic country dance was in progress with most of the onlookers' attention focused on the dance floor. She slipped out and wove her way through the chairs and pillars until she had put a respectable distance between herself and the retiring-room door.

'Cousin Tallie, may I ask you something?'

It was William, appearing at her side as though by magic. Tallie blinked at him, still too shaken by what had just taken place to focus properly. 'William? Not you as well? It is too much!'

Chapter Twenty

Nicholas sauntered casually out of the retiring room just in time to see Tallie turn from William, fumble in her reticule for her handkerchief and disappear into the sitting-room which had been set aside for ladies.

He laid a none-too-gentle hand on his cousin's shoulder. 'And just what have you said to Tallie to upset her?'

'Damned if I know,' William retorted defensively. 'All I said was that there was something I wanted to ask her and she said, "Not you as well? It is too much" or some such nonsense. Then her eyes filled up with tears and off she bolted!' He looked aggrieved. 'I only wanted to ask her to dance the boulanger. I know I'm not that good a dancer, but no one has ever burst into tears before when I asked them.'

Nick eyed the firmly closed leaves of the sitting-out-room door, a faint and uncharacteristic line forming between his brows. 'I suspect she thought you were about to propose.'

'Propose? Propose what?' William crooked a finger at a passing waiter, secured a glass of champagne, then choked on the first sip. 'Not *marriage*?'

'Hmm.' Was that what Tallie thought? That there was a family plot for one of them to marry her because she had been compromised and if she did not marry him, then his cousin would step into the breach?

He regarded William, who was coughing indignantly, and administered a sharp slap on the back. 'Stop that racket. Is it so surprising? I've been dinning into her the fact that she has been compromised and will have to marry someone.'

'Well, why isn't she marrying you?' William enquired in a whisper, casting a hasty glance round to see if anyone had noticed their conversation. 'You compromised her. And she's in love with you.'

'What?' Nick thundered, fortunately under cover of the opening chords of the boulanger, then dropped his voice hastily. 'Of course she isn't. If she were, she wouldn't have turned me down.' Or given me such an effective summing up of my thoroughly unsatisfactory character, he thought grimly. His mind flinched at the memory of her bitingly expressed opinions—cold, controlling, aloof, amused

at the antics of lesser mortals. Apparently pleasant enough to kiss.

William gave an unmannerly snort of disbelief. 'The pair of you are going about like April and May, for goodness' sake!' Nick regarded him incredulously. 'Very well, not quite like that, I suppose, but one can feel it in the air when the two of you are together. A certain something.'

'What you can feel is irritation on my part and wilful bad temper and obstinacy on hers.' And enough erotic attraction to light kindling, Nick ruefully acknowledged. Could Tallie possibly be in love with him? Surely not, or why on earth refuse him? He shook his head as though shaking off an irritating fly. William was hardly a connoisseur of the tender passions—paying him any heed on the subject was madness.

And if anyone was running mad it was Nicholas Stangate, Lord Arndale. He had given himself two weeks to change Tallie's mind and now he was even further from understanding that mind than he had been at seven o'clock that morning. Damn it, was it only that morning that she'd lain in his arms, in his bed? He felt his body tightening at the memory and trampled ruthlessly on the recollection of soft, warm, naked… 'Boiled fish.'

'What?'

God, he *was* losing his mind if that was the best he could do to conjure up the most unerotic thought possible. 'Never mind, I was thinking aloud. Best go and find Aunt Kate and tell her Tallie is not feeling well. She'll probably want to take her home.'

William began to weave his way through the guests. Nick was vaguely conscious of him leaving, but his eyes stayed on the closed door of the sitting-out room. Provokingly independent, charmingly outrageous, worryingly courageous. All those descriptions fitted Talitha Grey. Marriage to her would certainly never be boring. His involuntary smile faded at the memory of the handkerchief she had held to her eyes as she vanished into the room. He had never seen her cry before, surely? Oh, yes, he had, he recalled with a pang of conscience. Once when he had knocked the breath out of her and once when some sharp remark he had made had caused her eyes to fill with bravely suppressed tears. At the thought of her distress something tightened hard in the pit of his stomach. Had he been harassing her? Pushing her too far? Or was it just that the last twenty-four hours were enough to undermine the spirits of anyone, however resolute?

Tallie sniffed resolutely and waved away the sal volatile that Miss Harvey, a fellow débutante, was helpfully attempting to press into her hand. 'Thank you, no, I am quite all right. It was just that someone stood on my toe—so very painful! I quite thought he had broken it, and my eyes were watering. No, no, I assure you, you are most kind...'

Would the wretched girl never go away? Tallie wiped her eyes, smiled with more than a hint of gritted teeth and at last, thankfully, Miss Harvey turned away, only to swing round at the door with renewed offers of assistance.

'No, nothing you can do. *So* kind of you...' And it was kind, Tallie acknowledged to herself. And poor William had probably meant nothing more than to ask her to dance, or if she wanted a drink. Her nerves were on edge, she was overtired, that was all. In the morning after a good night's sleep all would be in proportion again. Nicholas would accept his *congé* with good grace, Aunt Kate would stop worrying and she could slip away down to Putney to see Zenna's proposed schoolhouse for a few days' peace and quiet. Then she could return and spend the last weeks of the Season enjoying herself before slipping quietly out of Society for ever.

'Talitha dearest, whatever is the matter!' It was Lady Parry, all of a flutter, waving aside the attendant and seizing Tallie's hands in hers as she plumped down on the sofa next to her.

'Nothing, Aunt Kate, I am just a little tired, that is all.'

'I should never have agreed to this madcap scheme of Nicholas's, not so soon after…after last night. You must be emotionally drained, you poor child. Come along, I have told William to order up the carriage; we'll send it back for the men later and they can stay and play cards and flirt to their hearts' content. Why they do not flag with exhaustion I do not know—I am quite worn out.'

'Possibly because you do not stay abed until past noon the next day, ma'am,' Tallie suggested lightly. She would raise the idea of a trip to Putney on their way back, then she could try to sleep, at least knowing that was settled.

Clucking under her breath at the indolent and dissipated ways of modern young men, Lady Parry swept Tallie out of the sitting-out room and scanned the crowds. 'Goodness knows where Agatha Mornington has got to—probably flirting with the Lord Chief Justice.'

'Surely not?' Despite herself Tallie was entertained at the thought.

'Well, they do say she had an *affaire* with him in their youth,' Lady Parry confided, then recalled to whom she was speaking and added firmly, 'All silly gossip, of course. Now, where has William got to?'

At length the ladies found themselves safely in their carriage, Tallie having found the opportunity for a rapid whispered apology to William. 'I am so sorry I was short when you tried to speak to me, I am just so tired this evening.' The effect of her green eyes, still swimming with unshed tears, was more than enough to reduce him to a stammered assurance that he had noticed nothing, nothing at all out of the way, and of course she must be tired.

Lady Parry disposing her furs, reticule and fan about her on the broad expanse of green velvet, was less easy to fob off. 'You poor child! What a dreadful couple of days you have had of it.' Although Tallie could not see her face, she was aware of a shift of mood, a sharpening of interest. 'Now, has Nicholas had the opportunity to speak to you?'

'Yes, ma'am.'

'And?'

'And what, ma'am?'

'Has he proposed to you?'

'Lord Arndale has kindly explained to me that I am ruined, hopelessly compromised and must marry him, yes.'

'And?'

'In the face of such a tender declaration I felt no compunction in declining,' Tallie replied, somewhat more tartly than she had intended.

'Oh, foolish boy! I had no thought that he could express himself so badly! What on earth is he about? When I consider how much address he has...'

'Possibly too much, dear ma'am. I think Lord Arndale expects the weaker sex to fall in at once with whatever he proposes, whether it is a walk in the park, the best place for their investments or his opinion on their marriage prospects. I, however, do not choose to dance to his lordship's tune and, as I have already explained to him, I have no intention of marrying and never have had.'

'But, Talitha, do consider...'

'I agree, dearest Aunt Kate, that I am indeed compromised. Should I be intending to marry, it would put me in the most delicate of situations for I would need, in all honour, to confess everything to a prospective husband. And,' she added with a wry laugh, 'I suspect he would remain a contender for my hand for not a moment after hearing that confession. But I have not the slightest desire to take a husband, so it does not arise.'

'Oh, Tallie, how can you not wish to marry? And Nicholas is the most eligible of men.'

'Why, certainly, ma'am, if one is concerned only

with title, wealth, intelligence, looks and a ready address. I am foolish enough to wish only for a husband, be he ever so humble, who loves me and tells me so. I am most unlikely to find such a soul mate, and his lordship, to do him justice, does not perjure himself with false declarations of emotions he does not feel.'

'Oh, dear,' Lady Parry said dismally. Even in the fitful light cast by the flambeaux as they passed Tallie could see her shoulders droop. 'This is not what Miss Gower and I dreamed about for you.'

'You thought that I should marry Lord Arndale?' The words were out before she could help herself. Surely the two ladies could never have dreamed that their protégée would attach the interest of the eligible Nicholas Stangate, Lord Arndale?

'Well, you always seemed so…different, so independent.' Lady Parry was obviously struggling to articulate what the two friends had plotted so deviously. 'And Nicholas is inclined to be so cool and so much in command of everything. We thought—' she broke off in confusion '—we thought you would do him good, shake him out of that control, make him enjoy himself.'

'I would have thought,' Tallie said drily, 'that Lord Arndale was more than capable of enjoying himself without any help from us.'

'You mean his mistresses and so forth,' Lady Parry remarked, apparently rendered indiscreet by the darkness. Tallie felt incapable of enquiring what *so forth* meant. 'Well, of course, but there too he is in control. By all accounts he is perfectly fair, very generous, but he needs shaking up a little in my opinion.'

'Well, I doubt if being turned down by me will be an adequate shock,' Tallie observed. It was a most peculiar sensation, having this intimate discussion about Nick in the dark. It was almost like talking to herself and it most certainly did not feel real. 'I must confess, Aunt Kate, I did overhear you both discussing his marriage plans. Being turned down by an eligible young lady would, I imagine, administer the appropriate salutary shock. Being spurned by a shockingly eccentric milliner is unlikely to do more than sting his pride.'

'Oh, dear.' Lady Parry sighed. 'I appear to have made a mull of everything.'

'Do not say so!' Tallie impetuously moved to sit next to her patroness and hugged her. 'I have had a lovely time, truly. And I could not have hoped for a warmer welcome than you and William have given me. It is an experience I will always treasure, but I am not cut out for this sort of life. If you will allow me, may I borrow the carriage to go down to Putney tomorrow to stay with Miss Scott? She thinks she has found the perfect house for her school and wants me to approve it.

'If I stay perhaps a week, then Lord Arndale will forget all this nonsense about having to marry me and I can come back and finish the Season, if you will allow.'

'Of course you may have the carriage.' The vehicle drew up outside the house as Lady Parry spoke and she continued as the groom helped her down. 'And of course you must finish the Season. I cannot imagine how I am going to get along without you; I have had so much pleasure from your company.'

'And I from yours, dearest adoptive Aunt.' Tallie kissed Lady Parry on the cheek as they stood in the hall, blinking in the light of the many-branched candelabra that Rainbird had set on the side-table. 'Thank you so very much.'

Tallie managed to escape the next morning with her portmanteau without an encounter with Nicholas—who, as she had predicted to Lady Parry—had kept to his room until noon. Had Tallie known it, her haste to escape was quite unnecessary. His lordship was far too old a hand at games of cat and mouse to press his suit so soon after the ball. He partook of a leisurely luncheon before strolling round to Clifford Street to visit his tailor, then made his way to his club and passed a pleasant afternoon apparently immersed in the news-sheets and keeping half an ear open for gossip about Mr Hemsley's fall from grace.

His quarry, meanwhile, sank back against the squabs with a sigh, which might have been either relief or regret, and watched the bustling street scene as it passed. How long was it since she had counted every penny before considering whether to take a hackney carriage? Not so many weeks, and here she was taking for granted the luxury of a private carriage with liveried servants at her beck and call.

Tallie took a firm grip on her imagination, which was wistfully conjuring up images of a certain grey-eyed gentleman, and thought fondly of dear Miss Gower, whose kindness had led her to pluck an anonymous young lady out of her genteel poverty and establish her in comfort and elegance. The smile that curved Tallie's lips at the memory of the doughty old lady faded as she wondered how many other young women the City held who were forced to make their own way in a hostile world, most of them without the benefits of upbringing and education she had received.

The germ of an idea began to form as the carriage

drove into the country near Little Chelsea; by the time it had reached the village of Fulham her eyes were positively sparkling. *Yes! This is what I can do...* Tallie knew next to nothing about the advanced theories of education that Zenna held so dear, but she did know what sort of start in life an impoverished young woman needed, and it was not just young ladies fallen on hard times who required help.

The pretty view of the Thames from Putney bridge passed unnoticed, and when the coachman drew up in front of the tall double-fronted house just off the High Street in Putney Tallie was so lost in thought that the groom had to cough to draw her attention to the fact that he had been patiently holding the door open for her for some moments.

'I am so sorry,' Tallie apologised, stuffing her tablets and pencil into her reticule and jumping down. 'I had an idea. Zenna! Have you been watching for me? I am sorry not to have given you more notice.' The friends embraced, then Tallie allowed herself to be shown into the house.

'What do you think of it?' Zenna asked anxiously. 'The country air is so pleasant, and it is not too far from town, I thought...'

'Is it big enough?' Tallie demanded, staring around her with furrowed brow.

'Big enough? But I was worried that you would

think it too big!' Zenobia broke off, torn between relief and puzzlement. 'There are two wings at the back that do not show from the road. I had thought perhaps a dozen young girls and a dozen older ones. There is ample room for that and for classrooms and rooms for the assistant mistresses, a dining hall, a suite of rooms for me and servants' rooms. The kitchens are rather antiquated, but a new close range and a little work and they will be perfectly acceptable.'

'No, it needs to be bigger.' Tallie took her friend's arm and began to march towards the stairs. 'Can we manage to accommodate another dozen or so girls? Not fee-paying ones, but poor girls who would benefit from a good education? And a suite for me as well.'

'Well, there *is* room, we might have to do more work on the left-hand wing, I suppose.' Zenna dug her heels in and they stopped abruptly at the foot of the stairs. 'But who is going to pay for these girls? And why do you want a suite of rooms? Surely you are going to marry Lord Arndale?'

'I am going to pay for them and, no, I am not going to marry Nicholas or anyone else. I am ruined and I intend to devote myself to the education and advancement of deserving girls.'

Chapter Twenty-One

'Ruined?' Zenna squeaked. 'How? Who by?'

'Really, Zenna,' Tallie chided, starting to climb the stairs. 'Do you not mean "by whom"?'

'You know perfectly well what I mean,' Zenna said fiercely, running to catch up. 'I suppose it was Lord Arndale, and why are you not marrying him? You might be…I mean…'

'Expecting a child?' Tallie stopped on the landing and surveyed the doors opening off it. 'This will need some redecoration, will it not? No, I am not in any danger of that. It appears that one can be quite effectively ruined without any of the supposed pleasures one might expect in the process.'

'Talitha Grey!' Zenna stopped dead in front of her and wagged a finger. 'Stop sounding flippant and as if you do not care. I know you better than that, remember. Why will you not marry Lord Arndale, for goodness' sake? You are in love with the man after all.'

'But he is not in love with me,' Tallie replied briskly. 'And I have no intention of finding myself married to a man who will be making the best of things by regarding me as a cross between an unpaid housekeeper, a hostess for his entertaining and a brood mare.' She paused and added with a rueful smile, 'And not necessarily in that order!'

'Tallie! I am certain Lord Arndale would never—'

'Oh, he would be perfectly charming, I am sure, and I would live a life enriched with every comfort and elegancy.' She broke off to push open a door. 'These rooms are very spacious for the second floor, are they not?

'The children would be a joy, of course,' she added somewhat absently, 'although I would prefer it if their father had married me because he loved me, not first and foremost because he had compromised me.'

They had arrived at the end of the corridor and Tallie started to climb the narrow stairs in front of her. 'Where does this go?'

'To the attics and down to the kitchens. Tallie, do stop and come and sit down and have some luncheon and tell me why you will not marry his lordship. What has upset you so?' Zenna regarded her friend's set face. 'Now, this minute, Tallie! Or I swear I will write to Lord Arndale and demand to know what he has done to you.'

Miss Zenobia Scott was not given to making threats she would not carry out. Tallie allowed herself to meet her friend's eyes for the first time that day and smiled ruefully, finding it difficult to prevent her lip quivering.

'Very well, Zenna,' she capitulated meekly, following her down the twisting servants' stair to the ground floor.

'Mrs Blackstock is staying with her cousin, but the lady kindly lent me two of her maids so that I could stay here for a few days and assess the house better. The owner is proving so co-operative that I think he must be having trouble disposing of such a large establishment. That gives me hope we can drive a hard bargain.'

She tugged the bell-pull and spoke a few words to the maid who appeared in answer. 'There, something will be ready in ten minutes. Now sit down, Tallie, please, and tell me what has occurred.'

Taking a deep breath, Tallie repeated the tale she had told Lady Parry the day before. It was easier the second time round and without Nick there it was considerably less embarrassing. She was also far more frank with her friend about exactly what had happened when she awoke in Nick's bedroom.

'Oh, my goodness,' Zenna said weakly, her eyes round with shock. 'And his lordship did not...'

'No.'

'Goodness,' she repeated. 'I would have thought that his lordship is quite...er...that is, he is very...'

'Very,' Tallie agreed drily.

Zenna digested this for a moment. 'And he does desire you?'

'So it would seem. But then, most men appear to have very passionate desires. It means nothing in particular to them. It is certainly no basis for a marriage.' Tallie turned to her friend, suddenly fierce. 'I have no intention of sharing my husband with his mistress, however much Society may turn a blind eye to that sort of behaviour.'

'It appears to be almost expected in Society marriages,' Zenna agreed sadly. 'But are you so sure he does not love you?' She bit her lip, obviously searching for some hopeful comment. 'Perhaps he is shy and...no, perhaps not.'

'I cannot imagine the circumstances in which Nicholas Stangate would be shy,' Tallie said with a smile at the thought. 'Besides, he tried every argument to point out to me just how necessary this match is. If he loved me, surely that was when he should have told me?'

'You would think so, but men are unaccountable beings,' Zenna mused, breaking off at a tap on the door. 'That will be luncheon ready. We will serve ourselves, so we can continue talking.'

The meal was set out in a charming parlour at the back of the house, giving Tallie the opportunity to admire the garden.

But Zenna was not to be diverted. 'So how have you left things? Surely you cannot avoid meeting Lord Arndale if you are continuing to reside with Lady Parry?'

'He has wagered me that I will agree to marry him within two weeks of yesterday.'

'He is very sure of himself!'

'He is indeed, which is why I want you to promise me that you will not admit him here if he calls. A few days' peace will allow me to think about how I can best dissuade him from this.' Zenna looked doubtful, but Tallie persisted. 'Promise me, Zenna!'

'Very well,' her friend agreed. 'Beside our friends and tradespeople, I will admit prospective parents only.'

That provoked a laugh from Tallie. 'Come now, Zenna! Even for someone as confident as you, that is carrying expectation too far, is it not?'

'It is not impossible,' Zenna retorted, passing a plate of ham across the table. 'I have confided my intentions to a number of people and I do think this house will prove suitable. Now, tell me more calmly about this idea of yours to admit young women of no means. How can we afford it?'

'I will pay their fees. We cannot take many, I quite realise that, but even a few who leave with the skills to manage their own small business, or become governesses or companions—surely that is better for them than struggling in poverty when they have the intelligence and the spirit to do better for themselves?'

Zenna looked thoughtful. 'Yes, you are right. Think what a difficult situation you or I would have been in if we had tried to make our own way in the world with no education.' She delved into her reticule for the set of tablets and pencil that inevitably accompanied her. 'This has given me much to think about and will change some of my calculations.' She sucked the end of her pencil thoughtfully. 'How many girls do you think we should start with?'

Tallie, who had begun by using her idea as a defence against having to think about Nick and how miserable she felt, found herself drawn deep into Zenna's plans and how they could be adapted to accommodate her 'special students', as Zenna called them.

* * *

Dinner time found the pair of them still hunched over the dining table surrounded by sheets of paper, Zenna's tablets long exhausted. Rough sketch plans of each floor with scribbled notes about alterations jostled with lists of everything from subjects to be taught to bed linen required.

They continued during the meal until Tallie spilled gravy on Zenna's tabulated curriculum for the youngest girls.

'Enough!' she announced, mopping it up. 'I am too tired to concentrate any more. In fact, if you will excuse me, Zenna, I will go direct to my bed. I declare I had no idea that education would be such an exhausting undertaking.'

Her friend, who had been prepared to carry on talking until she dropped if that helped keep the haunted look from Tallie's eyes, nodded encouragingly. 'What a good idea. I will just make sure the maids have locked up and then I will not be far behind you.'

Tallie fell asleep instantly, hardly stirring when Zenna slipped into the other side of the big bed they were sharing.

But her slumber was racked with nightmares and she tossed and turned, muttering under her breath until poor Zenna seriously considered taking a pillow and the counterpane and trying to sleep on the chaise longue in the front parlour.

In consequence, it was two heavy-eyed young ladies who regarded each other over a very late breakfast. 'What were you dreaming about?' Zenna demanded bluntly, draining her second helping of hot chocolate and reaching for the pot to refill her cup. 'It was like sharing the bed with a basket of puppies.'

Tallie rubbed her aching brow and tried to recall. 'I was in class and you were telling me to write on my slate "I will marry Lord Arndale" one thousand times. And when I refused you turned into him and he shouted at me that I was ruined and must go and stand in the corner and disobeying him was no way to learn ancient Greek. And I would not do that either so he took me in his arms and...'

'Yes?' Zenna's chocolate cup tilted dangerously.

'...said he would have to kiss me until I could do all my irregular verbs.'

'I am sure I would never have learned mine if that was the penalty for disobedience,' Zenna observed dispassionately.

'Zenna!'

'Well, he is extraordinarily attractive, and if you do not want him...'

'I do want him! But not on his terms, so there is no use in teasing me—I am not refusing him on a whim.'

They both chased their sweet rolls around their plates in a desultory manner.

'I suppose I should sort out those papers from yesterday,' Zenna observed, making no move to do so.

'Hmm. It is a nice day; perhaps we should look at the garden.' Tallie too stayed sitting at the breakfast table.

Suddenly Zenna pushed back her chair and got to her feet. 'I know what will blow the cobwebs away. Come along, up to the attics.'

'That's more likely to cover us in cobwebs,' Tallie grumbled, but she submitted to being urged towards the back stairs and climbed up behind Zenna to the very top.

'There!' Zenna flung open the door to reveal light-filled, spacious rooms opening one after another. 'There is a mansard roof,' she explained, gesturing at the high ceilings and big windows. 'It is unconventional, but I thought of having my rooms up here. There is room for both of us, in fact—a bedroom each, two dressing-rooms and a big sitting-room.'

Tallie nodded, catching her enthusiasm.

'But the space is not the best thing, just look at the view.' Zenna flung open a window and, ducking slightly, stepped out onto the leads. Without thinking Tallie followed her, then clutched the window frame with a gasp.

Because of the design of the roof there was a flat walkway, perhaps five foot wide, running around the edge of the roof before it sloped up steeply to its flat top. The edge was bounded by a stone balustrade at about waist height and, even with her back to the window, Tallie could see the wide view across the rooftops of Putney to the sparkle of the river beyond.

Careless of the height, Zenna perched on the balustrade and called, 'Come and see. It is quite safe, the stonework is sound.' She glanced back over her shoulder, and saw Tallie's face. 'Oh, I am sorry, I had forgotten about your fear of heights.'

'It is very foolish of me,' Tallie said firmly, making herself let go of the window frame and stand up. 'The view is indeed lovely and I think the rooms would be delightful.' Her stomach heaved, but she managed to fix a smile on her face, wondering what she could do to lure Zenna off the parapet and away from that dreadful drop.

In the event Zenna hopped off with as little concern as she would have shown getting up from a chair and leaned over, heedless of the effect on the elbows of her gown. 'Oh, look, a carriage has drawn up. Now who can that be?' She leaned further, oblivious of Tallie's squeak of alarm. 'Not Mrs Blackstock, for it is not a hackney carriage. I know—it must be Lady Whinstanley, she was most interested when I told her about my plans and she has a house somewhere near.'

'You had better run down, then,' Tallie managed to say. 'It would never do to keep her waiting.' To her immense relief Zenna straightened up and ducked back through the window.

As the sound of her footsteps diminished down the stairs Tallie began to back into the room, eyeing the balustrade warily as though it might leap at her and toss her over. Then something stopped her. Quite what it was she could not decide, but the sound of Nick's voice calmly telling her she could step out onto that nightmare of a ledge at Mr Harland's house mixed with the hasty apology that Zenna had made when she remembered her fears.

Nick had had to put himself at great risk by having to coax and support her along that ledge. Zenna was doubtless regretting her plan for converting this lovely space into rooms because she knew Tallie was scared of the height.

She made herself step out again, clinging to the

window frame as she had before. At least she was certain this was a genuine fear and she was not indulging herself in order to draw attention, or have a man protect her. Here she was alone and as terrified as she had been at the studio. But if she could only manage to conquer the fear enough to stand out here and admire the view with Zenna, that would be something.

She held on to the window and looked up, studiously following a bird in flight until it began to swoop down. That was all right; she could look at the tree tops. She dropped her eyes further and her stomach lurched with them, but after perhaps five minutes carefully gazing at the distant prospect she felt able to let go of the window and walk up and down the wide ledge.

This was so successful that she even let her eyes stray to the parapet and its broad top. It was far wider than any stool she had ever sat upon. How proud of her Zenna would be if she could sit on that or even just lean against it. Her stomach lurched again.

Tallie closed her eyes and began to pace up and down, repeating out loud, 'I will not give in, I will *not*.' She put out a groping hand and found the parapet, edged towards it and, with her face screwed up into a scowl of grim determination, eyes still tight shut, started to hitch one hip up onto the broad top as she had seen Zenna do.

The voice shouting 'No!' hit her almost at the same moment as the arms that seized her, dragged her round and off the parapet.

She screamed, opened her eyes and saw her worst nightmare, the wide view spinning around her. She was falling, helpless…

With another shriek Tallie hit the steep slope of the Mansard roof, her breath crushed out of her by the body that pinned her there. Hands pressed her face to a broad chest, fingers laced desperately in her hair and a voice, a familiar voice sounding utterly unfamiliar, repeated words that made no sense at all.

Tallie stopped flailing and trying to find breath to scream and heard incredulously what Nick Stangate was gasping into her hair, against her face.

'My love, my darling…no…I am sorry, I will not harass you any more, I promise, my love…only promise me you will never do anything like that again. Tallie, my heart, I will never come near you, if only you'll promise me…'

She gave up trying to push him away and reached to fasten her hands in his hair, forcing his head back so she could gaze incredulously into Nick's face.

His eyes were wild, dark, his expression vulnerable as she had never seen it.

'What did you call me?' she managed to whisper.

'My love.' His voice was hoarse. 'Tallie darling, I never meant to hound you until you would do something so desperate…'

'You thought I was going to jump?' Of course, that must have been what it looked like. 'Oh, no Nick, I was just trying to sit on the ledge, like Zenna did. She was so disappointed that I might not want to share her rooms up here because of the height. I was only trying to conquer my fear.'

He slowly straightened his arms until he was standing with her trapped by them, her back against the near-vertical slope of the roof. He closed his eyes and Tallie saw the tension ebb out of him. 'Of all the damn fool, witless ideas,' he said, his voice shaking. Then he caught hold of himself and the grey gaze was furious on her face. 'You could have been killed, you could have become dizzy, fallen. You were all by yourself up here. It was the most hen-witted…'

Tallie swallowed and enquired meekly, 'Did you call me *your love*?'

'Yes.' The glare faded. 'Tallie, my darling, never, never do anything like that to me again. You have taken years off my life—in fact, I will probably wake up tomorrow with white hair.'

'Very distinguished,' Tallie murmured, the growing bubble of happiness welling up inside her, threatening to burst and leave her speechless. 'Did you mean it when you called me that?'

'Of course I meant it.' Nick touched a cautious finger to her cheek. 'Your face is dirty. Did I hurt you just now?'

'No, I do not think so. Nick, why did you not tell me? You made me all those arguments about why I had to marry you and never mentioned the one thing—the only thing—that matters to me.'

'I had no idea that I loved you,' he admitted, regarding her ruefully. 'Not an inkling. I knew I desired you, but that seemed to blind me to what else I was feeling.' He shook his head, apparently trying to explain things to himself as much as to Tallie. 'I knew I worried about you and you infuriated me and puzzled me. I wanted to protect you and I wanted to make passionate love to you—and half the time I wanted to shake you. How was I to know I was in love with you? I have never been in love before.'

'Neither have I.'

'Then you do love me? After what I've done to you? Embarrassed you in the street, pried into your life, disapproved of your friends, kissed you in the most improper way, compromised you...'

'...looked after me, saved my reputation, fought for me, made me laugh, made me want to behave in the most abandoned and outrageous manner?'

'Then why would you not marry me when I asked you, you little wretch?'

Tallie regarded him in loving exasperation. 'What, agree to marry a man who was lecturing me on how I was ruined and *had* to marry him? Marry a man whom I had just overheard telling his aunt all about his now useless plans to marry a well-connected nice young Society miss?'

'Ah, I can see that would be a consideration.' Nick regarded her steadily, all the amusement gone from his eyes. 'It would have been a terrible mistake, that nice young Society miss. I would have been bored in a month. What I want—what I *need*—is a beautiful, scandalous, argumentative milliner.'

'Is that a proposal, my lord?'

'That is a proposal, Miss Grey. Will you do me the honour of becoming my wife?' Nick stepped back, leaving her free, as though he did not want to constrain her answer any more than her person.

Tallie dropped a neat curtsy. 'Thank you, my lord. I accept with all my heart.'

The sensation that this must be a dream—an impossible, wonderful dream—was swept away as Nick swooped and caught her up in his arms, carried her through into the attic and, setting her on her feet, proceeded to kiss her with a thoroughness that even the most torrid dream could not conjure up. This was indeed real.

Tallie finally managed to free herself and hold him off with both hands hard on his chest. 'Nick, tell me truly, will your family be very shocked at such a misalliance? Because if they will be I could not bear to be the cause of any coldness between you.'

'My aunt loves you already, William adores you like a sister, my assorted great-aunts and great-uncles who have yet to meet you will congratulate me upon securing such a charming bride and my dear mama, who is nursing a collection of completely imaginary ailments in Bath, will dote upon you. And, besides, I have a clinching argument.'

Tallie regarded the twinkle in his eyes with some suspicion. 'And what might that be?'

'The economy of having a wife who can make her own hats. Why, I need give you but a fraction of the dress allowance I would otherwise have to.'

'You beast!' Tallie seized a cushion off the moth-eaten sofa, which comprised the furnishings of the attic room, and swung wildly at Nick with it. He retaliated with its companion and the space was instantly a snowstorm of dust and feathers. Almost unable to breath with giggles and sneezes Tallie landed a telling blow just as the door swung open to reveal Zenna, a look of horror on her face.

'Oh, no!' she wailed and promptly burst into tears. Tallie had never seen her with so much as a dampness in her eye; appalled, she dropped her cushion and ran to put her arms around her friend.

'Zenna dearest, what is wrong?'

'I thought…I thought I was doing the right thing letting Lord Arndale in,' Zenna hiccupped miserably. 'I thought he really loved you, and all the time he just wanted to ravish you and you had to beat him off…'

'Ravish her…!'

'Do be quiet, Nick, can you not see that Zenna is upset? We were having a pillow fight, Zenna darling, that is all. He does love me, we are going to get married.'

'Truly?'

'Truly.' Tallie regarded her friend's pink-faced embarrassment severely as she scrabbled in her pocket for her handkerchief. 'But what were you about letting Nick in? You promised me that you would not.'

'I asked him if he would send his daughters to my

school,' Zenna stated, blowing her nose defiantly. 'And he said of course he would—so that makes him a prospective parent. And you agreed I might let those in.'

'We would, would we not, my darling?' Nick enquired.

'Would what?' Tallie was too amazed at Zenna's duplicity to follow his question.

'Send our daughters here.'

'Our daughters? Oh!' Tallie gazed at Nick, the blush spreading up her face. 'You would like daughters?'

'Two daughters and two sons seems a reasonable sort of number to me, but naturally it is something I feel we should discuss at considerable length.'

'Excuse me,' Zenna said with some firmness, her schoolmistress expression back on her face, the effect only marred by a very pink nose. 'I should point out that this is a most improper conversation and that we should go downstairs, Talitha. I am sure his lordship will have many things to arrange and will be calling upon you on your return to London tomorrow. I will accompany you.'

Nick gave way with grace in the face of such a formidable front. His bow on the dusty threshold was a model of deportment and his face serious as he said, 'You are entirely correct, Miss Scott. Miss

Grey, I will call tomorrow afternoon if you will permit.'

He then spoiled the effect, much to Tallie's delight, by seizing her by the shoulders and kissing her lingeringly on the lips. 'Darling Tallie, I adore you.' And he was gone.

Chapter Twenty-Two

The new Lady Arndale sat up nervously against the pile of lace-trimmed pillows in her big bed. Her bed, her suite of rooms, her house. Heronsholt, hazy in the evening light, a mass of grey stone and warm red tiles, the impression of a classical frontage and a hint of more chaotic wings behind.

But Nick had given her little opportunity to study the house nestling in its woods overlooking a sweeping Hertfordshire valley. He had ushered her past a confusing number of bowing and curtsying servants, delivered her into the hands of the beaming housekeeper and announced that dinner was required within the hour.

When she had joined him in the dining room there was a full contingent of footmen and an impressive butler to face. Tallie sent a look of pure panic down the length of polished mahogany to where Nick was getting to his feet and met his eyes.

They were steady, confident, approving. Her chin went up and she returned the look with a smile that was suddenly calm. Her footmen, her butler—and she was not going to be intimidated by any of them.

Nick was at her side, holding her chair and she smiled up at him. 'Thank you, my lord.'

'Thank you, my lady,' he whispered back. 'Tomorrow we will have three leaves taken out of the table and will dine in comfort.'

But tonight he wanted her to impress the servants, she could tell. He had told her all their names on the journey from London, a dreamlike journey after the equally dreamlike wedding ceremony and the wedding breakfast organised on a lavish scale by Lady Parry. Flashes of memory came back to her: Millie looking radiant as she sang at her first private engagement, Mrs Blackstock in earnest discussion with Mr Dover as she explained the problems of finding reliable servants for three lodging-houses and Zenna shamelessly cornering Society ladies and lecturing them on the advantages of an education for girls at her select new seminary.

Nick had dealt with her obvious inexperience of managing a large household and her nervousness about the staff not by referring to it, but simply by giving her the information she would need.

'Thank you, Partridge,' she had said firmly, turning to the waiting butler. 'You may serve now.'

But coping with the servants was one thing—that merely needed acting and a show of self-confidence until she acquired the real thing. Of all her new acquisitions, there was one that could not be dealt with in such a way. Her new husband.

Tallie swallowed, pulling the sheets up to her chin before she realised what she was doing and turned them down again. *He has kissed you countless times*, she chided herself. *You have been in bed with him, for goodness' sake. He has seen you naked. You have seen him, if it comes to that. Why so shy now?*

If Nick had not been so restrained and proper for the four interminable weeks before their wedding, she might not have felt so nervous. But he had acted with the most scrupulous propriety, which unnerved her to the point where she almost convinced herself he was regretting the entire thing and was not in love with her after all. Then she would catch his gaze, see the passion burning in his eyes, hear the tenderness in his voice and she no longer doubted him.

A board creaked outside the door to her dressing-room. It opened onto a tiny lobby and then into his suite. Tallie swallowed, folded her hands over the crumpled wreck of the sheet edge and attempted to look calm. There was a scratch on the panels and the door opened to reveal her husband clad in a splendid dressing-gown of heavy crimson silk, his feet disconcertingly bare.

'You look very small in that big bed,' he observed, leaning one shoulder against the doorframe. 'Is it comfortable?'

Tallie's voice vanished into a squeak. She coughed and tried again. 'Very, thank you.' Why did he not come in?

'I wondered if perhaps you were very tired and would prefer it if I stayed in my room tonight.'

For a moment a ripple of relief ran through her. She would not have to face the horrible possibility that she might not please him tonight. Tomorrow she would be rested, not so tense. A good night's sleep would surely banish this quivering, feverish feeling that had been spreading through her limbs ever since she had placed her hand in his at the altar.

She opened her mouth to agree and heard herself say, 'Oh, no, Nick, no. I am not so very tired.' Before she could correct herself he was at the bedside, flipping back the covers to reveal her modestly clad in the long nightgown of fine cambric that she had nervously chosen to wear. With one hasty, appalled glance she had rejected the dozen or so outrageous pieces of nonsense that Lady Parry had encouraged her to buy and which her new maid had spread out for her choice.

'Very restrained,' Nick observed. 'How does it come off?'

'Er…over my head.'

'And are you very fond of this garment?' His long fingers were toying with the chaste satin ribbon which gathered the neckline.

'No. Why?'

In answer Nick simply took the neck edges in both hands and ripped the nightgown firmly from top to toe, leaving Tallie naked. Before her hands could grasp the edges again he bent down, scooped her up and strode back towards the door. 'I have been having the most improper thoughts about doing this since the first moment I saw you in Harland's studio.'

'You have?' Tallie gasped, wrapping her arms around his neck as they swept through both dressing-rooms and into the master bedroom.

'Hmm.' Nick's voice was a throaty growl of anticipation that sent an answering echo through her. 'And your hair…' He set her on her feet, tugged at the ribbon that was tying her hair back and swept the freed mass out over her shoulders with both hands. 'And that scent of jasmine has been haunting me.' He buried his face in her hair and Tallie found herself pressed against the warm sensual silk. It slid across her naked skin. She shivered and instantly Nick cupped her face in his hands and looked intently down at her.

'Are you cold? No? Then are you frightened?'

'Um, a little bit,' Tallie admitted. Nick seemed so big, so dominant, so possessive.

'Did Aunt Kate say anything to you?'

'Only that it would be all right and you were much too experienced to make a mull of it.'

'Oh, did she?' Nick said indignantly. 'And did you find that reassuring?'

'Not very.'

'Then let me assure you, Tallie, that I am not experienced in bedding virgins and I intend this to be the first and last time I do so. So we are going to have to muddle through this together and try not to make a mull of it jointly.' She suppressed a little snort of amusement and he smiled. 'That is better. Now, then, where were we?'

Fortunately that appeared to be a rhetorical question, for Tallie very much doubted that she could come up with a coherent answer. She burrowed closer against him as though to cover her nakedness with his robe and found that her fingers—quite of their own volition—were untying the knot of the sash. The edges fell apart and she was against Nick's body.

Tallie froze, absorbing sensations, recalling how it had felt when she had woken in his bed and was held in his arms. This was different. For a moment she was puzzled, then realised that, standing, she was pressed against Nick in a slightly different way. She could rest her head on his shoulder, which meant she could let her lips graze against the side of his neck where the pulse beat so hard. The strangely exciting friction of his chest hair against her softness was the same; she wriggled and caught her breath at the way his breath caught in turn.

And like this, tight against him, there was no mistaking the extent to which she had aroused him.

'Tallie,' Nick murmured against her hair.

'Mmm?'

'Let me kiss you.' She tipped back her head and his hands came up to her shoulders to push off the wreck of her nightgown. The fine cambric whispered to the floor as he bent to her lips and Tallie responded, opening to him, yielding to the demands of tongue and lips until suddenly this was no longer enough and the aching, throbbing feeling inside built into a clamorous demand that she could no longer pretend she did not understand.

Nick seemed to sense the change in her. He bent, caught her up in his arms, laid her on the bed. With one fluid movement he had shrugged out of his robe and was on the bed at her side.

Tallie swallowed, struggled to calm her breathing, still the turmoil that racked her. Then the world seemed to stop as she met Nick's eyes. She had thought she had seen love in them before. She had glimpsed admiration, desire, love. But what she saw now took her breath away. There were all those things in the deep grey gaze, but mixed with them was awe, tenderness, strength and an aching vulnerability.

'I love you,' he whispered.

'I love you too,' she answered and saw the vulnerability vanish, showing her the banked fires of controlled desire behind the gentleness. And suddenly she did not want him to treat her like a fragile butterfly cupped in his hands, for the desire was welling up in her too, threatening to overwhelm her. 'Love me, Nick. I will not break.'

Even then he was careful, controlled. She learned to surrender to him, to his clever hands, to his mouth, to the heat and strength of his body until her own was arching in supplication beneath his. When he entered her Tallie was already so tense with the passion he had been building for her that the momentary pain passed in a flash to be replaced with an explosion of sensation.

Tallie cried out, her hands locked about Nick's neck, her head thrown back on the tumbled pillows, her entire body and mind swept by a crashing wave of sensation.

Slowly, slowly she came to herself, marvelling at the weight of him capturing her so powerfully, so tenderly. Then she realised that he still possessed her, filled her, completed her and her newly awakened body quivered around him.

'Oh, my love.' Nick's eyes were on hers as she smiled tremulously up at him. 'My beautiful, beautiful Talitha.' And he began to move again, thrusting, possessing until she found that she was no longer just marvelling at the feel of him within her but that her body was responding, answering his. That extraordinary sensation was building again inexorably, even more overwhelmingly. She drowned in his eyes, convinced she was going to shatter now, break into pieces.

Then as her body convulsed around him again she heard his cry and saw, as her vision blurred, the expression of triumph and love and utter completion that transformed his face.

Tallie woke slowly, languorously. She stretched, reached out a hand as one or other of them had done at intervals throughout that incredible night—and found the bed empty. Her groping hand found only the warm rumpled hollow where Nick had lain. Tallie opened her eyes, blinking in full daylight and lay looking up at the underside of the bed canopy while she thought about just how new and strange her body felt.

It was as though every muscle was sleek and polished, as though her skin had been oiled and as if she should stretch and purr like a cat instead of simply sitting up in bed. She compromised, wriggling up against the pillows, arching her back and raising her arms in a long, luxurious stretch.

Her husband was standing across the room from the bed, reaching up to turn a small key in a hole in the panelling. As he heard her move he turned and smiled at her. Tallie felt her heart give a sharp beat. Loved and loving, that was how she felt, how she knew she would always feel with Nick.

'Good morning, my lady wife.'

'Good morning, my lord.' He had not troubled to pull on his robe and Tallie regarded him unashamed and admiring. 'What are you doing? That panelling is new, is it not?'

Nick turned back and opened what she could now see was a pair of doors above the dado level, then stepped aside to repeat the action on the next length of wall.

Tallie gasped. Revealed by the opening doors was a large oil painting, a scene of a classical temple with a nymph placing an offering before the altar.

'But that is one of Mr Harland's canvases…' She swung her feet out of bed and ran to Nick's side as he opened one panel after another. 'And that, and that one and that is the Diana picture! Nick, have you bought all the paintings he did with me as the model?'

In answer Nick swept a hand around the room. The locked panels were open to reveal six scenes of the ancient world, each with the slender blonde-haired figure of the new Lady Arndale gracing it. 'It seemed the safest way of keeping them from prying eyes, and, when I saw them, how could I resist?'

He watched, hardly conscious of the smile on his face as he regarded his wife walking slowly around the room gazing up at the luminous pictures, her hands pressed to her flushed cheeks. Each image was lovely, but none matched the real woman he knew. For a moment he shivered at the thought of how he would be feeling now if she had refused him. To possess those still images and know that he had lost the one being who completed him as a person. Unbearable.

Tallie turned slowly to face him and he felt his

spirits soar again, the unthinkable vanishing in the warmth of her smile. 'There is still one space.' She gestured at the central panel between the windows.

The half-formed idea he had entertained but never thought through came to his lips before he could check it. 'Perhaps you could…no.' No, the idea of his Tallie exposed to the eyes of any other man again, even the apparently sexless Harland, was unbearable. Then he saw her face and could not have felt worse if he had struck her.

'Tallie, darling, I am sorry, I would not have you go through that again for anything. I am a thought-less beast.' He caught her in his arms, burying his face in her hair. *Damn it!* This business of being in love was far harder than he had ever imagined. You opened up your every thought and feeling to another and they to you—and that made it so easy to hurt them. He was aware of her slender body shaking against him. He had made her cry.

'Tallie, sweetheart… You are *laughing.*' She struggled to get her expression under control. 'You were teasing me?'

Instantly she looked all contrition. It was incred-ible the way she could hide every feeling or let down every barrier and expose her soul to him. 'I am sorry. It was just your face when you were con-templating it, and then instantly you came all over-possessive. I think perhaps people would expect a nice conventional portrait of both of us for the main reception rooms, but I have a much better idea for this wall.'

'Yes?' Nick said cautiously, telling himself that he had better learn fast how to deal with this infuriating minx of a new wife before she ran rings around him.

'It was Mr Harland's suggestion, and I have to admit that I have thought of it often since he made it.' Nick waited, hands on hips. 'He said, the first time he saw you—when I, of course, did *not* see you—that he would like to paint you as Alexander the Great. I found it a powerful image,' Tallie added reflectively.

'Alexander? I suppose I must be flattered, but you do not want a picture of a man in armour in the bedchamber, surely?'

'Oh, no, not in armour.' For some reason Tallie was edging away from him round the edge of the bed. 'In the antique style, carrying a shield and sword and wearing sandals.'

'And what else?'

'Why, nothing at all.'

'You little wanton! You expect me to pose naked for some da—blasted artist?'

'Why not? What is sauce for the goose...'

Nick stared at her. The thought that Tallie could think of him with quite the same physical admiration that he thought of her—in fact, *had* thought about the image Harland had conjured up with a no-doubt idle suggestion—that was powerfully erotic. He felt his body tighten and stir and caught the spark of wicked acknowledgement in his wife's eyes.

'Madam, this gander is not for plucking. And if you need any convincing about just who is master in this house, I am afraid I am just going to have to show you all over again.' He grinned as she dodged laughing away from his reaching arm and then tumbled of her own accord onto the big bed, stretching out her hands to him.

'Of course, my lord, if you dislike the idea we will say no more about it…'

Nick let himself be pulled down onto the bed then rolled Tallie over to hold her trapped tightly beneath him. 'For some reason, my adorable new wife, I suspect that this show of meek obedience is just that—show. I have no doubt that I am going to be cajoled, lured and tricked into Harland's studio.'

Tallie attempted a hurt pout and only succeeded in looking adorably flustered. 'Do you mind?'

'Not in the least. I fully anticipate years of enjoyment from your wiles, my love—and from attempting to take your mind off further schemes. Like this, my very dearest love...'

And Tallie, gasping with delight in his arms, could only murmur against his lips, 'I do love you so, Nick. So very, very much. And for ever.'

* * * * *

Mills & Boon® Online

Discover more romance at
www.millsandboon.co.uk

- 🌹 **FREE** online reads
- 🌹 **Books** up to one month before shops
- 🌹 **Browse our books** before you buy

...and much more!

For exclusive competitions and instant updates:

 Like us on **facebook.com/romancehq**

 Follow us on **twitter.com/millsandboonuk**

 Join us on **community.millsandboon.co.uk**

Visit us Online — Sign up for our FREE eNewsletter at **www.millsandboon.co.uk**

WEB/M&B/RTL4/LP